U0032590

用英文遊台灣

透過 **50** 篇對話情節、
超過 **650** 個中英對照的
「趴趴走好用句」，
學習**台灣風土特產**等
各色說法。

（附贈2片CD）

黃玟君◎著

繼《用英文寫台灣》之後，
玟君老師又一在聯合報
教育版受歡迎專欄。

自序——

「我愛台灣！」

　　我生長於台灣，可是老實說，就像許多土生土長的台灣人一樣，我除了知道台北有個世界高樓101、台灣最長的河流是濁水溪，其實並不特別瞭解台灣。不過自從於94年8月應《聯合報》之邀，開始在教育版寫了「笑談時事英語」* 及「用英文遊台灣」專欄後，我總算可以理直氣壯地告訴大家：「我愛台灣」！

　　為什麼呢？因為我以前總是認為台灣的新聞千篇一律、了無新意，結果接下「笑談時事英語」專欄重任，「被迫」開始認真鑽研台灣新聞、笑談時事後，竟發現台灣還有許多能夠博君一笑的政治新聞和社會新聞！習慣關心台灣的一切後，我儼然成為「台灣新聞達人」：舉凡詐騙電話(telephone scam/fraud)、靜坐抗議(sit-in protest)、買票文化(vote-buying culture)、馬屁文化(brown-nosing culture)、金錢外交(money diplomacy)、禽流感(avian flu)、狗仔隊(paparazzi)、爆料者(Deep Throat)……，甚至連時令節慶，如尾牙(year-end party)、清明節(Tomb Sweeping Day)、划龍舟競賽(dragon boat racing)……，我都可以用中、英文一次說清楚，講明白！

　　專欄的讀者反應熱烈，隨後於95年9月，我便開始跟著廣大的《聯合報》讀者「用英文遊台灣」。當初寫作最大的目的，

便是希望台灣讀者可以藉由專欄的幫助，大肆向外國友人宣揚台灣的美。時光荏苒，不知不覺我們已經由北到南、再由南到北、甚至連外島都走透透了！也因為這個專欄，我現在對台灣各地的風景名勝、文化習俗、美食小吃、甚至歷史典故……，都可以如數家珍！

令我驚訝的是，「用英文遊台灣」專欄不僅讓許多台灣讀者在招待外國友人時有個參考依據，更讓不少外國友人在全台趴趴走時，多了絕佳的英文資訊。這麼說起來，我的「愛台灣」絕對實至名歸呢！

可見「愛台灣」不僅要嘴巴說，還要用英文說；除了用英文說，還要起而行、帶著外國友人一起趴趴走，真正實踐「用英文遊台灣」！如此一來，不僅增加了自己的英文能力，也因此替台灣的國民外交盡了一份心力，這就是真正的愛台灣。

這本「用英文遊台灣」收集了一年來刊登在聯合報的50篇專欄文章，每篇文章另附上單字、片語解說，另外在每篇的最後還附上十二句「趴趴走好用句」，讓大家面對外國友人時不會詞窮。不過因為英文能力的增加還需靠讀者自己的「產出」，因此在閱讀「趴趴走好用句」時，請大家先將中文句子以英文說出或寫出，測驗一下自己的英文能力，而不要直接看答案喔！

最重要的，English is for communication，學英文就是要溝通，在我們將台灣的美告訴外國友人時，一定要確保對方知道我們在講什麼，同樣的，當外國友人問我們關於台灣的種種時，我們也要聽懂才有辦法作國民外交。因此我特別撰寫「聽

說技巧大公開」一章，盼能對長期對英語有「聽不懂、說不清」困擾的讀者有所幫助。另外，在本書每篇中，我也挑出一個句子，標明相對應的聽說技巧，期望能幫助讀者學以致用，更上一層樓！

　　最後感謝《聯合報》駱焜祺先生以及台灣師大呂燕妮小姐對此書的大力協助。

　　現在就讓我們一起「用英文遊台灣」、愛台灣！

黃玟君

---

　　*「笑談時事英語」專欄已於95年9月結集成書，書名為《用英文寫台灣》（聯經出版）。

目次

聽說技巧大公開

　　很多台灣人在使用英語時最大的問題都出在「聽不懂、說不清」──既聽不懂外國人連珠炮般的字句，自己講出來的英語也令人聽攏無。喜歡聽英文歌的人通常也會有這樣的困擾：自己明明很努力的字正腔圓，卻似乎永遠跟不上CD裡歌詞的速度……。為什麼會這樣呢？

字正腔圓的英語？

　　你相信嗎？學生時代老師無時無刻叮嚀的，要我們將每個子音、母音發清楚的英語，可能正是我們無法和外國人溝通、無法跟得上英文歌的主因呢！讓我們先來舉個國語的例子：現在的年輕人都知道，國語裡的「就醬子」是「就這樣子」的偷懶省略版，講出來沒有台灣人會聽不懂，但如果你有一天心血來潮跟朋友字正腔圓地說「就──這──樣──子」，相信他也會熊熊嚇一跳吧！

　　這就像如果有個外國人和你說：Thank you for your help！，你卻很字正腔圓地回答「Not—at—all—」，而不是偷懶省略的 nadedol /naDəDɔl/＊，對方應該也會感到很吃驚吧！所以說，英

＊　　音標中的/D/為彈舌音的唸法，細節請參照本章中「彈舌音」處。

語要講得道地、說得親切、甚至要能聽得懂，有時還真的需要摒棄字字分明、字正腔圓的精神呢！

有了這樣的心理準備，接下來我們就要來談談台灣人在英語聽說上的三大罩門：

(一)連音

(二)削弱音

(三)彈舌音

瞭解了這三種英語人士的發音方式，你的發音與聽力便會從此無往不利！

越偷懶越能學好英語？

我們都知道，說英語時，除了要掌握單字的發音，尚要顧及「單字與單字組成句子」時的發音。在英語句子中，單字與單字之間會互相產生許多「干擾」的作用，進而形成我們剛剛提及的「連音」、「削弱音」、「彈舌音」，造成許多聽不懂、說不清的困擾。至於這三大問題，究其根本，便在於「偷懶」。

為什麼呢？因為一般人在日常生活講話時最主要的目的是「溝通」，而溝通首重簡單迅速，為了講得快、講得多，很多字便會黏成一團、甚至削弱不見。再者，一般人講話不可能每字每句的音調、速度都保持不便，而是會根據句子中要強調的、不強調的字而有快慢輕重、高低起伏，如此才能抑揚頓挫，時而溫柔，時而鏗鏘。

因此如果你想將英語說得道地，很多時候便得適時在該偷

懶的時候偷懶。信不信由你，如此一來你便能夠既偷懶、又把英語學好呢！

聽說第一大罩門：連音

說到連音，這可是許多台灣學生學英語時心中永遠的痛。為什麼呢？因為很多人就曾經在考聽力時、或在和外國人交談時，將 Aunt Bella 聽成 umbrella、將 rub us 聽成 Robert 呢！

為什麼明明兩個字、甚至三個字的英文，我們會以為只有一個字呢？關鍵就在於「連音」。因此現在讓我們好好探究一下「連音」最常發生的三個原因：

(一)子音 + 母音

(二)子音 + 子音

(三)子音 + /y/ 的變音

一、子音 + 母音

發音規則：前一個字的字尾是「子音」、後一個字的前面是「母音」，則產生連音。

在進入重點之前，請你先唸一下這個句子：

Stand up, please.

在例子中，stand up 的 /d/、/ʌ/ 會產生「連音」。為什麼呢？大家都知道，英語中母音可以單獨形成音節，因此不需要子音的配合便能發聲。相反的，英語中的子音，在絕大多數的情況下並不能單獨成就一個音節，因此「子音」必須找到它的媽媽「母音」，母子連心，結合成一個「音節」來發音。

　　所以原本分開的兩個字，如果前一個字的字尾是「子音」、後一個字的前面是「母音」，「子音」與「母音」碰在一起，便會產生「連音」。

　　如果你將上面的那個句子以「沒連音」與「有連音」的方式各唸一次，就會發現兩者差異頗多！這就是我們在聽外國人講話時，最容易搞不懂的地方。

　　現在請你將書中的片語試著用「連音」唸一次，然後聆聽 CD 中的唸法：

❖ **left out** (**p.18**)

❖ **rake in** (**p.18**)

❖ **in the eyes of** (**p.26**)

　　試著用「有連音」和「沒連音」的方式各唸一次，差別是不是很大呢？

　　你或許會問：那我以後每次看到一個英文句子，要不要運用上面所說的「連音」規則，一一把「連音」找出來後再開口講呢？答案是「當然不需要」啦！其實所有的發音規則都不需死背，你只要多說英語，且在說英語時多多偷懶，「連音」便可以自然形成！

二、子音 + 子音

　　發音規則：前一個字字尾的子音與後一個字前面的子音相同，則產生連音。

　　在說明連音的第二個規則前，請你先唸這個句子：

Here's the bus station.

上面的例子中，bus station 的兩個 /s/，會產生「連音」。這種連音出現的情況在「前一個字字尾的音與後一個字的前面音一樣」時。

遇到這種情況時，你當然不需要很辛苦的將兩個相同的音發兩次囉！基於懶散原則，你只要發一次便可，但必須加長其「長度」。為什麼呢？因為人家本來真的有兩個音啊！

以上面的 bus station 為例，你該不會刻苦耐勞到把 bus station 的兩個 s 換氣唸兩次吧！其實你只要唸一次就可以了，然後記得將 s 稍稍加長。

讓我們接著多練習一些例子。請你將本書的三個句子片語試著用「連音」唸一次，然後聆聽 CD 中的唸法：

❖ **old days**（**p.18**）

❖ **Museum of Fine Arts**（**p.122**）（/v/ 與 /f/ 在這裡屬同類型的音，因此適用此項規則）

❖ **prehistoric culture**（**p. 298**）

三、子音 ＋ **/y/** 的變音

發音規則：當子音 /t/、/d/、/s/、/z/ 與 /j/ 碰在一起時，便會產生連音及變音。

在進入這個發音規則前，請先試著唸唸以下句子：

Can't you do it?
Did you do it?
I miss you.
He's gone for all these years.

要注意：這裡的 can't you、did you、miss you、these years 已經不再是分開的 /kænt ju/、/dɪd ju/、/mɪs ju/、/ðiz jɪrz/，而是連起來並且變音的 /kæntʃu/、/dɪdʒu/、/mɪʃu/、/ðiʒɪrz/！這種「連音＋變音」在英語中十分常見，就是 /t/、/d/、/s/、/z/ 這幾個音與 /j/ 碰在一起時，所產生改變：

/t/ + /j/ → / tʃ /
/d/ + /j/ → / dʒ /
/s/ + /j/ → / ʃ /
/z/ + /j/ → / ʒ /

讓我們接著多練習一些例子。請你將本書的三個句子試著用「連音」的方法唸一次，然後聆聽 CD 中的唸法：

❖ **Sadness your ass!** (p.18)
❖ **Which kind would you like?** (p.58)
❖ **Don't you worry.** (p.338)

聽說第二大罩門：削弱音

除了「連音」，台灣學生學英語的另一痛是「削弱音」，因為許多喜歡跟著英文歌哼哼唱唱的人最常遇到的問題便是「跟不上」，而這個「跟不上」，十之八九和「削弱音」有關！

能不能練好「削弱音」關乎著你能不能將英語講得更道地，也關係著你能不能真正聽懂外國人到底在說些什麼。可是偏偏「削弱音」在英語中出現的次數與花樣超多，令人眼花撩

亂！不過別擔心，只要你秉持剛剛學「連音」」的精神，以偷懶為目的，就可以輕鬆搞定它。以下便是「削弱音」幾個常出現的地方：

　　(一)子音 + 子音*
　　(二)wanna 與 gonna
　　(三)and 的削弱
　　(四)削弱音的選擇

一、子音 + 子音

　　發音規則：當兩個不同的子音碰撞在一起時，前面的子音會被削弱。

　　在進入重點前，請先唸以下的單字及字組：

checkbook
pipeline
send to

　　在上面的例子裡，單字 checkbook 的 /k/ 、pipeline 的 /p/ 、以及字組 send to 的 /d/ 會發生「削弱音」，為什麼呢？因為這三個子音的後面分別碰上了另一個子音 /b/、/l/ 與 /t/，而「削弱音」最常發生的情形，便是兩個子音碰撞在一起時。當「子音」與「子音」狹路相逢，為避免衝突，會將前面的那個子音

---

　　*　　這裡的「削弱音：子音 + 子音」與前面所提的「連音：子音 + 子音」不同。「削弱音」的宗旨是「兩個子音碰在一起，前面的子音倒楣」；「連音」的宗旨則是「兩個相同的子音碰在一起時，兩個音會連在一起」。

削弱。

　　不過要小心的是，「削弱」並非「削去」，所以我們並不能將這些前面的子音完全刪去不唸，而是必須將這個音的長度、嘴型、舌頭位置……等表現出來。也就是說，我們雖然不發出前面子音的「音」，卻必須保存它的「長度」及「發音方式」。

　　所以當我們唸 checkbook 時，雖然 ck 的 /k/ 不見了，/k/ 所代表的長度、嘴型、舌頭位置還是要表現出來。而發 pipeline 時，/p/ 雖然不發音，可是它畢竟還是存在，我們必須把它表現出來，所以在我們發這個字的前半部 / paɪp / 與後半部 / laɪn / 之間，必須將嘴唇合併，作出 /p/ 的長度、嘴型、舌頭位置。

二、wanna 與 gonna

　　發音規則：當 want to 與 going to 唸得很快且偷懶時，便會變成 wanna 與 gonna。

　　相信許多喜歡聽英文歌曲的讀者常在歌詞中看到 wanna 與 gonna 兩個字，查遍字典卻找不到它們的蹤跡，事實上這兩個怪字的拼法便來自「削弱音」的規則。首先請唸以下的兩個短句，唸的時候盡量將速度加快：

I want to go.

I am going to go.

　　怎麼樣？唸的速度變快後，有沒有覺得其中的 want to 及 going to 好像「變音」了呢？其實 wanna 是 want to 的「削弱音」、而 gonna 是 going to 的「削弱音」：

| want t<u>o</u> | → | want t<u>a</u> | → | wanta | → | wanna |
| /ʊ/ | | /ə/ | | /ə/ | | |

| going to | → | gointo | → | gointa | → | gonna |
| /ŋ/ /ʊ/ | | /n/ | | /ə/ | | |

　　want to 的 to 之所以會從 /tu/ 變成 / tə /，主要是因為 to 是不定詞，不是句子重音的所在，所以 /ʊ/ 會被削弱成比較好發的 / ə /*。因此如果你將唸得慢而重的 want to，改唸成快且輕的音，便會變成 wanna 了！

　　而 going 這個字的結尾是鼻音 –ing / ɪŋ /，之所以會從 / ŋ / 變成 /n/，也是因為這是個「非重音」音節，因此我們會將發起來比較費力的 / ŋ / 改成較不費力的 /n/。

　　讓我們接著多練習一些例子。請你將書中的 want to 與 going to 試著用「削弱音」的方法唸一次，然後聆聽 CD 中的唸法（句子中畫底線處為削弱音的所在）：

✤ **They didn't <u>want to</u> stay.**（p.154）

✤ **What are we <u>going to</u> eat tonight?**（p.74）

✤ **I'm never <u>going to</u> let you sit in front again!**（p.266）

　　除了常見的 wanna 與 gonna 外，類似的「削弱音」還有下列幾個：

| got to | → | gotta |
| /gɑt tu/ | | /gɑDə/ |

---

* 　英文中最容易發的音、亦即既輕鬆又不費力就可以發出來的母音是 / ə /，因此講話時若碰到「非重音」位置的母音，英文便有個傾向將它們都發成最不費力的 / ə /。

ought to	→	oughtta
/ɔt tu/		/ɔDə/

out of	→	outta
/aut ʌv/		/auDə/

　　要注意的是，以上的這些字除了受到「削弱音」的影響，也受到「彈舌音」的影響（我們在下一節中會討論）。不過你只要記得，在遇到這些字時，將它們從「慢而重」改唸成「快且輕」的音，就可以渾然天成了！

三、and 的削弱

　　發音規則：and 因為是連接詞，不是句子重音的所在，所以 / ænd / 會削弱成 / ənd /。

　　下面這些字組，你會怎麼唸呢？

rock'n'roll
big'n'little
cream'n'sugar

　　這些字中間的「'n'」其實就是連接詞 and，所以 rock'n'roll、big'n'little、cream'n'sugar 分別是 rock and roll、big and little、cream and sugar 的「削弱音」，不信請看：

and	→	and	→	an
/ænd/		/ənd/		/ən/

　　and 因為是連接詞，不是句子主要意義及重音的所在，所

以 / ænd / 會削弱成 / ənd / ，加上字尾的 /d/ 常常會因為與後面接的子音碰撞而被犧牲，堂堂的 / ænd / 就變成 / ən /。如果再加上「母音+子音」的連音，堂堂的 rock and roll 就會變成 rock'n'roll / rɑkənrol / 了！

　　現在請你將本書三個詞組試著用「削弱音」的方法唸一次，然後聆聽 CD 中的唸法：

✤ **shops and restaurants** (**p.242**)

✤ **bread, and soup** (**p.250**)

✤ **fresh and scrumptious** (**p.250**)

　　在句子中，其他常出現、且最容易被削弱的字還有以下這幾個：

have →	**have** →	**have**
/hæv/	/həv/	/əv/
	for →	**for**
	/fɔr/	/fə/
	or →	**or**
	/ɔr/	/ə/
would have →		**would've**
/wʊd hæv/		/wʊdəv/
could have →		**could've**
/kʊd hæv/		/kʊdəv/
might have →		**might've**
/maɪt hæv/		/maɪtəv/

must have →	must've
/mʌst hæv/	/mʌstəv/

　　究其原因，都是因為上面這些字在句子中通常扮演不太重要的角色，處於「非重音」音節，因此常常會被講話的人犧牲。

　　現在請你將書中句子試著用「削弱音」的方法唸一次，然後聆聽 CD 中的唸法（句子畫底線處為削弱音產生的地方）：

❖ **But I <u>have to</u> say, Kenting really is a lot of fun.**（p.266）

❖ **This place is also ideal <u>for</u> bird- and butterfly-watching.**
　(p.322)

❖ **The market stays open until about 2 <u>or</u> 3 am.**
　(p.2)

❖ **Who <u>would have</u> thought that fire and water can coexist?**
　(p.210)

❖ **They <u>must have</u> already used up all the shells?**（p.362）

四、削弱音的選擇

　　經過了前面「削弱音」的規則及例句，相信你已經發現到，並不是所有的音都適用於「削弱音」的規則，最明顯的例子便是 /s/，它不論處在英語句子的何處，都不會被削去，例如：

Mary want<u>s</u> to go abroad.

They need pencil<u>s</u> to write.

　　以上這兩句 wants 與 pencils 的 /s/ 與 /z/，後面接的都是子

音，根據「削弱音」的規則，「子音 + 子音」的第一個子音必須被削弱，但是在上述的兩個例子中，我們卻無論如何必須把 s 清楚的發出來，為什麼呢？

原來 s 具有英文文法上重要的意義功能，例如大家所熟知的文法規則：「第三人稱單數現在式動詞必須加 s」、且「複數名詞後面必須加 s」，所以這麼重要的 s，是無論如何不會消失的！

不過同樣具有文法功能的「過去式」及「過去分詞」等，在碰到「削弱音」時，該如何解決呢？例如以下的兩個句子：

> **He pick<u>ed</u> up the books.**
> /t/

> **I ask<u>ed</u> them for help.**
> /t/

在第一個句子中，picked 的 ck /k/ 根據規則理應被削弱（子音 + 子音，第一個子音會被削弱），而其後的 ed /t/ 則不被削弱，因此理所當然的保留了其文法意義上的重要性（在此為「過去式」）。而且在第一句中，根據「連音」的規則，ed /t/ 還會與 up 的 u / ʌ / 產生連音，出現 picked up / pɪktʌp / 的現象：

> **picked up　→　piedup**
> /pɪkt ʌp/　　　/pɪtʌp/

而在第二個句子中，asked 的 k /k/ 根據規則理應被削弱，其後的 ed /t/ 則不被削弱，因此也符合我們對其文法重要性的期待（在此為「過去式」）。只不過 ed /t/ 遇到另一個子音 th / ð /，因此 /t/ 的音或多或少會被削弱一點：

> **asked them → asthem**
> /æskt ðɛm/ /æsðɛm/

讓我們接著多練習一些例子。請你將以下詞組唸一次，然後聆聽 CD 中的唸法：

* **baked sandwich** (p.2)
* **all packed close together** (p.90)
* **shaved ice** (p.2)

聽說第三大罩門：彈舌音

在前一節講到削弱音 wanna 時，細心的讀者或許會有疑問：

> **want to → want ta → wanta → wanna**
> /ʊ/ /ə/

為什麼第三個步驟的 wanta 會變成第四個步驟的 wanna？wanta 的那個 t 到底跑哪兒去了？還記得我們當時是如何解決這個問題的嗎？我們說：「如果你將唸得慢而重的 want to，改唸成快且輕的音，便會變成 wanna 了」。這段話，就是「彈舌音」的精髓。

發音規則：*當 /t/、/d/ 在一個母音或 r 之後、且在另一個非重音的母音之前，一個比 /t/ 或 /d/ 更不費力氣的「彈舌音」/D/ 便會產生。

---

* 　由於「彈舌音」最常出現在兩個母音之間，因此很多人為了省麻煩，將「彈舌音」的規則修改為「兩個母音中間的 /t/ 與 /d/ 便會變成彈舌音」，以方便記憶！

在進入重點之前，請你先唸以下的字與字組，唸的時候盡量唸快一點、偷懶點：

better

had it all

當你將以上的字唸快、唸偷懶時，便會自然而然產生「彈舌音」。「彈舌音」（一般用音標 /D/ 表示）顧名思義，就是「藉由舌頭的快速滑動或彈動所產生的音」，這是美式英語的一個重要特色。發音時，當 /t/、/d/ 在一個母音或 r 之後、且在另一個非重音的母音之前，一個比 /t/ 或 /d/ 更不費力氣的「彈舌音」/D/ 便會產生。

我們知道，發 /t/ 或 /d/ 時，你必須將舌尖「用力」抵在上排齒齦處，並在瞬間將嘴裡的空氣往外釋放，因此要好好的發 /t/ 與 /d/，是需要花些力氣的。/D/ 則不然，你只須把舌頭在上排齒齦處「輕輕」滑過、彈一下，就可以了。

/t/ 與 /d/ 之所以會變成 /D/，是因為它後面接的是一個「非重音」的母音，既然非重音，我們自然而然就會發出較不費力氣的「彈舌音」。要注意的是，/D/ 不只出現在單字本身，亦會出現在字組間！遇到這種情形，我們只要將整個字組看成一個大單字（例如將 had it all 看成 haditall），則同樣可以利用我們的規則找出「彈舌音」。

現在你應該會明白以前國中學的 not at all，為什麼會唸成「怪腔怪調」的 nadedol /nɑDəDəl/ 了！

讓我們接著多練習一些例子。請你將本書的四個詞組唸一

次，然後聆聽 CD 中的唸法（圈起處為彈舌音的所在）：

* **water**（**p.306**）
* **ready**（**p.194**）
* **quiet at night**（**p.18**）
* **sad about**（**p.18**）

單字與句子的重音規則

　　大家都知道，一個單字有重音及非重音，同樣的，單字串起來成為一個句子時，也有重音及非重音。這種重音及非重音的字、詞交錯組織起來的英語，唸起來便會快慢交織、抑揚頓挫；不然若完全速度一致、大小聲一樣，便有如和尚唸經了！在此我們分別就單字與句子的重音規則做一說明：

　　在講重音規則前，我們要先知道「重音」有何特色。所謂的「重音」，指的是一個句子、字組或單字中，有以下三個特色的音：

　　（一）特別強調

　　（二）音調較高

　　（三）音節長度較長

　　因此當你看到一個單字的某個音節標有重音符號，你便必須將這個音節特別強調、將音調提高、將音節長度拉長。例如以下幾個本書當中的單字，重音的音節絕對具有此三個特色，若不清楚這些單字的發音，請聆聽CD（單字中標示處即為重音因節所在）：

* **vege`tarian**（**p.12**）

✤ **coloni`zation（p.20）**

✤ **vol`canic（p.84）**

✤ **manu`facturing（p.148）**

　　說完了單字的重音規則，現在來談談句子的重音及音調的高低起伏。英文句子的重音基本上就是句子中會重讀的那幾個字。一般來說，英文句子也如單字般，包含一堆「重讀字」及「輕讀字」（或稱「非重讀字」），這些字在一個句子中交互出現，如此形成了英語的特色，那便是我們說的「節奏感」。

　　你要如何說出有「節奏感」的英語？英語中的重音及音調規則其實很簡單，那就是「重要的字重讀、不重要的字輕讀」。這句話雖聽起來有點「理所當然」，但一個句子中，到底哪些是「重要的字」、哪些是「不重要的字」？

　　要談到英文中重要與不重要的字，我們要先瞭解這些字的「詞性」。英文裡有許多不同的詞性，包括：名詞、動詞、介詞、助動詞、形容詞、冠詞……。其中最重要的詞性有以下六種：

　　(一)名詞

　　(二)動詞

　　(三)形容詞

　　(四)副詞

　　(五)疑問詞*

＊　　所謂的「疑問詞」，就是疑問句中詢問「何人」、「何時」、「何處」、「何事」、「為什麼」與「如何」的 who、when、where、what、why、how。這些疑問詞因為肩負了我們講話時「取得對方重要資訊」的責任，所以當然很重要，必須重讀。

(六)指示代名詞*

這些字或詞在英文裡稱作「內容字」（content words），是表達句子意義的關鍵所在，所以最重要。既然重要，當我們講到這些字時，便要「重讀」。

至於句子中其他的詞性，如代名詞、助動詞、冠詞、介詞、連接詞……等，則稱為「功能字」（function words）或「結構字」（structure words），它們既然不是意義關鍵的所在，重要性便不如之前的「內容字」，因此可以「輕讀」。

現在讓我們來整理、比較一下這兩種須重讀及輕讀的詞類：

須重讀的字

Content Words 「內容字」	例字
名詞	dog；table；flower
動詞	run；like；read
副詞	quickly；broadly
形容詞	happy；comfortable
疑問詞	who；what；why；where；what；how
指示代名詞	this；that；these；those

---

* 　　另外，我們說話時，指稱事物的 this、that、these、those 就是所謂的「指示代名詞」，它們在英文句子中也十分重要，因此也須重讀。

須輕讀的字

Function/Structure Words 「功能字」／「結構字」	例字
(人稱)代名詞及其受格	I；you；he；she；him；her；they；them；we；us
(關係)代名詞	who；which；that
冠詞	a；an；the
介詞	of；to；at；for；in；on
連接詞	and；but；so；or
所有格	his；her；their；our
助動詞	can；do；will；has；have
to be 動詞	is；are

　　現在讓我們接著練習一些本書的例子。請你將以下兩個句子根據輕重音的規則唸一次，然後聆聽 CD 中的唸法(標重音的單字為句中必須重讀的字)：

❖ **We can `also `visit the `National `Theater and the `National `Concert `Hall while we're `there. (p.50)**

❖ **A `typical `basin `town, it is `surrounded by `mountains on `four `sides and is `known as a "`mountain `city." (p.154)**

CD
1-1

基隆廟口小吃
Keelung Temple
Space（Miaokou）Snacks

Robert: My goodness. This place is **packed**!

Taike: Well, of course! This is the **world-renowned** Keelung Miaokou night market!

Kitty: Alas, these stands are **filthy** and **stinky**; you probably won't like the food here.

Robert: Not really—actually, the foods here look very... er, interesting! Hey, what's that **round** stuff?

Taike: Oh, that's my favorite greasy rice cake. Right next to it is baked sandwich, and then tempura, oyster omelet, spearfish stew, shrimp and meat stew, shaved ice; and of course the one and only pot side scrapings soup!

Robert: Yummy yummy! I've heard that the tasty specialties in Keelung include not only snacks, but also **seafood** and traditional **pastries**...

Taike: Right. There are fishing ports and fish markets along the seashore of Keelung, so the seafood here is super fresh. Besides, pastries such as **egg yolk shortcake**, green bean cake, and pineapple cake are also very famous.

Robert: So should we start with the first stand and eat all along the street?

Kitty: There's nothing special about **roadside stands**, Robert. If you want to **sample** different kinds of food, why don't you try the **buffet restaurant**?

Robert: But the dishes at the high-class buffet place you took me to yesterday were **lukewarm**. On the other hand, the vendors here prepare the food right in front of you, and everything is well-cooked. This is actually more **sanitary** and free of **disease-causing germs**...

Taike: Robert, my friend, you're sounding more and more like my brother! There are 200 food stands here, and the market stays open until about 2 or 3 am. Eat to your heart's content, and this **round** is on me!

羅波：我的媽呀，真是人擠人！

邰克：當然囉，這裡可是名聞遐邇的基隆廟口夜市呢！

高貴：唉呀，這些小吃攤又髒又臭，你大概吃不慣啦。

羅波：不會呀，其實這裡的東西看起來很……有趣呢！喂，這圓圓的東東是啥？

邰克：啊，那是我最愛的油粿，隔壁這攤是碳烤三明治，再來是天婦羅、蚵仔煎、旗魚羹、蝦仁肉羹、泡泡冰，啊，還有獨一無二的鼎邊銼！

羅波：好吃好吃！我聽說基隆好吃的特產除了小吃，還有海鮮和糕餅……

邰克：對呀，基隆海岸沿線有許多漁港和漁市，所以海鮮超新鮮的。這裡的蛋黃酥、綠豆糕，和鳳梨酥也都很有名耶！

羅波：那我們要不要從第一攤開始沿路吃呢？

高貴：唉呀，羅波，路邊攤有什麼好吃的，如果你喜歡嘗試多種口味，何不去飯店自助餐？

羅波：可是昨天妳帶我去的高級自助餐的東西都溫溫的。這裡的小吃現煮現吃，而且都熟到冒泡，這樣其實更衛生，而且也沒有會致病的怪細菌……

邰克：羅波，你真是越來越像我兄弟了！好，這夜市共有兩百家小吃，營業到凌晨兩、三點，你愛吃什麼就點什麼，這攤全算我的啦！

單字 ····· 🔊

- ✤ **packed**（adj.）擠滿人的；客滿的
- ✤ **world-renowned**（adj.）世界知名的
- ✤ **filthy**（adj.）污穢的
- ✤ **stinky**（adj.）發惡臭的
- ✤ **round**（adj.）圓形的
- ✤ **seafood**（n.）海鮮
- ✤ **pastry**（n.）糕餅；餡餅
- ✤ **egg yolk shortcake** 蛋黃酥
- ✤ **roadside stand** 路邊攤
- ✤ **sample**（v.）品嚐；體驗
- ✤ **buffet restaurant** 「吃到飽」餐廳
- ✤ **lukewarm**（adj.）微溫的
- ✤ **sanitary**（adj.）衛生的
- ✤ **disease-causing**（adj.）致病的
- ✤ **germ**（n.）細菌
- ✤ **round**（n.）一回合；一局

片語與句型

- ✤ **one and only**：獨一無二的
  - 例 Ladies and gentlemen, let's welcome the one and only Frank Sinatra!（女士先生，讓我們歡迎獨一無二的法蘭克・辛那塔！）

❖ **right in front of...**：就在……(眼)前
　　right (adv.) 不偏不倚地；正好；就
　　例 I can't believe he treated me like that right in front of everyone!（我不敢相信他竟然在所有人面前這樣對我！）

❖ **be free of...**：沒有……；不用
　　例 This meal is free of charge.（這頓飯不用錢。）

❖ **stay open until...**：營業到……
　　例 This restaurant stays open until midnight.（這家餐廳營業到午夜。）

❖ **... to one's heart's content**：盡情地……
　　例 They got together and talked and laughed to their hearts' content.（他們聚在一起聊天、開懷大笑。）

發音小技巧

Keelung's former name is "Jilong"(rooster's cage); it is a bay-type deep-water port.

基隆的舊名是「雞籠」（雞的籠子），是海灣型的深水港。

● 趴趴走好用句

1.　基隆終年水氣豐富、潮濕多雨，因此有「雨港」之稱。

Keelung is misty, humid, and rainy all year round, and is thus nicknamed The Rainy Port.

2.　基隆港三面環山，一面臨海，是台灣三大國際港之一。

Keelung Harbor, one of the three largest international harbors in Taiwan, is surrounded on three sides by mountains and faces the open sea on the fourth side.

3.　旅客在白天可以遊覽基隆港四周的古蹟或島嶼，晚上可以到基隆廟口夜市大快朵頤。

During the day, tourists can visit the historical sites and islets around Keelung Harbor; at night, they can feast on a wide selection of food at the Keelung Miaokou night market.

4.　「海洋大學」的校園介於山和海之間，校門外就是太平洋。

The National Taiwan Ocean University campus is ensconced between the mountains and the sea. Its main gate overlooks the Pacific Ocean.

5.　早期的「八斗子海濱公園」附近是軍事重地，並不開放民眾進入，但現已成為觀光地區。

In the early days, the area near Badouzih Coastal Park was a military site closed to the public. It has now become a tourist destination.

6. 「八斗子海濱公園」有一個寬廣的木製觀景平台，適合觀賞基隆海景和夕陽。

Badouzih Coastal Park has a wide wooden sightseeing balcony where one can enjoy Keelung's ocean view and sunset.

7. 「和平島」位於基隆港的北端，本來是個小島，現在已經和台灣本島連在一起。

Heping Island is located to the north of Keelung Harbor. Originally a small island, it is now connected with the mainland of Taiwan.

8. 「基隆廟口夜市」的攤販都有按順序編號，而且有統一的招牌和管理。

Keelung Miaokou night market stalls are identified by serial numbers. They also have uniform store signs and central management.

9. 「中正公園」是市民們平常休閒的最佳去處。

Zhongzheng Park is the locals' favorite place to relax.

10. 「碧砂漁港」是著名的觀光漁市，有兩棟建築，分別是「漁市場」和「飲食街」。

Bisha Fishing Port is a well-known tourist-oriented fish market. It comprises two buildings: a fish market and a food court.

11.　「碧砂漁港」附近的海產店販賣各式各樣的漁產，包括遠洋、近海、養殖魚類。

The seafood restaurants near Bisha Fishing Port supply all kinds of deep-sea, coastal and cultured marine harvests.

12.　「望幽谷」（又稱「忘憂谷」）是一片翠綠的谷地，夜晚很適合欣賞漁火。

Wangyou Valley(otherwise known as Carefree Valley)is a verdant expanse of countryside, great for admiring the fishing boat lights at night.

大稻埕與迪化街
Dadaocheng and Dihua Street

Robert: Ouch! My feet hurt like hell. I can't walk any longer!

Kitty: You're such a **wimp**! How bad can a **foot massage** be?

Robert: Well, since we've got a full **schedule** today, I thought the massage was going to help me walk **farther**, and it would give me a chance to help the blind **masseurs**, too. But that's all right. I may not be able to walk, but I can always eat.

Taike: We're at Dihua Street! Stores here sell Chinese **herbs**, **preserved** dry food, and **canned** foods, such as mushrooms, dry fish, **tree fungi**, and dry **sliced cuttlefish**. Are you interested in trying them?

Robert: Dry sliced cuttlefish—are they those **chewy** little things? I might **choke** to death.

Kitty: This is one of the oldest towns in Taipei City. The European-style buildings, as well as traditional industries such as stores selling bamboo products, **rice-husking mills**, **incense** shops, and **lantern** stores still make this place very special!

Taike: Wait, I know where to take you—the Xiahai City God Temple.

Robert: Why, does the temple offer **tasty Buddhist**-style **vegetarian** dishes?

Taike: Nope. The temple serves as a **matchmaker** for single males and females who gather to **pray** for a happy marriage.

Robert: Then let's hurry! Maybe three of us would be lucky enough to find our **better halves** at the temple!

Kitty: Well, the foot massage really did work, judging from your speed!

羅波：唉呦喂，我的腳痛死了，根本不能走路了啦！

高貴：你真的很沒用耶！腳底按摩有那麼痛嗎？

羅波：唉，我本來想，今天行程滿檔，做個腳底按摩可能會讓我走更遠，而且還可以幫助那些盲人師傅⋯⋯。不過沒關係，腳不中用嘴巴還中用啦。

邰克：這裡是迪化街耶，店裡賣的都是中藥、乾貨和罐頭，例如香菇、魚乾、木耳、魷魚絲等，你有興趣吃嗎？

羅波：魷魚絲，就是很「潤」的那種東東嗎？我可能會噎死耶。

高貴：不過這裡是台北市最古老的市區之一，加上歐風建築及竹器行、碾米廠、香舖、燈籠店等傳統行業，還是別有一番風味的啦！

邰克：啊，我知道該帶你去哪了─霞海城隍廟。

羅波：怎樣，廟裡有好吃的素食齋菜嗎？

邰克：不是啦，那個廟是專門給未婚男女拜的，祈求好姻緣的啦！

羅波：那我們趕快去拜！運氣好的話，說不定我們三個都會在廟裡遇到自己的另一半！

高貴：從你跑的速度看來，腳底按摩還是有用的嘛！

單字

- **wimp** (**n.**) (口語) 窩囊廢
- **foot massage** 腳底按摩
- **schedule** (**n.**) 時程表；進度表
- **farther** (**adv.**) 更遠地
- **masseur** [mæˋsɝ] / **masseuse** [mæˋsɝz] (**n.**) (男/女) 按摩師
- **herb** (**n.**) 草藥
- **preserved** (**adj.**) 保存的
- **canned** (**adj.**) 裝於罐頭內的
- **tree fungus** [ˋfʌŋɡəs] 木耳 (複數 **fungi**)
- **sliced** (**adj.**) 切片的
- **cuttlefish** (**n.**) 墨魚
- **chewy** (**adj.**) 有嚼勁的；不易嚼碎的
- **choke** (**v.**) 哽住；塞住
- **rice-husking mill** 碾米廠
- **incense** (**n.**) 香
- **lantern** (**n.**) 燈籠
- **tasty** (**adj.**) 美味的；可口的
- **Buddhist** [ˋbudɪst] (**adj.**) 佛教的
- **vegetarian** (**adj.**) 素食的
- **matchmaker** (**n.**) 媒人
- **pray** (**v.**) 祈禱
- **better half** 另一半

片語與句型

❖ **hurt like hell**：（口語）痛得半死
　㉄ My head hurt like hell this morning!（我今天早上頭痛得要死！）

❖ **judge from...**：由……判斷
　judge（v.）判斷
　㉄ He's fairly well off, judging from what he's wearing.（從他的衣著判
　斷，他過得很好。）

發音小技巧 🔊

At the end of each year, Dihua Street holds a "Lunar New Year Bazaar."

迪化街每年在歲末舉辦「年貨大街」活動。

趴趴走好用句

1. 早年的「大稻埕」曾經是重要的通商口岸，也是台北市的精華所在。

   Dadaocheng was once an important trading port, as well as one of the choicest areas in Taipei.

2. 導演侯孝賢的電影「最好的時光」，其中第一段是以「大稻埕」為背景。

   Dadaocheng served as a backdrop to the first scene in director Hou Hsiao-Hsien's movie Three Times.

3. 迪化街不但是大稻埕最早的市街，也是大稻埕商圈的核心。

   Dihua Street is not only the oldest city street in Dadaocheng, it is also situated at the core of the Dadaocheng shopping district.

4. 迪化街從清朝末年以來，就是乾貨、茶葉、中藥和布匹的批發集散地。

   Since the late Qing Dynasty, Dihua Street has been a wholesale commercial center for dry goods, tea leaves, Chinese medicine, and cloth.

5. 「霞海城隍廟」在日據時期常舉辦臺灣北部最大的迎神賽會。

   During the Japanese occupation, the Xiahai City God Temple frequently held the largest god reception parades in northern Taiwan.

6.　「永樂市場」是布匹的批發集中地，部分店家還可以為顧客量身裁製旗
　　袍。

Yongle Market is a cloth wholesale center. Some stores even tailor cheongsams for their clients.

7.　迪化街的中藥行林立，從城隍廟一路延伸到民生西路口。

Chinese medicine shops abound on Dihua Street. The stores stretch from City God Temple on the one end to Minsheng West Road on the other.

8.　迪化街的房屋是台灣典型的「店舖加住宅」建築形式；門面不寬，但屋
　　身向後延伸很長。

Buildings on Dihua Street are typically classic Taiwanese shop-residence combinations. Although not wide, these buildings stretch inwards for quite a distance.

9.　迪化街是台北市目前保存最完整的老街，雖然裡面現在有許多具現代風
　　格的房屋。

Dihua street is currently the best-preserved old street in Taipei City, although it is now adorned with a fair number of modernist buildings.

10.　迪化街的北段有許多西式樓房，使用紅磚建造。

Several Western-style red brick buildings can be found on the northern section of Dihua Street.

11. 在迪化街的中段和南段，有許多仿巴洛克式的房屋，外觀華麗繁複。

Extravagant quasi-Baroque buildings grace the central and southern sections of Dihua Street.

12. 「台北偶戲館」常舉辦布偶戲劇教學課程及掌中戲（即布袋戲）、皮影戲的表演。

The Puppetry Art Center of Taipei frequently hosts such events as puppet drama teaching classes, hand puppet shows and shadow shows.

CD
1-3

九份與金瓜石
Jiufen and Jinguashi

Robert:　Wow, Jiufen is nice and quiet at night, totally different from the **bustling** and noisy **crowds** during the day!

Kitty:　Yeah, this place is always packed on weekends; it's totally **commercialized**. You can only experience its simple lifestyle from the old days during the night, after the tourists are gone.

Taike:　But I think the **winding** old streets are still filled with plain and simple human culture. And the **herbal cakes** and **taro balls** are exceptional!

Robert:　I thought the old Jinguashi **mines** that we visited this afternoon were something special. I actually felt a trace of **sadness** while visiting the Crown Prince **Chalet** and the **ruins** of the Gold Zen Temple.

Taike:　Hey, you've never been **governed** by Japan, so what are you all sad about?

Robert:　The **brochure** of the Gold Ecological Park said that during the period of Japanese **colonization**, all the gold **mined** from here was sent to Japan. Also, it's sad that Jiufen was **prosperous** because of a **gold rush** but then **faded** with the **decline** of gold mining activities.

Kitty:　And the saddest part is that you were totally left out from this **gold-digging** business!

Taike:　Well, perhaps this is why the film A City of Sadness is such a sad movie.

Kitty:　Sadness your ass! With so many tourists visiting here, the shop owners are **thrilled** to rake in all their money. Who in his right mind wouldn't be happy?

羅波：哇，九份的夜晚好謐靜，與白天的嘈雜完全不一樣！

高貴：是呀，這裡週末時總是人擠人，完全的商業化，只有在晚上遊客
離開後，才能感受它純樸的舊日生活風貌。

邱克：不過我覺得曲折的老街還是有質樸的人文風情啦，尤其草仔粿和
芋圓超好吃的！

羅波：我倒覺得今天下午參觀的金瓜石礦坑很特別，看到「日本太子賓
館」及「黃金神社」遺址，讓我有一絲絲的悲情。

邱克：喂，你又沒被日本人統治過，悲情個啥咧？

羅波：這個「黃金博物園區」的簡介有說，日據時代時，被開採出來的
大量黃金全都被輸往日本啊。而且這地方因為採金而繁華，卻也
隨著採金事業的沒落而蕭條，當然很悲情啦！

高貴：最悲情的是你竟然沒有恭逢其盛，趁機淘金賺一筆！

邱克：咦，或許這就是電影「悲情城市」之所以悲情的原因喔。

高貴：悲情個鬼啦！現在遊客這麼多，商家賺得笑呵呵，誰還會悲情
咧？

單字

- **bustling** (**adj.**) 忙亂擾攘
- **crowd** (**n.**) 群眾
- **commercialized** (**adj.**) 商業化的
- **winding** (**adj.**) 彎曲的；迂迴的
- **herbal cake** 草仔粿
- **taro ball** 芋圓
- **mine** (**n.**) 礦
- **sadness** (**n.**) 悲傷
- **chalet** [ʃæˋle] (**n.**) 木造小屋
- **ruins** (**n.**)(複數)遺跡
- **govern** (**v.**) 統治
- **brochure** [broˋʃur] (**n.**) 小冊子；手冊
- **colonization** (**n.**) 殖民
- **mine** (**v.**) 開採(礦物)
- **prosperous** (**adj.**) 繁榮的
- **gold rush** 淘金熱
- **fade** (**v.**) 消弱；消退
- **decline** (**n.**) 衰退；式微
- **gold-digging** (**adj.**) 淘金的
- **thrill** (**v.**) 使感到興奮或激動

片語與句型

❖ **be filled with...**：充滿……

　　例 Her life is filled with love and laughter.（她的生活充滿愛與歡笑。）

❖ **a trace of...**：一絲絲的

　　trace (n.) 一絲絲；少量

　　例 The police were unable to find any trace of drugs in his apartment.（警察在他的公寓找不到一絲絲毒品。）

❖ **be left out**：被排除在外

　　例 I feel left out every time I go out with them.（每次與他們出去，我都感到不受重視。）

❖ **rake in（the money）**：（口語）大量地賺（錢）

　　例 They put up an online shopping website, hoping to rake in money.（他們架設了個購物網站，希望能賺大錢。）

發音小技巧

Keelung Mountain, situated between Jiufen and Jinguashi, is an extinct volcano 588 meters above sea level.

「基隆山」海拔588公尺，位於九份與金瓜石之間，是一個死火山。

趴趴走好用句

1. 九份因為電影「悲情城市」在此拍攝後，成為民眾懷舊的熱門旅遊景點。

   Jiufen became a hotspot for nostalgic tourists after serving as the backdrop to the movie A City of Sadness.

2. 金瓜石在「黃金博物園區」開通後，遊客大量湧入。

   Tourists flocked to Jinguashi in droves when the Gold Ecological Park opened to the public.

3. 「昇平戲院」是台灣最早的戲院，以前是九份居民的休閒中心。

   Shengping Theater is Taiwan's oldest theater, and was once the leisure getaway of local Jiufen residents.

4. 「金瓜石車站」蒐集了不少文史資料及珍貴照片。

   Jinguashih Station preserves a sizable collection of literary and historic information as well as priceless photographs.

5. 「日本太子賓館」是1922年日本人為了迎接皇太子來台灣，仿效日本皇室建築而興建的木造房屋。

   The Crown Prince Chalet, a wooden structure fashioned after the Japanese royal residence, was built by the Japanese in 1922 to welcome the crown prince to Taiwan.

6.　「黃金神社」當時供奉了礦山的守護神，也是日據時代日本人的信仰中心。

During the Japanese occupation, the Gold Zen Temple enshrined the guardian god of the mines and served as a religious center for Japanese.

7.　「黃金神社」年久失修，目前只剩下「鳥居」及神社的水泥柱和祭壇。

After years of neglect, the only remnants left from the original Gold Zen Temple are the torii, the cement posts and the altar of the shrine.

8.　金瓜石的「銅山公園」是第二次世界大戰的英軍戰俘營。

Jinguashih's Tongshan Park was an internment camp for English POWs during World War II.

9.　金瓜石旅遊景點包括「黃金博物園區」、黃金瀑布、本山五坑、台金公司遺址、茶壺山、陰陽海等。

Tourist attractions in Jinguashih include the Gold Ecological Park, the Golden Fall, Benshan Fifth Tunnel, Taiwan Metal Mining Company, Teapot Mountain, and Yingyan Sea.

10.　「黃金博物園區」裡的「黃金博物館」內，有一個兩百公斤的金磚，是世界最大的金磚。

There is a 200-kilogram gold block, the largest in the world, in the Museum of Gold at the Gold Ecological Park.

11. 茶壺山海拔約580公尺，遠看像一只沒有把手的茶壺，故又稱為「無耳茶壺山」。

Teapot Mountain rises 580 meters above sea level and resembles a handleless teapot when seen from a distance; hence its nickname, Earless Teapot Mountain.

12. 結束金瓜石、九份之旅後，可以走濱海公路到「碧砂漁港」一帶吃海鮮。

Round off your trip to Jinguashih and Jiufen by indulging yourself with a seafood feast at the Bisha Fishing Port.

淡水
Danshui

Kitty: Look, here is the "Hongmao **Castle**," the **historical** site in Danshui with historical meaning! It was built by the Spanish in 1629 and later **restored** by the Dutch.

Robert: But it was **originally** called "**Fort** San Domingo..."

Taike: Well, that's because you foreigners are all red-haired. That's why we Taiwanese call it the "Red-Hair **Fortress**."

Robert: Yeah right! But not ALL foreigners are red-haired; like my hair is **blonde**!

Taike: Stop **whining**! It's like we Asians ALL look alike in the eyes of you **pointed**-nosers!

Robert: Well, go ahead and call me a pointed-noser. What's wrong with a pointed nose? Kitty has been talking about getting a **nose job**!

Kitty: Hey, leave me out of this! Well, this castle is more than 300 years old and is listed as a first-**grade*** historical site.

Robert: And what's that red **brick** building across the **lawn** and garden?

Kitty: Oh, it used to be the British **Consulate**. The old Oxford College and former **residence** of Dr. Mackay are also in the neighborhood.

Taike: Later we can go enjoy the cool sea breeze and the **spectacular** sunset, and then off to the Old Street for fish balls, A-ghey, iron eggs, fried shrimp rolls, and fish **crisps**.

Robert: And then to Fishermen's **Wharf** to take the **ferry** ride between Danshui and Bali!

Taikei: In your dreams, pointed-noser!

高貴：看，這就是擁有歷史意義的淡水「紅毛城」！它是在1629年由西班牙人建造，然後由荷蘭人修建的。

羅波：可是它原本的名字明明叫「聖多明哥城」呀……

邱克：那是因為你們外國人都紅頭髮啦，所以我們台灣人管這個城叫紅毛城。

羅波：是喔，又不是所有外國人都是紅頭髮，像我就是金頭髮呀！

邱克：別抱怨了，我們亞洲人在你們阿豆仔眼中還不是通通一個樣！

羅波：哼，儘管叫我阿豆仔，鼻子高有什麼不好？不然高貴幹嘛整天說她要去隆鼻？

高貴：喂，別扯到我啦。這城堡有超過三百年的歷史，而且被列為一級古蹟耶！

羅波：過了草坪和花園的那棟紅磚建築物是啥？

高貴：喔，那曾是英國領事館。這附近還有個舊牛津學堂及馬偕博士以前的住所。

邱克：我們等會兒可以去淡水吹海風，看夕陽，然後去老街吃魚丸、阿給、鐵蛋、炸蝦捲，還有魚酥！

羅波：然後還要去「漁人碼頭」坐往返淡水和八里的渡輪！

邱克：想得美喔，阿豆仔！

*「一級古蹟」又可稱為 Class I historical site

單字

✤ **castle**（**n.**）城堡

✤ **historical**（**adj.**）歷史性的

✤ **restore**（**v.**）修復

✤ **originally**（**adv.**）原本地；最初

✤ **fort**（**n.**）城堡；堡壘

✤ **fortress**（**n.**）要塞

✤ **blonde**（**adj.**）金髮的

✤ **whine**（**v.**）哀鳴；發牢騷

✤ **pointed**（**adj.**）尖的

✤ **nose job**（口語）隆鼻；鼻子塑形手術

✤ **grade**（**n.**）等級

✤ **brick**（**n.**）磚

✤ **lawn**（**n.**）草地

✤ **consulate**（**n.**）領事館

✤ **residence**（**n.**）住宅

✤ **spectacular**（**adj.**）壯觀的

✤ **crisp**（**n.**）酥脆的東西；油炸薄片

✤ **wharf**（**n.**）碼頭

✤ **ferry**（**n.**）渡船

片語與句型

* **in the eye(s) of...**：在……眼中
  例 Beauty is in the eye of the beholder.（情人眼裡出西施。）
* **go ahead...**：儘管……
  例 Go ahead and do it—I don't care!（儘管去做吧—我才不在乎呢！）
* **off to...**：到……去
  例 They rushed to the shop and then off to the nearby pub.（他們急急忙忙去商店，然後到附近的酒吧）。

發音小技巧 🔊

Danshui has always been a commercially developed, culturally rich area where Western shops and ancient relics abound.

淡水自古以來便是個商業發達、文化活動興盛的地區，有許多洋行和古蹟。

● 趴趴走好用句

1. 淡水背倚大屯山，面對台灣海峽，是台灣島最早開發的地區之一。

   Facing the Taiwan Strait and backed by Datun Mountain, Danshui was one of the first areas in Taiwan to be developed.

2. 淡水的中正路是最熱鬧的街，有海鮮餐廳、小吃、老街、古董店、藝品店等。

   Zhongzheng Road is the busiest street in Danshui. Here you can find everything from fresh seafood and snacks to old streets, antique shops and handicraft stores.

3. 淡水的著名小吃包括淡水魚丸、魚酥、炸蝦捲、鐵蛋、阿給等。

   Famous Danshui snacks include Danshui fish balls, fish crisps, fried shrimp rolls, iron eggs and A-ghey.

4. 「阿給」是在油炸豆腐中塞入冬粉，糊上魚漿後，再蒸熟。

   A-ghey is made by stuffing deep-fried tofu with green bean noodles, then covering the combination with a coat of fish sauce and steaming it.

5. 淡水有渡輪來往對岸的八里之間，是當地人往來兩地的交通工具。

   Ferries travel across the river to Bali and back again, serving as transportation for local commuters.

6.　「關渡大橋」外觀鮮紅，橋上設有觀景步道，是淡水鎮明顯的地標。

Guandu Bridge, the most striking landmark in Danshui Township, is a bright red structure equipped with a sightseeing walkway.

7.　淡水的「祖師廟」與萬華的祖師廟供奉同一尊黑面祖師爺。

The Zushi Temple in Danshui and its namesake in Wanhua venerate the same black-faced Zushi Master.

8.　「淡江大學」為中國宮殿式的建築，要進入校園，必須爬上132階的「克難坡」。

The architecture of Tamkang University is modeled after a Chinese palace. One has to climb all 132 steps of the Overcome Difficulty Slope to reach the campus.

9.　加拿大出生的馬偕牧師在西元1872年來臺，在淡水傳教、定居。

Canadian-born minister George Leslie Mackay, who came to Taiwan as a missionary in 1872, made Danshui his home.

10.　馬偕牧師是第一個在台灣北部傳教的長老教會牧師。

Dr. Mackay was the first Presbyterian minister to preach in northern Taiwan.

11.　「漁人碼頭」有許多漁船及遊輪，因此常成為電視廣告拍攝的場景。

With its many fishing boats and ferries, Fisherman's Wharf has become a popular filming location for TV ads.

12.　「漁人碼頭」位於淡水河出海口的右岸，最著名的景點是百公尺長的木棧步道。

Fishermen's Wharf, best known for its hundred-meter-long boardwalk, is located to the right of the mouth of the Danshui River.

烏來
Wulai

Robert: The Atayal people's traditional **tribal** dances and ceremonies were very interesting!

Kitty: Yeah, it sure was interesting. It actually got more interesting after you joined them with your break dancing **moves**!

Robert: Really, you think so? Great! Is the black face **tattoo** part of the Atayal culture?

Kitty: Yes, it is. It's a traditional **rite**, and it is said that having a face tattoo can help bless your **descendants**.

Taike: Wulai is my favorite! **Streams**, **waterfalls**, hot **springs**, cherry blossoms, **maple** leaves, **railcars**, **aborigine** singing and dancing...

Robert: I agree. These fried river fish and shrimp are wonderful, as is this bamboo tube rice. And the pork-on-the-**slate** is unique!

Taike: Bro, let's toast each other with this **millet** wine. Bottoms up!

Robert: But this millet wine smells pretty strong...

Taike: You beer-drinking **chicken**! Then how about this millet mochi? It's Wulai's **specialty**!

Robert: But I don't eat **sticky** and chewy stuff for fear that I'll choke.

Kitty: Don't push him. Anyway, it wouldn't be good to enjoy the hot springs with a full stomach. The water here comes in two types, **carbonate** and **sodium bicarbonate**, and both are believed to be good for treating **gastric ailments** and **moisturizing** the skin. It's exactly what I need!

Robert: And can we try the cable car?

Taike: But I'm afraid of heights...

Robert: So, who's the chicken now?

羅波：剛剛那段泰雅族的傳統部落舞蹈和儀式真有趣！

高貴：是很有趣啊，尤其是你加入他們大跳霹靂舞之後，就更有趣了。

羅波：真的嗎？太棒了！不過黥面是泰雅族的傳統嗎？

高貴：沒錯，那是一種傳統儀式，據說可以保佑子孫。

邱客：我最喜歡烏來了。小溪、瀑布、溫泉、櫻花、楓葉、觀光台車、山地歌舞……

羅波：是啊，這炸溪魚溪蝦和竹筒飯真不賴，石板豬肉也很特殊！

邱克：我們兩兄弟乾一杯小米酒吧！乾杯！

羅波：不過這酒聞起來很烈耶……

邱克：只敢喝啤酒的膽小鬼！那你嚐嚐這小米麻糬好了，這可是烏來的名產喔！

羅波：可是我不吃黏黏有嚼勁的東西耶，怕會噎著。

高貴：算了，你別逼他。吃太多東西等會兒泡溫泉也不舒服。這裡的溫泉有碳酸泉和碳酸氫鈉泉兩種，可以治胃病，也可以滋潤皮膚呢！正合我的需要！

羅波：那我們可不可以坐高空纜車？

邱克：但我有懼高症耶！

羅波：喂，現在誰是膽小鬼啊？

單字

- **tribal**（adj.）部族的；部落的
- **move**（n.）招式；動作
- **tattoo**（n.）刺青
- **rite**（n.）儀式
- **descendant**（n.）子孫
- **stream**（n.）小河；溪流
- **waterfall**（n.）瀑布
- **spring**（n.）泉水
- **maple**（n.）楓樹
- **railcar**（n.）台車（或稱 trolley train）
- **aborigine** [ˌæbəˈrɪdʒəni]（n.）原住民
- **slate**（n.）石板
- **millet**（n.）小米；稷
- **chicken**（n.）(俚語)膽小鬼
- **specialty**（n.）招牌商品
- **sticky**（adj.）黏的
- **carbonate**（n.）碳酸鹽
- **sodium bicarbonate** 碳酸氫鈉
- **gastric**（adj.）胃的
- **ailment**（n.）(輕微的)疾病
- **moisturize**（v.）使有濕度；滋潤

片語與句型

* **toast... with...**：以……乾杯；敬(酒)
  * 例 She toasted everyone with a cranberry juice.(她以小紅莓汁與每個人乾杯。)

* **for fear that...**：害怕會……
  * 例 The little boy sleeps with his parents for fear that the ghost will come to him at night.(這小男孩和父母一起睡，因為怕鬼會在晚上找他。)

* **push someone**：逼迫某人
  * push (v.) 強迫；催逼
  * 例 He pushed me into this chaos.(他將我逼進這團混亂之中。)

發音小技巧

Wulai Township is situated to the southeast of Taipei City, at an average of 900 meters above sea level.

烏來鄉位於台北市的東南方，平均海拔900公尺。

● 趴趴走好用句

1.　烏來在數百年前是泰雅族山胞狩獵的場所。

Wulai once served as a hunting ground of the Atayal tribe several hundred years ago.

2.　烏來是泰雅族語「冒煙的熱水」之意。

In the Atayal language, the word Wulai means "steam gushing from hot springs."

3.　烏來四面環山，年平均溫度約攝氏21度。

Wulai is surrounded by mountains on all four sides and enjoys an average temperature of 21 degrees Celsius.

4.　烏來以台車、溫泉、瀑布、雲仙樂園，以及原住民文化聞名。

Wulai is known for railcars, hot springs, waterfalls, Yun Hsien Holiday Resort, and aboriginal culture.

5.　烏來的「觀光台車」原本是用來運輸木材的，現在已成為旅客登山遊覽的交通工具。

Wulai's "tourist railcars" were originally used to transport timber but have now become a way for tourists to sightsee in the mountains.

6. 烏來一年四季都吸引人——春季賞櫻、夏季戲水、秋季賞楓、冬季泡湯。

Wulai is attractive all year round—you can see the cherry blossoms in the spring, play in the water in the summer, see the maple leaves in the fall, and immerse yourself in the hot springs in the winter.

7. 「烏來溫泉」溫度很高，約攝氏80度左右，水質清澈透明，可泡可飲。

The temperature of the Wulai hot springs, at approximately 80 degrees Celsius, is very high. The hot spring waters are clear and transparent, and can be both drunk and bathed in.

8. 烏來著名的小吃有炸溪蝦、山蘇、山苦瓜、山藥、石板豬肉、竹筒飯，以及其他原住民特有美食。

Famous Wulai delicacies include such aboriginal specialties as fried river shrimp, bird's nest fern, wild bitter gourd, yam, pork-on-the-slate, and bamboo tube rice.

9. 「竹筒飯」是將糯米裝入竹筒內，用香蕉葉封口，然後火烤或蒸煮。

Bamboo tube rice is made by grilling or steaming a bamboo shoot filled with glutinous rice and sealed with banana leaves.

10. 「雲仙樂園」位於新店溪上游，有山谷、溪流、湖泊，還有各種動物、植物。

Yun Hsien Holiday Resort, located upstream along the Xindian River, has valleys, streams, and lakes as well as a variety of plants and animals.

11.　烏來的「高空纜車」全長共382公尺，高、低相差165公尺，可乘載91人。

Wulai's cable railway is 382 meters long, rises 165 meters and can transport 91 passengers at a time.

12.　「松蘿湖」是高山湖泊，由於終年都在雲霧繚繞中，因此又被稱為「夢幻湖」。

Songluo Lake is an alpine lake perennially surrounded by clouds and mist, and is thus also known as Menghuan（Fantasy）Lake.

06

CD
1-6

台北101與信義商圈
Taipei 101 and the Xinyi Business District

Robert: Wow, this is the world's tallest building, Taipei 101, the new **landmark** in Taiwan!

Kitty: Yeah, isn't it **fascinating**? This **tower** includes an office area, an **observatory**, and a six-floor retail mall with shops, restaurants, a bookstore, and other **attractions**.

Robert: It's **awfully** high. What if an **earthquake** hits?

Kitty: Don't worry. The tower is designed to **endure** earthquakes above seven on the Richter scale, or even super typhoons! You can say that this building is the most **technologically** advanced **skyscraper constructed** to date!

Taike: Yeah, and I heard that the **exterior** of the building **resembles** a bamboo **stalk** and is **studded** with copper **ingots**, the **currency** used in ancient China by **royalty**. Look, there are eight of them, one every eighth floor.

Robert: Does the number "eight" **symbolize** good fortune in Chinese?

Taike: You're pretty smart! Pretty much this entire building is **fraught** with **symbolism** of financial success!

Robert: I know, you see, Kitty can't wait to spend her money! But this place is like every other American mall—there's nothing special about it!

Kitty: Well, I'll sure shop till I drop. Meanwhile, you guys can **stroll** around the Xinyi shopping area nearby. You can visit Warner Village **Cinemas**, the Shin Kong Mitsukoshi department stores, the Taipei World Trade Center and so on. This area is definitely Taipei's newest **burgeoning** business district!

羅波：哇，這就是世界最高樓、台灣新地標「台北101」！

高貴：是啊，很棒吧？這大樓包含了辦公區、觀景台，以及六層樓的購物商場，裡面有商店、餐廳、書店，以及其他好玩的東西。

羅波：可是它這麼高，地震來了怎麼辦？

高貴：別擔心，這高樓的設計可以抵擋芮氏七級以上的地震，甚至超級大颱風！這大樓可以說是利用目前最先進的科技所打造的！

邱克：對呀，聽說它的外觀一節一節的，形狀像竹子，而且還鑲有銅鑄錢，這是古代中國皇室所用的貨幣。你看，總共有八個銅鑄錢，每八層有一個。

羅波：中文的「八」代表「發發發」啊？

邱克：算你聰明，總而言之，這整棟樓就象徵著發大財啦！

羅波：是啊，高貴已經等不及去花錢了！不過這裡面就像美國所有的購物商場一樣，沒什麼特別的！

高貴：嗯，我要血拼到虛脫。你們兩個可以去這附近的信義區逛逛，像是華納威秀影城、新光三越、世貿中心等等。這裡可是台北最新、發展最快的商業區呢！

單字 ·····

🔊

- ✤ **landmark**（**n.**）地標
- ✤ **fascinating**（**adj.**）迷人的；令人神魂顛倒的
- ✤ **tower**（**n.**）高樓；塔
- ✤ **observatory**（**n.**）觀測站；瞭望台
- ✤ **attraction**（**n.**）吸引人的事物
- ✤ **awfully**（**adv.**）（口語）非常地；很
- ✤ **earthquake**（**n.**）地震
- ✤ **endure**（**v.**）忍受
- ✤ **technologically**（**adv.**）科技上地
- ✤ **skyscraper**（**n.**）高樓大廈
- ✤ **construct**（**v.**）建造
- ✤ **exterior**（**n.**）外部的
- ✤ **resemble**（**v.**）和⋯⋯相似
- ✤ **stalk**（**n.**）莖；幹
- ✤ **stud**（**v.**）釘以飾釘
- ✤ **ingot** [ˋɪŋgət]（**n.**）鑄錢
- ✤ **currency**（**n.**）貨幣
- ✤ **royalty**（**n.**）皇族；王室
- ✤ **symbolize**（**v.**）象徵；代表
- ✤ **fraught**（**adj.**）滿載的
- ✤ **symbolism**（**n.**）象徵；記號
- ✤ **stroll**（**v.**）閒逛；散步

❖ **cinema**（**n.**）電影院
❖ **burgeoning**（**adj.**）急速發展的

片語與句型

❖ **What if...**：如果……怎麼辦？
　⑩ What if he decided to quit? What should we do then?（他如果決定放棄怎麼辦？我們屆時該如何做？）
❖ **to date**：到目前為止
　⑩ It is said that the San Diego International Airport is the largest airport to date.（據說聖地牙哥國際機場是目前最大的機場。）
❖ **shops till someone drops**：逛到倒地為止
　drop（v.）（因精疲力盡）倒下
　⑩ It's the annual sale again—let's shop till we drop!（又是一年一度的週年慶了—我們逛到掛吧！）

發音小技巧 🔊

Taipei 101 is 508 meters high, with 101 floors above ground and five underground.

「台北101」高508公尺，地上有101層、地下有五層。

● 趴趴走好用句

1. 「信義計畫區」是新興的商業區，也是目前台北最繁華、時髦的商圈。

    The Xinyi planned district is a burgeoning business center. It is also the busiest, most fashionable shopping district in Taipei at the moment.

2. 「信義計畫區」包括台北101、市政府、世貿中心、國際會議中心、紐約紐約購物中心、新光三越百貨、新舞台、君悅飯店等。

    The Xinyi planned district includes Taipei 101, the Taipei City Hall, the Taipei World Trade Center, the Taipei International Convention Center, New York New York, the Shin Kong Mitsukoshi department stores, Novel Hall, and the Grand Hyatt Taipei.

3. Neo19 和「誠品書店」旗艦店皆位於「信義計畫區」，是台北時尚男女的聚會地點。

    Neo19 and the flagship store of Eslite Bookstore, popular hangouts for Taipei's fashionable crowd, are situated in the Xinyi planned district.

4. 「台北世貿中心」有商品展覽、海外貿易、會議服務及旅館餐飲等四大功能。

    The four main functions of the Taipei World Trade Center are product exhibitions, overseas trading, conferencing services, and hotel accommodations and dining.

5. 「台北金融大樓」，即「台北101」，緊鄰台北市政府。

    Taipei 101, otherwise known as the Taipei Financial Center, is located in the vicinity of the Taipei City Government.

6.　　「台北101」是目前世界上最高的大樓，造價高達五百八十億元台幣。

Taipei 101, the tallest building in the world to date, cost NT$58 billion to build.

7.　　「台北101」由國際知名的建築師李祖原負責設計與監造。

The world-renowned architect C.Y. Lee was in charge of the design and construction of Taipei 101.

8.　　「台北101」的外形呈竹節型，向上延伸，象徵步步高昇。

Taipei 101 was designed to resemble an unfolding bamboo shoot, signifying continual progress.

9.　　「台北101」擁有世界最快的電梯，每分鐘以高達1,000公尺的速度上升。

Taipei 101 is equipped with the world's fastest elevator, which travels upward at a top speed of 1,000 meters per minute.

10.　　「台北101」的B1至四樓是購物中心；六樓至八十四樓為辦公大樓。

A shopping mall occupies the space from the first underground floor to the fourth floor; the sixth to 84th floors are offices.

11.　「國父紀念館」是座仿中國宮殿式的建築。

The National Sun Yat-sen Memorial Hall is a piece of Chinese palace-style architecture.

12.　「國父紀念館」外的大廣場很適合戶外運動、休閒。

The expansive square outside the National Sun Yat-sen Memorial Hall is an ideal place for outdoor sports and leisure.

CD
1-7

忠烈祠與中正紀念堂
The Martyrs Shrine and
Chiang Kai-shek Memorial Hall

Robert: Wow, after watching the **guard**-changing **ceremony** at the Martyrs **Shrine**, I definitely feel more **manly**!

Kitty: Yeah, right. After seeing you **secretly** touching the guard, I definitely feel more like a **criminal**.

Robert: But those guards were so **rigidly** trained! They stood like **expressionless statues** and remained unmoved even after I **poked** them.

Taike: Robert, since you're so **disrespectful** to Taiwanese soldiers, I'll have to send you to Chiang Kai-shek Temple to **kowtow** to Chiang's **bronze** statue!

Robert: You mean the Chiang Kai-shek **Memorial** Hall? I've been dying to go there! I've heard that its **architecture** was **inspired** by Tientan in Beijing, and the four sides of the structure are similar to those of the **pyramids** in Egypt. Best of all, the material is white **marble**...

Kitty: Yes, the entire building uses the colors of red, white, and blue to **represent** the Taiwanese flag and the spirit of "freedom, **equality**, and **brotherhood**."

Robert: So **touching**! I have tears in my eyes...

Kitty: We can also visit the National Theater and the National Concert Hall while we're there. Also, there are always various activities taking place in the **plaza**, like **marching band** shows, **cheerleading** performances and things like that.

Taike: Cheerleaders? Let's go right now!

Kitty: Wait, let's go to the nearby Grand Hotel and enjoy **high tea** first!

羅波：哇，看了忠烈祠的衛兵交接儀式，我覺得自己更像男人了！

高貴：是呀，你剛剛偷摸衛兵之後，我覺得更像犯人了。

羅波：可是他們真的經過嚴格訓練耶，像個面無表情的雕像，連我戳他們都紋風不動。

邰克：羅波，你對台灣軍人這麼不敬，我要罰你去中正廟向蔣公銅像敬禮！

羅波：你是說「中正紀念堂」嗎？我好想去喔，聽說那建築是從北京天壇來的靈感，而且四面的建築和埃及的金字塔很像。最棒的是建築材料是白大理石……

高貴：是呀，那整個的建築是紅、白、藍，代表台灣的國旗及「自由、平等、博愛」的精神。

羅波：真感人，我都快哭了！

高貴：我們可以順便去國家戲劇院和國家音樂廳走走，而且廣場常常有人舉行不同的活動，像是學校樂隊表演、啦啦隊表演等等。

邰克：有啦啦隊？那我們現在就去！

高貴：等一等，我們先去旁邊的圓山飯店喝英式下午茶啦！

單字

- ✤ **guard**（**n.**）守衛
- ✤ **ceremony**（**n.**）儀式；典禮
- ✤ **shrine**（**n.**）祠堂
- ✤ **manly**（**adj.**）有男子氣概的
- ✤ **secretly**（**adv.**）秘密地
- ✤ **criminal**（**n.**）罪犯
- ✤ **rigidly**（**adv.**）嚴格地
- ✤ **expressionless**（**adj.**）面無表情的
- ✤ **statue**（**n.**）雕像
- ✤ **poke**（**v.**）戳；刺
- ✤ **disrespectful**（**adj.**）無禮的；不敬的
- ✤ **kowtow**（**v.**）磕頭
- ✤ **bronze**（**n.**）青銅
- ✤ **memorial**（**adj.**）紀念的；追悼的
- ✤ **architecture**（**n.**）建築式樣；結構
- ✤ **inspire**（**v.**）給予靈感
- ✤ **pyramid** [ˈpɪrəmɪd]（**n.**）金字塔
- ✤ **marble**（**n.**）大理石
- ✤ **represent**（**v.** ）表現；呈現
- ✤ **equality**（**n.**）平等
- ✤ **brotherhood**（**n.**）兄弟情誼
- ✤ **touching**（**adj.**）動人的

✤ **plaza**（**n.**）廣場

✤ **marching band** 樂隊

✤ **cheerleading**（**adj.**）啦啦隊的

✤ **high tea**（英式）下午茶

片語與句型

✤ **be dying to...**：超想要……

　㉄ John loves Mary very much and is dying to meet her parents.（John 很愛 Mary，十分希望能見見她父母。）

✤ **has tears in one's eyes**：十分感動

　㉄ She had tears in her eyes when watching the movie.（看那電影時，她眼睛泛淚光，十分感動。）

✤ **take place**：發生；舉行

　㉄ The carnival took place last weekend.（嘉年華會上週末舉行。）

發音小技巧 🔊

People frequently come together at the Chiang Kai-shek Memorial Hall square to exercise.
/ks/

「中正紀念堂」的廣場常成為群眾運動的集會地點。

● 趴趴走好用句

1. 「中正紀念堂」的正牌樓「大中至正門」是台北市區內最大的牌樓。

   Dazhong Zhizheng Gate, the main entrance into Chiang Kai-shek Memorial Hall, is the largest entrance archway in all of Taipei City.

2. 「中正紀念堂」的下層大廳設有文物展示室、中正藝廊等。

   You can find exhibition rooms and the Zhongzheng Art Gallery on the lower level of the main hall.

3. 「國家戲劇院」及「國家音樂廳」皆為金黃色調的中國傳統建築。

   Both the National Theater and the National Concert Hall are golden-hued traditional Chinese buildings.

4. 「國家戲劇院」及「國家音樂廳」時常舉辦藝文表演活動。

   The National Theater and the National Concert Hall frequently host artistic and cultural events.

5. 「中正紀念堂」佔地25萬平方公尺，有廣場、迴廊、庭院、池塘等景觀。

   The Chiang Kai-shek Memorial Hall covers 250,000 square meters and features such scenic spots as squares, galleries, courtyards, and ponds.

6.　「中正紀念堂」內部有許多庭園造景，池塘內飼養錦鯉，是十分著名的景
　　點。

Garden landscaping is evident throughout the Chiang Kai-shek
Memorial Hall. The pond, inhabited by variegated carp, is an
extremely well known scenic attraction.

7.　「忠烈祠」建於西元1969年，是為了紀念抗日犧牲的軍人所建的。

The Martyrs Shrine was constructed in 1969 to commemorate the
soldiers who sacrificed their lives for the country during the Sino-
Japanese War.

8.　「忠烈祠」外觀仿北京故宮的「太和殿」，十分雄偉壯麗。

The Martyrs Shrine, a tremendously grand and elegant structure, was
built to resemble the Hall of Supreme Harmony in Beijing's Palace
Museum.

9.　「忠烈祠」每小時的衛兵交接儀式，常吸引大批遊客參觀拍照。

The hourly guard-changing ceremony at the Martyrs Shrine often
attracts scores of picture-taking tourists.

10.　「士林官邸」早期是先總統蔣公的住所。

The Shilin Presidential Residence was the home of former President
Chiang in its early days.

11.　「圓山飯店」外觀是中國是宮殿建築，是世界十大旅館之一。

The Grand Hotel, an example of Chinese palace-style architecture, is among the world's ten biggest hotels.

12.　「台北故事館」的外觀有如西洋童話故事裡的糖果屋。

The Taipei Story House resembles in appearance the candy houses found in Western fairy tales.

08

CD
1-8

故宮與士林夜市
The National Palace Museum and Shilin Night Market

Robert: Wow, that National **Palace** Museum is really something!

Kitty: Yeah, the Museum **houses** the world's greatest and most **priceless treasures** of Chinese art. Many Taiwanese don't even know it was listed as one of the world's five greatest museums!

Robert: True. This **pamphlet** says that its collection of **artifacts** includes almost 700,000 pieces whose age range covers almost the entire five-thousand-year Chinese history... After seeing all these, I do feel more "cultured" now!

Kitty: Yep. After seeing all this **jadeware**, **bronzeware**, **pottery** and **porcelain** along with all the **sculpture**, **calligraphy**, paintings, **embroidery**, etc, it feels pretty romantic to see the traditional, elegant Chinese garden here at Chi-Shan Garden!

Taike: Seeing this huge, **plump variegated carp** is making my stomach **rumble**. Robert, which kind would you like— **braised** or steamed?

Kitty: You're such a Taike! You only care about gobbling up anything that can either fly, **crawl**, or swim.

Robert: But I'm getting hungry as well. Anything good to eat around here?

Taike: Let's go to the world-renowned Shilin Night Market! It's a favorite among Taiwanese students. We can have panfried **dumplings**, little-cake-in-big-cake, Shilin **sausages**, Shandong duck heads, frogs-laying-eggs, **wok**-fried **squid**, and tomatoes in **ginger** juice. They're all extremely delicious!

羅波：哇，故宮真了不起！

高貴：是呀，故宮收藏了全世界最多、最無價的中華藝術寶藏；很多台
　　　灣人甚至不知道它名列世界五大博物館之一呢！

羅波：對啊，這簡介上說故宮珍藏了歷代古物將近七十萬件，年代橫跨
　　　五千年的中國歷史……。看完後讓我覺得自己似乎更有文化了！

高貴：是啊，看完那麼多玉器、銅器、陶瓷、雕刻、字畫、刺繡……，
　　　現在來「至善園」看看這些高雅的中國傳統庭園也挺浪漫的！

邱克：尤其是看到這麼多又肥又大的錦鯉，害我肚子都開始咕咕叫了！
　　　羅波，你說紅燒好還是清蒸好？

高貴：你真的很台耶，每次看到天上飛的、地上爬的、水裡游的，就只
　　　想到吃的。

羅波：不過我肚子真的也餓了。這附近有啥好吃的？

邱克：啊，去「士林夜市」，世界知名的喔，而且是台灣學生的最愛
　　　耶！那裡的水煎包、大餅包小餅、士林大香腸、山東鴨頭、青蛙
　　　下蛋、生炒花枝、蕃茄沾薑汁都超正點的！

單字 ‥‥‥

- **palace**（n.）宮殿
- **house**（v.）收藏；儲存
- **priceless**（adj.）非常貴重的；無價的
- **treasure**（n.）寶藏
- **pamphlet**（n.）小冊子
- **artifact**（n.）古物
- **jadeware / jade ware**（n.）玉器
- **bronzeware / bronze ware**（n.）銅器
- **pottery**（n.）陶器
- **porcelain** [ˋpɔrslɪn]（n.）瓷器
- **sculpture**（n.）雕像
- **calligraphy** [kəˋlɪɡrəfɪ]（n.）書法
- **embroidery**（n.）刺繡藝品
- **plump**（adj.）豐腴的
- **variegated**（adj.）五顏六色的
- **carp**（n.）鯉魚
- **rumble**（v.）（肚子）咕嚕咕嚕響
- **braise**（v.）燉煮
- **crawl**（v.）爬行
- **dumpling**（n.）水餃狀食物
- **sausage**（n.）香腸；臘腸
- **wok**（n.）（中國式）炒鍋

✤ **squid**（n.）花枝；魷魚
✤ **ginger**（n.）薑

片語與句型

✤ **be such a...**：真是個……
　⑩ Andre is such a jerk—he is dating three women at the same time.（Andre 真是混蛋—他腳踏三條船。）
✤ **gobble up**：狼吞虎嚥
　gobble（v.）狼吞虎嚥
　⑩ She gobbled up the food like she hadn't eaten in weeks.（她狼吞虎嚥，好像好幾星期沒吃東西一樣。）

發音小技巧 🔊

The Shilin Night Market offers an expansive selection
of food and products that are both attractive and affordable.
　　　　　　　　　　　　　　　　/ks/

士林夜市販賣的物品種類眾多，各式小吃應有盡有，而且物美價廉。

● 趴趴走好用句

1. 士林夜市以陽明戲院為中心，範圍包括文林路、大東路與大南路。

The Shilin Night Market centers on Yangming Theater and encompasses Wenlin, Dadong, and Danan Roads.

2. 士林夜市裡有大塊炸雞排的創始店，以及香味撲鼻的水煎包、蔥油餅。

Shilin Night Market is home to the pioneer plus-size chicken cutlets as well as to the very fragrant pan-fried dumplings and fried spring onion pancakes.

3. 士林夜市的「藥燉排骨」湯鮮肉美，一年四季都可以大快朵頤。

The scrumptious broth and meat of spareribs stewed in herbal soup found in the Shilin Night Market can be enjoyed all throughout the year.

4. 士林夜市賣的衣服、鞋子、飾品配件都是當前最流行的款式。

The clothes, shoes, and accessories sold in Shilin Night Market are the latest trends in the market.

5. 「國立故宮博物院」位於外雙溪，是一座中國宮殿式的建築。

The National Palace Museum, located in Waishuangxi, is a Chinese-style palace architecture.

6.　台灣的故宮與美國的大都會博物館、英國的大英博物館、法國的羅浮宮、俄羅斯的隱士盧博物館並列世界五大博物館。

The National Palace Museum in Taiwan has been named as one of the five greatest museums in the world, the others being the Metropolitan Museum of Art in the US, the British Museum in the UK, the Louvre in France, and the Hermitage in Russia.

7.　故宮的收藏品中，大多數來自昔日中國的皇室。

Most of the items in the National Palace Museum came from Chinese imperial collections.

8.　故宮從民國九十年起，展覽館局部開放民眾攝影，不過不可使用閃光燈。

Since 2001, photography has been allowed in certain sections of the National Palace Museum exhibition halls, although using a flash is still not permitted.

9.　故宮院內提供包括中、英、法、德、日、西、韓等七國語言的專業導覽。

The National Palace Museum provides professional guides in seven languages, namely Chinese, English, French, German, Japanese, Spanish, and Korean.

10.　「國立臺灣科學教育館」可以讓親子一起動手探索科學現象。

The National Taiwan Science Education Center gives families a chance to discover scientific phenomena hands-on.

11.　「至善園」融合中國傳統的庭園建築理念，展現出樸實悠閒的情趣。

Chi-Shan Garden, infused with traditional Chinese garden architectural concepts, exudes a simple and leisurely atmosphere.

12.　「張大千先生紀念館」是張大千生前的住所。

The Chang Dai-chien Memorial Residence was Chang Dai-chien's home during his lifetime.

龍山寺與華西街
Longshan Temple and Huaxi Street

Robert: Wow, so many people are burning **incense** and **candles** here!

Kitty: Yeah. Longshan Temple was built during the Qing **Dynasty** in the fifth year of the Qianlong emperor, and it is for **worshipping** Avalokitesvara* and other **divine** spirits.

Robert: Hmm... The doors, **beams**, and **pillars** are so beautifully **decorated**. Look, there are also pairs of bronze dragon pillars in the front and middle halls! And the wood **sculptures**—so **exquisite**!

Taike: Yeah, on the first and fifteenth days of each month in the **lunar** calendar, visitors come here for worship ceremonies. There are also temple activities during various traditional **festivals**.

Kitty: Rumor has it that during World War II, the main hall of this temple was **bombed**, **ruining** the entire building, and yet the Buddha statue **remained untouched**. Therefore the temple is said to be **unbelievably efficacious**!

Robert: Then I'll ask for Buddha's **blessing** to protect us from having a motorcycle **accident**!

Kitty: Knock on wood... jinx!

Taike: Just let him worship. He's gonna have snake blood and snake meat soon, and who knows, he might not make it to tomorrow!

Robert: What? Are you talking about the well-known "Snake **Alley**?"

Taike: It's Huaxi Street! Hey, don't you want to see the snake shops that **demonstrate** snake **processing** and snake fights? Besides, with so many herb shops and Buddhist **article** stores around here to protect you, your chance of dying is very slim!

羅波：哇，這裡的香火鼎盛呢！

高貴：是啊，「龍山寺」建於清朝乾隆五年，拜的是觀音以及其他的神明。

羅波：嗯，這門、樑、柱子都裝飾得好漂亮。喂，前殿和中殿還有銅鑄的龍柱耶。還有這木雕……，真是美呆了！

邱克：是啊，每月的初一、十五，廟裡都有拜拜的儀式，而且傳統節慶時都會舉辦廟會活動。

高貴：聽說第二次世界大戰的時候，這裡的正殿曾被砲火擊中，殿堂全毀了，可是神像卻絲毫無損，所以這裡的神明超靈的！

羅波：那我趕快來拜一拜，請神明保佑我們這陣子騎機車不會出車禍！

高貴：呸呸呸，烏鴉嘴！

邱克：讓他拜一拜也好啦，因為等會兒他要吃蛇血蛇肉，說不定撐不到明天，哈哈！

羅波：什麼？你說的是那有名的「蛇街」嗎？

邱克：是「華西街」啦！喂，難道你不想看殺蛇和蛇打架嗎？再說，這附近還有許多草藥店和佛具店，這麼多東西保護你，你死不了啦！

*「觀音」又稱 Quan Yin

單字 🔊

* **incense**（n.）香
* **candle**（n.）蠟燭
* **dynasty**（n.）朝代
* **worship**（v.）崇敬；參拜
* **divine** [də`vaɪn]（adj.）神的；神聖的
* **beam**（n.）橫樑
* **pillar**（n.）柱子
* **decorate**（v.）裝飾
* **sculpture**（n.）雕刻；雕刻品
* **exquisite**（adj.）絕妙的
* **lunar**（adj.）陰曆的
* **festival**（n.）慶宴
* **bomb**（v.）轟炸
* **ruin**（v.）毀壞
* **remain**（v.）保持（某種狀態）
* **untouched**（adj.）原原本本的；未被碰觸的
* **unbelievably**（adv.）令人難以置信地
* **efficacious** [ɛfə`keʃəs]（adj.）靈驗的；有效的
* **blessing**（n.）祝福；祝福的話
* **accident**（n.）（汽車）事故
* **alley**（n.）小巷
* **demonstrate**（v.）示範；表演

* **processing**（n.）處理
* **article**（n.）貨物；商品

片語與句型

❖ **protect someone from...**：保護某人不受⋯⋯
　⑳ She tries protect her children from getting hurt by her husband.（她試著保護小孩不受她丈夫的傷害。）

❖ **knock on wood**：確保好運、趕掉壞運（的說法）
　⑳ The rain looks like holding off, knock on wood.（雨看起來不會下，希望如此啦！）

❖ **make it**：成功；完成某事（此處 **make it to tomorrow** 意為「活到明天」）
　⑳ The test looks very difficult, and I am not sure if I will make it this time.（這考試看起來很難，我不知道這次是否會通過。）

❖ **the chance is slim**：機會很小
　slim（adj.）細微的；渺茫的
　⑳ The chance for them to win the championship is very slim.（他們要贏得冠軍的機會十分小。）

發音小技巧 🔊

Longshan Temple hosts temple fairs during holidays,
such as a lantern display for the Lantern Festival.

龍山寺在各式節慶都會舉辦廟會活動，例如元宵節的花燈大展。

● 趴趴走好用句

1. 龍山寺除了供奉觀音，也供奉媽祖、文昌帝君、關公、福德正神等神明。

   Aside from enshrining Avalokitesvara, Longshan Temple also honors such gods as Matsu, Wen Chang Di Jun, Guan Gong, and Earth God.

2. 「華西街觀光夜市」是享譽國際的觀光夜市，以蛇肉、蛇湯、蛇酒最為著名。

   Huaxi Street Tourist Night Market is a world-renowned tourist night market best known for its snake meat, snake soup, and snake wine.

3. 「華西街觀光夜市」有許多腳底按摩店及情趣商店。

   Huaxi Street Tourist Night Market abounds with foot massage parlors and sex toy shops.

4. 龍山寺旁邊有著名的「青草巷」，附近的大理街則有台北規模最大的成衣批發市場。

   The famous Herbal Lane is located alongside Longshan Temple, and neighboring Dali Street is home to the largest-scale wholesale market for ready-made clothes in Taipei.

5. 「植物園」園內有一千六百多種世界各地的植物。

   The Taipei Botanical Garden houses more than 1,600 plant species from all over the world.

6. 「植物園」內除了溫室，最著名的莫過於荷花池。

The second most popular attraction within the confines of the Taipei Botanical Garden, after the greenhouse, is the lotus pond.

7. 「國立歷史博物館」典藏許多古物，如青銅器、唐三彩、歷代錢幣等。

The National Museum of History boasts an expansive collection of antiques, such as bronzes, Tang tri-color glazed ware, and coins from various eras of generations past.

8. 「西門町」在民國五、六十年代是全台灣最熱鬧的地區，現在則成為青少年、哈日族的聚集地。

Ximending was the busiest district in all of Taiwan in the 60s and 70s. It has now become a place where teenagers and fervent followers of Japanese pop culture come together.

9. 「西門町」有著名的阿宗麵線，也有學生們最愛的大頭貼機。

Ximending is home to the famous A Zong Mien Xian as well as the purikura machines so popular among students.

10. 「西門町」是明星宣傳活動、以及漫畫／電玩角色扮演的最佳場所。

Ximending is just the place for celebrity promotional activities as well as cosplay events.

11.　「西門町」融合日式、美式、中式的風格，也是年輕人表現自我風格的場所。

Ximending is an elaborate mix of Japanese, American, and Chinese influences. It is also a place where teenagers display their uniqueness.

12.　「紅樓劇場」是一座紅磚造的八角形洋式建築，也是一座說唱劇場。

The Red House Theater is a Western-style octagonal red-brick structure used as a theater for musical narrative performances.

10

CD
1-10

卡拉OK與台北美食
Karaoke and Taipei Delicacies

Robert:　Wow, that really felt good—I haven't been **shouting** and **screaming** for a long time. Kitty, I can't believe you've got such a nice voice!

Kitty:　Well, let's just say I get lots of practice! Don't you know going to KTVs is one of Taipei **residents**' favorite **pastimes**?

Taike:　Don't you have KTV in the US?

Robert:　In America, we mainly have **karaoke** bars—you know, the ones where someone sings up on a **stage** in front of a group of strangers.

Kitty:　Then the Taiwanese **private**-room style is more fun— at least you don't have to worry about being **hissed** or **booed**.

Robert:　But you kept covering your ears the whole time I was singing! Well, never mind. After all that singing, I'm **starving**. What are we going to eat tonight?

Kitty:　I'm not sure—you're such a big **eater**.

Taike:　Well, we can go to Tienmu for **exotic** foreign food, to Ximending for street-**stall** snacks, or to Yongkang Street and the East District shopping area for **upscale cuisine**, then off to Fuxing South Road for rice **congee** and small **side dishes** in the middle of the night, and finally to Yonghe for **soy milk**, baked **sesame** cakes and fried **breadsticks** early in the morning.

Robert:　They all sound wonderful! Let's go climb the stairs of Taipei 101 first, and then enjoy the **foodfest**!

羅波：哇，真是痛快，我好久沒有鬼吼鬼叫了。高貴，想不到妳歌喉這
麼美妙！

高貴：因為我常常練歌啊！你不知道上KTV唱歌是台北人最喜歡的休閒
活動之一嗎？

邱克：難道美國沒有KTV嗎？

羅波：美國幾乎都只有卡拉OK吧，就是一個人在台上唱，台下坐一大堆
不認識的人那種。

高貴：那還是台灣的包廂式比較好玩，至少不用擔心會被噓下來。

羅波：可是我剛才唱歌時妳還不是一直搗耳朵！算了，唱完歌肚子也餓
了。今晚吃啥？

高貴：不知道耶……，你食量那麼大。

邱克：嗯，我們可以去天母吃異國美食，也可以去西門町吃路邊攤，或
者去永康街及東區吃高檔的，半夜還可以去復興南路吃清粥小
菜，一大早再飆去永和喝豆漿、吃燒餅油條。

羅波：聽起來都很棒耶，那我們先去爬台北101的階梯，再去享受美食大
餐！

單字 ⚫⚫⚫⚫⚫ 🔊

- ✣ **shout** (**v.**) 大喊大叫
- ✣ **scream** (**v.**) 尖叫
- ✣ **resident** (**n.**) 居住者
- ✣ **pastime** (**n.**) 消遣；娛樂
- ✣ **karaoke** (**n.**) 卡拉 **OK**
- ✣ **stage** (**n.**) 表演台
- ✣ **private** (**adj.**) 私人的；隱密的
- ✣ **hiss** (**v.**) 發出噓聲
- ✣ **boo** (**v.**) 發出噓聲嘲笑
- ✣ **starving** (**adj.**)（口語）飢餓的
- ✣ **eater** (**n.**) 吃東西的人
- ✣ **exotic** [ɪgˋzɑtɪk](**adj.**) 異國的
- ✣ **stall** (**n.**) 小攤子
- ✣ **upscale** (**adj.**) 高級的；高消費的
- ✣ **cuisine** [kwɪˋzin](**n.**) 菜餚；烹飪風格
- ✣ **congee / porridge** (**n.**) 稀飯
- ✣ **side dish** 小菜
- ✣ **soy milk** 豆漿（或稱 **soybean milk**）
- ✣ **sesame** [ˋsɛsəmɪ](**n.**) 芝麻
- ✣ **breadstick** (**n.**) 麵包棒
- ✣ **foodfest** (**n.**) 大餐

片語與句型

✤ **never mind**：算了；別在意
　例 Would you go buy the food for the cookout?... Never mind—I will do it myself.（你可不可以去買野餐要吃的食物？……算了，我自己去買。）

✤ **off to...**：到……去
　例 They rushed to the shop and off to the nearby pub.（他們急急忙忙去商店，然後到附近的酒吧）。

發音小技巧

The Taipei East District frequently plays host to all sorts of launch events and celebrations.

台北東區經常舉辦各式發表會及慶祝活動。

● 趴趴走好用句

1. 永康商圈以永康公園為中心，範圍包括永康街、麗水街、金華街等。

   The Yongkang Street shopping district centers on Yongkang Park and encompasses Yongkang, Lishui, and Jinhua Streets.

2. 永康商圈原先有許多台灣和大陸各省的小吃與餐廳，現在多了許多異國美食和咖啡館。

   The Yongkang Street shopping district was once home to Taiwanese and regional mainland Chinese snack stalls and restaurants. They have now been replaced by exotic bistros and coffee shops.

3. 「鼎泰豐」和「冰館」是永康商圈最有名的美食聖地，兩家店永遠大排長龍。

   The lines never cease at DinTaiFung and Ice Monster, two of the best-known food meccas in the Yongkang Street shopping district.

4. 「鼎泰豐」的小籠包、小籠湯包，以及元盅雞湯是中、外遊客的最愛。

   DinTaiFung's steamed pork dumplings, steamed mini pork dumplings with soup, and steamed chicken soup are well-loved favorites of visitors local and foreign alike.

5. 「冰館」夏天的「新鮮芒果冰」、冬天的「新鮮草莓冰」最受顧客喜歡。

   Ice Monster's jumbo mango ice and jumbo strawberry ice are crowd pleasers during the summer and winter months, respectively.

6. 天母位於陽明山山麓，區內有許多高貴住宅區及具有異國風情的商店。

Tienmu, located at the foot of Yangmingshan, features scores of upscale residential areas and exotic shops.

7. 天母早年有許多外國人士居住，因此呈現了多元的國際風貌。

In the early days, Tienmu was home to large numbers of foreign nationals, which accounts for its diverse, international style.

8. 天母國際商圈多集中在中山北路六、七段和天母東、西路附近。

The Tienmu International Circle refers to the area around sections 6 and 7 on Zhongshan North Road and Tienmu East and West Roads.

9. 「天母運動場」每逢週末或大型比賽總是擠滿人潮。

Tienmu Sports Park is usually packed during weekends and major game days.

10. 台北「東區」多年來是繁華的商業、娛樂重地，是台北人最愛的逛街地點。

For years now, the Taipei East District has been a major business and entertainment district and a favorite shopping destination among Taipei residents.

11. 台北「東區」有許多著名的購物中心，例如 Sogo 百貨、明曜百貨、微風廣場、誠品書店等。

The Taipei East District boasts a multitude of popular malls, including Sogo, Ming Yao Department Store, Breeze Center, and Eslite Bookstore.

12. 台北市復興南路上有一整排的清粥小菜餐廳。

There is an entire row of stalls selling rice congee and small side dishes along Taipei's Fuxing South Road.

CD
1-11

陽明山與北投
Yangmingshan and Beitou

Robert: Look, I've been sweating like crazy! Wow, Yangmingshan National Park is **phenomenal**!

Taike: Yep, it is truly the **backyard** of Taipei.

Kitty: You know, February and March are the "flower season" here, and the burst of **azaleas** and **cherry blossoms** are amazing. The **volcanic terrain** is also well known for its abundance of butterflies.

Robert: Yes, I've heard that there are **crater** lakes, **sulfur fumaroles**, and **geothermal energy** here.

Kitty: Yes. Like Xiaoyoukeng nearby, it is filled with volcanic **fissures** that **spew** steam from the **bowels** of the earth, forming **clusters** of sulfur **crystals**.

Taike: After we wear ourselves out mountain climbing, we can try the wild vegetables grown on the mountains of Yangmingshan, and then go enjoy the hot springs in Beitou.

Robert: Are you talking about the "Male Haven" Beitou? I've heard there are traditional Japanese **geisha** and **Nakashi** there!

Kitty: You're talking about the Beitou of forty years ago, a place for a life of **luxury** and **dissipation**, feasting and **revelry**. Beitou is very cultural now!

Taike: Speaking of "cultural," should we visit the Beitou Hot Spring **Museum**?

Kitty: Sure, and after that, you two **stinky** rats can go wash yourselves off in the public pool while I enjoy my spa in the hotel!

羅波：看，我流好多汗呢……哇，陽明山公園真是漂亮！

邱克：是呀，陽明山可是台北的後花園呢。

高貴：你知道嗎，二月和三月是陽明山公園的花季，杜鵑和櫻花盛開，美到不行。這公園還是火山地形，蝴蝶超多的。

羅波：是呀，我聽說這裡有火口湖、硫磺噴氣孔及地熱咧。

高貴：嗯，像附近的「小油坑」因為佈滿了火山裂縫，因此蒸汽會從地底深處噴出，形成硫磺結晶叢呢！

邱克：爬山爬累了，我們可以吃吃這裡的野菜，然後去北投泡溫泉。

羅波：啊，是不是俗稱「溫柔鄉」的那個北投？我聽說那裡有傳統的日本藝妓及那卡西喔。

高貴：你說的是四十年前夜夜笙歌、燈紅酒綠、紙醉金迷的北投啦，人家北投現在可是很文化的呢！

邱克：很有文化，那是不是說我們一定要去「溫泉博物館」走走啊？

高貴：當然，而且等會兒泡溫泉時，你們兩個臭男生去公共池洗一洗，至於我呢，當然是去飯店做SPA囉。

單字

- ❖ **phenomenal**（**adj.**）非凡的
- ❖ **backyard**（**n.**）後院
- ❖ **azalea** [əˋzeljə]（**n.**）杜鵑花
- ❖ **cherry**（**n.**）櫻桃；櫻桃樹
- ❖ **blossom**（**n.**）(果樹的)花
- ❖ **volcanic**（**adj.**）火山的
- ❖ **terrain**（**n.**）地域；地形
- ❖ **crater**（**n.**）火山口
- ❖ **sulfur**（**n.**）硫磺
- ❖ **fumarole**（**n.**）噴火口
- ❖ **geothermal energy** 地熱
- ❖ **fissure**（**n.**）裂縫
- ❖ **spew**（**v.**）吐出；噴出
- ❖ **bowels**（**n.**）(複數)內部；中心
- ❖ **cluster**（**n.**）叢集；團
- ❖ **crystal** [ˋkrɪst!]（**n.**）結晶體
- ❖ **geisha**（**n.**）(日本)藝妓
- ❖ **Nakashi**（**n.**）那卡西
- ❖ **luxury**（**n.**）奢侈豪華
- ❖ **dissipation**（**n.**）放蕩
- ❖ **revelry**（**n.**）狂歡喧鬧
- ❖ **museum**（**n.**）博物館
- ❖ **stinky**（**adj.**）發惡臭的

片語與句型

* (**sweat**) **like crazy**：(口語)(流汗)超多（**like crazy** 亦可用 **like hell**，例如 **hurt like hell** 為「痛得半死」）

  ⑩ Gosh, my stomach hurts like crazy.（天啊，我的肚子超痛的。）

* **be well known for...**：以……知名

  ⑩ This building is well known for its height.（這棟建築物以高度聞名。）

* **wear someone out**：使某人筋疲力竭

  ⑩ All the hiking and rock-climbing is wearing them out.（健行和攀岩讓他們都筋疲力竭。）

* **speak of...**：說到……

  ⑩ Speaking of music, when are you going to return the CD that I lent you?（說到音樂，你何時才要還向我借的 CD 啊？）

發音小技巧 🔊

Tourists enjoy boiling eggs in the hot water of Beitou's Geothermal Valley.

北投的「地熱谷」水溫高，許多遊客喜歡在這裡將生蛋煮熟。

趴趴走好用句

1. 「陽明山」早年因芒草叢生而被稱為「草山」。

Yangmingshan was once called Grass Mountain because of the Japanese silvergrass that grows there in abundance.

2. 「陽明山」為了紀念哲學家王陽明改名。

The name was changed to Yangmingshan to commemorate the philosopher Wang Yangming.

3. 「陽明山國家公園」原本是一位日本人的私人別墅，後來擴建，變成山林公園。

Yangmingshan National Park was once the private resort of a Japanese citizen. It was later augmented and transformed into a forest park.

4. 「陽明山國家公園」以各式各樣的花朵聞名，包括杜鵑、櫻花、茶花、桃花等。

The Yangmingshan National Park is known for the variety of flowers that grow there, including azaleas, cherry blossoms, camellias, and peach blossoms.

5. 陽明山附近有許多旅遊景點，包括竹子湖、擎天崗、小油坑遊憩區、草山行館、夢幻湖等。

There are plenty of travel hotspots around Yangmingshan, including Zhuzihu, Qingtiangang, Xiaoyoukeng Recreation Area, Grass Mountain Château, and Menghuan Pond.

6.　陽明山盛產各式野菜，土雞也十分著名。

Yangmingshan is abundant in wild vegetables, and the chickens raised there are renowned.

7.　文化大學是台灣的「最高學府」（雙關語）。

Chinese Culture University is the "highest educational institution" (pun intended) in Taiwan.

8.　「擎天崗」是一大片草原，春、秋兩季是最佳的造訪時間。

Qingtiangang is an expansive area of greenery. Spring and fall are the best seasons to visit this attraction.

9.　北投地區的溫泉從日據時代就很有名，其中的「北投溫泉博物館」現為三級古蹟。

The Beitou district's hot springs have enjoyed fame since the Japanese era. The Beitou Hot Spring Museum is recognized as a Class III historical site.

10.　到北投最方便的方式是搭乘捷運到新北投站，對面便是「新北投公園」。

The easiest way to reach Beitou is by taking the MRT to Xinbeitou Station, which is right across from Xinbeitou Park.

11.　捷運關渡站及紅樹林站之間的沿岸有一大片的紅樹林沼澤帶。

There is a long stretch of mangrove marshlands along the coast between the Guandu and Hongshulin MRT stations.

12.　「關渡自然公園」位於淡水河和基隆河的交接處，是候鳥的棲息地。

Guandu Nature Park, located where the Danshui and Keelung rivers combine, serves as a habitat for migratory birds.

CD
1-12

鶯歌與石門水庫
Yingge and Shihmen Reservoir

Robert: You're so good at making **pottery**, Kitty! Were you making a **chamber pot**?

Kitty: Are you kidding me? No, it's a **teapot**.

Taike: The Yingge **Ceramics** Museum was pretty cool. Although the tickets were a bit expensive, the free **hands-on** ceramics **workshop** was very nice.

Robert: Yeah, the old potters' street we were just at was very unique too. The shops which **produce** and sell pottery were all **packed** close together, and the **abundance** and the **diversity** of pottery were really something!

Kitty: That's why Yingge is also called the Taiwanese Jingdezhen!

Robert: So maybe we can all come here for the Yingge Ceramics Festival during the summer!

Taike: Sure, and after that we can visit Sanxia, the cultural center. The place is highly **valued** in culture and has many traditional **artisans** and **engravers**. We can **appreciate** the famous Zushi Temple with its **delicate engravings** and complex designs on the pillars.

Robert: Hey, this pool of yellow water right in front of us can't be the Shihmen **Reservoir**, can it?

Taike: Well, yes. We **purposely** took you here for the taste of the well-known "three ways of tasting the live fish."

Robert: Thanks a lot! But with the water so **turbid** and **cloudy**, are you sure the fish we'll be eating are really alive?

羅波：哇，高貴，妳真的好會拉胚喔！妳剛剛是在做夜壺嗎？

高貴：喂，你在開玩笑嗎，我是在做茶壺啦。

邰克：這「鶯歌陶瓷博物館」真不錯，門票雖貴了點，但還可以免費學做手拉胚。

羅波：是呀，剛剛我們去的陶瓷老街也很特別，製造和販賣陶瓷商品的店一家接著一家，各式各樣的陶瓷，種類豐富，真是好不熱鬧！

高貴：嗯，鶯歌也因此有「台灣景德鎮」之稱呢！

羅波：那暑假時我們可以來這裡參加「陶瓷嘉年華會」！

邰克：好啊，去完還可以順便去文化重心三峽。那裡有許多傳統藝師及雕匠，還有著名的祖師廟，我們可以好好欣賞它細緻的雕刻和複雜的柱石。

羅波：喂，眼前的這灘黃水不會就是「石門水庫」吧？

邰克：是呀，我們可是特地帶你來品嘗這裡赫赫有名的「活魚三吃」耶！

羅波：感恩啦！只不過這水這麼髒，你確定我們吃的真的是活跳跳的魚嗎？

單字 ·····

❖ **pottery**（n.）陶器

❖ **chamber pot** 夜壺；尿壺

❖ **teapot**（n.）茶壺

❖ **ceramics**（n.）窯業製品；陶瓷器

❖ **hands-on**（adj.）親自操作的；實習的

❖ **workshop**（n.）研習會；工作坊

❖ **produce**（v.）生產

❖ **packed**（adj.）擁擠的；塞得滿滿的

❖ **abundance**（n.）豐富；多量

❖ **diversity**（n.）多樣性

❖ **value**（v.）尊重；重視

❖ **artisan**（n.）工匠

❖ **engraver**（n.）雕刻師；雕工

❖ **appreciate**（v.）欣賞

❖ **delicate**（adj.）優美的；細緻的

❖ **engraving**（n.）雕刻作品

❖ **reservoir** [ˋrɛzəˏvwɑr]（n.）貯水池；水庫

❖ **purposely**（adv.）故意地

❖ **turbid**（adj.）混濁不透明的

❖ **cloudy**（adj.）混濁不清的

片語與句型

✤ **be good at...**：擅長於……
　例 She is good at volleyball and tennis.（她擅於打排球及網球。）
✤ **be something**：（口語）不簡單；了不起
　例 She took care of her family for the past 20 years, which is really something!（她過去二十年照顧家庭，真是了不起！）

發音小技巧

People can boat, swim, or fish in the Bitan Scenic Area in Xindian.

「碧潭風景區」位於新店，可以划船、游泳、釣魚等。

趴趴走好用句

1. 鶯歌的陶瓷工藝已有兩百年的歷史，早期的生產技術來自大陸的師傅。

   Yingge's pottery industry has a two-hundred-year history. The earliest production techniques were developed by Mainland Chinese masters.

2. 鶯歌的「陶瓷老街」，早期有許多窯廠，是鶯歌陶瓷業最早的聚集地。

   Yingge's Old Potters' Street, once lined with kilns and workshops, was the original home of Yingge's pottery industry.

3. 鶯歌有許多陶瓷藝品商店，但因需求量太大，很多產品並非當地出產。

   Ceramic shops abound in Yingge, but because of excessively large demand, many of their products are not manufactured locally.

4. 鶯歌的陶瓷主要可分為五類：藝術陶瓷、建築瓷、衛生瓷、日用瓷，以及工業用陶瓷。

   There are five types of Yingge ceramics: art ceramics, construction ceramics, sanitary ceramics, commodity ceramics, and industrial ceramics.

5. 「鶯歌陶瓷博物館」位於文化路，是全國第一座陶瓷專業博物館。

   The Yingge Ceramics Museum, located on Wenhua Road, is the country's foremost ceramic specialty museum.

6.　「鶯歌陶瓷博物館」除了有陶藝歷史的介紹，也常舉辦當代陶藝創作展覽及陶藝教學。

Aside from introducing the history of ceramics, the Yingge Ceramics Museum frequently hosts exhibitions on contemporary ceramics production as well as hands-on tutorials.

7.　「石門水庫」位於桃園縣龍潭鄉大漢溪的峽谷。

Shimen Reservoir is located in a gorge carved out by Dahan Stream in Taoyuan County's Longtan Township.

8.　「石門水庫」具有灌溉、發電、給水、防洪、觀光等五大功能。

The five main functions of Shimen Reservoir are irrigation, power generation, water supply, flood prevention, and tourism.

9.　「石門水庫」對台灣北部的農業、工業發展有貢獻。

Shimen Reservoir has contributed to the development of farming and industry in northern Taiwan.

10.　三峽「清水祖師廟」的建築、雕刻花了四十多年。

The construction and carving of Qingshui Zushi Temple in Sanxia took more than 40 years.

11.　三峽的「滿月圓森林遊樂區」因為山的形狀有如滿月而得名。

Sanxia's Manyueyuan forest recreation area got its name because of the way its mountains are shaped like a full moon.

12.　土城的「承天禪寺」是著名的佛教勝地，常有信徒沿著石階跪拜而上。

Tucheng's Chengtian Zen Temple is a well-known Buddhist mecca. Followers can usually be seen kowtowing their way to the top of the stone steps.

CD
1-13

新竹與北埔
Hsinchu and Beipu

Robert: Wow, Hsinchu is very windy!

Taike: Right. It's known for its frequent strong **monsoons** and is therefore nicknamed the "windy city." Don't take the wind lightly—it is said that the strong wind has **facilitated** the making of the famous Hsinchu rice noodles and **persimmon** cakes!

Kitty: Gee, the wind is so strong that my **delicate** skin will be dried up and **weathered** before the rice noodles!

Taike: Don't be such a **killjoy**. Don't you like the snacks in front of the City God Temple? The round dumpling with ground meat and the meatball soup go perfectly with each other!

Robert: Yes, they are a lot better than the Hakka cuisine we just had at Beipu. The dishes there were oily and salty. And the pork **intestine** with **shredded** ginger was so sour!

Taike: Hey, oily and salty stuff goes well with rice. And that way you don't have to prepare too many dishes and then be **wasteful**. **Frugality** is the traditional **virtue** of the Hakkanese.

Kitty: I also liked the old street area in Beipu, where cultural **relics** have been preserved **intact**.

Taike: Yeah. Beipu is **representative** of early Hakka culture. The nearby Lion's Head Mountain Scenic Area is also nice.

Robert: I didn't realize this region is full of culture! So should we stroll around the nearby alleys to experience the unique Hakka culture tonight?

Kitty: You guys go ahead. As for me, I'm going to walk around the Hsinchu Science Park to see if I could run into a "**millionerd**" there. If so, I might not have to work for the rest of my life, ha ha!!

羅波：哇，新竹的風真大！

邰克：嗯，新竹本來就以強勁的季風聞名，因此又稱「風城」。你可別
　　　小看這風喔，據說風的吹襲，使得這裡的名產新竹米粉和柿餅超
　　　級好吃呢！

高貴：哼，風這麼大，米粉還沒吹乾，我細嫩的肌膚都先風乾啦！

邰克：別這麼煞風景嘛，妳不覺得這城隍廟廣場的小吃很不錯嗎？肉圓
　　　和貢丸湯真是絕配！

羅波：嗯，比我們剛剛在北埔吃的客家菜好多了。那裡的菜又油又鹹，
　　　薑絲炒大腸又好酸喔。

邰克：喂，又油又鹹才下飯啊！這樣菜才不用煮太多浪費；節儉可是客
　　　家人的傳統美德耶。

高貴：我也喜歡北埔的舊街區，那裡的客家文化古蹟保存得很完整。

邰克：嗯，北埔是早期客家文化的代表之一。那附近的獅頭山風景區也
　　　很不錯。

羅波：我沒想到這地方還這麼有文化！那我們今天晚上要不要去附近的
　　　小巷子走走，體驗獨特的客家文化？

高貴：你們兩個去吧！我要去竹科附近逛逛，說不定能釣個呆呆科技新
　　　貴，這樣我下半生就不愁吃穿了，哈哈！

單字 ‥‥‥

✤ **monsoon** [mɑnˋsun] (**n.**) 季風

✤ **facilitate** (**v.**) 促進;助長

✤ **persimmon** [pɚˋsɪmən] (**n.**) 柿子

✤ **delicate** (**adj.**) 纖細的;柔軟的

✤ **weather** (**v.**) 曝曬;風化

✤ **killjoy** (**n.**) 掃興的人或物;煞風景

✤ **intestine** [ɪnˋtɛstɪn] (**n.**) 腸子

✤ **shred** (**v.**) 切成細條或碎片

✤ **wasteful** (**adj.**) 浪費的

✤ **frugality** (**n.**) 節儉

✤ **virtue** (**n.**) 美德

✤ **relics** (**n.**)(複數)遺跡

✤ **intact** (**adj.**) 完整的;無損害的

✤ **representative** (**adj.**) 代表性的;象徵的

✤ **millionerd** (**n.**)「百萬書蟲」(乃 **millionaire**＋**nerd**,意指身價不斐的科技人,但隱含嘲笑其只知工作、唸書,卻拙於社交之意)

片語與句型

❖ **be nicknamed...**：被取……綽號
　㋡ This dictator is nicknamed "The Beast" by his people.（這個獨裁者被人民取「野獸」的綽號。）

❖ **take something lightly**：小看……
　㋡ He will get into trouble if he takes this issue lightly.（他若小看這件事，將會惹上麻煩。）

❖ **go with...**：與……搭配；與……相配
　㋡ Your hat goes very well with your dress.（妳的帽子與洋裝非常相配。）

❖ **go ahead**：繼續進行；前進
　㋡ Why don't you go ahead? I'll catch up with you later.（你們繼續前進吧，我待會兒再趕上你們。）

發音小技巧 🔊

Hsinchu City's City God Temple, built during the Qing Dynasty, is a Class II historical site.

新竹市的城隍廟建於清朝，為二級古蹟。

● 趴趴走好用句

1. 「新竹科學工業園區」有數百家高科技廠商進駐，是北台灣的科技中心。

   Hundreds of high-tech businesses have set up camp in the Hsinchu Science Park, the technological core of northern Taiwan.

2. 「新竹科學工業園區」的主要產業包括半導體業、通訊業、電腦業、光電業、精密機械業，以及生物科技業。

   The businesses in the Hsinchu Science Park are mainly involved in the semiconductor, communication, computer, electro-optic, precision machinery, and biotechnological industries.

3. 「清華大學」校風優良，畢業生一直深受台灣企業界歡迎。

   National Tsing Hua University enjoys a good reputation. Its graduates have always been well received in Taiwan's business world.

4. 「清華大學」著名景點包括成功湖、昆明湖、梅園和梅谷等。

   Some of National Tsing Hua University's well-known attractions include Chenggong Lake, Kunming Lake, Mei Garden, and Mei Valley.

5. 「交通大學」位於新竹交流道旁，著名景點包括竹湖與竹園等。

   Located next to the Hsinchu interchange, the National Chiao Tung University boasts such popular attractions as Zhu Lake and Zhu Garden.

6.　「獅頭山風景區」地跨新竹縣與苗栗縣，以寺廟及客家文化著稱。

Lion's Head Mountain Scenic Area sits on the border between Hsinchu and Miaoli counties and is best known for its temples and Hakka culture.

7.　新竹縣的峨眉鄉有許多休閒農園、茶園，還保有傳統的農村風貌。

Hsinchu County's Emei Township features numerous leisure farms and tea gardens that have retained their traditional, earthy feel.

8.　「六福村主題遊樂園」位於新竹縣關西鎮，有著名的野生動物園。

Leofoo Village Theme Park, located in Guanxi Township, Hsinchu County, is the home of a famous wildlife park.

9.　「大霸尖山」位於新竹縣尖石鄉與苗栗縣泰安鄉之間，標高3,505公尺。

Dabajian Mountain, situated between Hsinchu County's Jianshi Township and Miaoli County's Taian Township, is 3,505 meters high.

10.　新竹縣湖口鄉的「湖口老街」建於民國四年，是台灣保存最完好的老街之一。

Hukou Old Street, located in Hsinchu County's Hukou Township and built in 1915, is one of the best preserved old streets in Taiwan.

11.　傳統的客家美食包括醃菜、板條、小炒、梅干扣肉等。

Examples of traditional Hakka dishes include pickled vegetables, flat noodles, stir-fry, and braised pork with preserved vegetables.

12.　新竹的特產包括：貢丸、米粉、烏龍茶、花生醬、金桔醬、柿餅等。

Examples of Hsinchu specialties include meatballs, rice noodles, Oolong tea, peanut butter, mandarin orange jam, and persimmon cakes.

CD
1-14

三義
Sanyi

Robert: Wow, check out this big-**bellied**, half-**naked** man!

Kitty: Well, that's Happy Buddha!

Robert: How about this **mean**-looking man with an **assault weapon** on his hand? Is he a **gangster**?

Taike: Hey, lower your voice—it's Guan Gong!

Robert: Oh, I see. Well, I have to say these **woodcarving** pieces are very **exquisite**!

Kitty: Sure. Sanyi is known for its woodcarving. The **craft** industry here has been in existence for more than one hundred years; it is the birthplace of Taiwanese woodcarving. This woodcarving street as well as the Wood **Sculpture** Museum are **must-sees**!

Taike: Now that we've seen all these woodcarving dragons, it's time to go somewhere else. We could go to the **nearby** Shengxing **Railway** Station, the **remains** of Longteng Bridge, Sanyi Train Station, Taian Hot Springs or someplace else.

Robert: Oh, I didn't know we were looking at dragons... I thought those **buck-toothed creatures** with **paws** were big snakes!

Kitty: Okay okay, let's visit the Longteng Bridge remains first. I've heard that the brick remains are considered a **masterpiece** of the art of Dutch **bricklaying** skills.

Taike: And after that I want to go visit the Shengxing Railway Station. It is the highest station of the North-South Railway, and the entire station is made of wood. Isn't that cool?

Robert: What, more wood?

羅波：哇，看這個半裸大肚男！

高貴：唉唷，那是彌勒佛啦！

羅波：那這個看起來很兇、手上還拿著武器的人是幫派份子嗎？

邰克：小聲點，那是關公啦！

羅波：喔，原來如此！不過這些木雕也做得太精巧啦！

高貴：當然，三義就是以木雕聞名。這裡的木雕業已有上百年的歷史，是台灣雕刻的鼻祖呢。這條木雕街和「木雕博物館」是一定要看的啦！

邰克：不過看了麼多隻木雕龍後，我想我們也該到別地方玩玩了，像是附近的勝興車站、龍騰斷橋、三義車站、泰安溫泉等等。

羅波：喔，原來我們一直在看的是龍，我還以為是有暴牙、長了爪子的大蛇呢！

高貴：好啦好啦，那我們先去龍騰斷橋好了，據說那裡留下來的殘磚仍是磚中極品，是荷蘭式的砌磚工法呢！

邰克：嗯，之後我想去勝興車站，因為它是南北縱貫鐵路上最高的車站，而且整座車站是用木頭建的呢，酷吧！

羅波：瞎米，又是木頭啊！

單字

❖ **belly**（**n.**）腹部

❖ **naked**（**adj.**）裸體的

❖ **mean**（**adj.**）刻薄的；兇的

❖ **assault**（**n.**）攻擊

❖ **weapon**（**n.**）武器

❖ **gangster**（**n.**）幫派份子

❖ **woodcarving**（**n.**）木雕

❖ **exquisite**（**adj.**）絕妙的

❖ **craft**（**n.**）工藝；技術

❖ **sculpture**（**n.**）雕刻

❖ **must-see**（**n.**）（口語）一定要看的東西

❖ **nearby**（**adj.**）附近的

❖ **railway**（**n.**）鐵道

❖ **remains**（**n.**）遺跡

❖ **buck-toothed**（**adj.**）暴牙的

❖ **creature**（**n.**）生物

❖ **paw**（**n.**）爪子

❖ **masterpiece**（**n.**）傑作

❖ **bricklaying**（**n.**）砌磚

片語與句型

❖ **check out...**：(口語)試試……；看看……
　例 Come and check out this cute little puppy!(快來看看這隻可愛的小狗！)

❖ **be in existence for...**：存在有……之久
　existence (n.) 存在
　例 This castle has been in existence for over 100 years.(這座城堡已經存在超過一百年了。)

Sanyi is located in Miaoli County; most of its residents earn their living by carving wood.

三義位於苗栗縣，當地居民多以木雕為業。

● 趴趴走好用句

1. 三義木雕的木材以樟木為主，另有檜木或檀香木等。

   While woodcarvings in Sanyi are mostly made of camphor wood, some are made with Chinese cypress or sandalwood.

2. 三義木雕的最大特色，在於木雕師傅擅長將木材根據原有的形狀，雕出自然生動的作品。

   The most distinguishing feature of Sanyi woodcarving is that the woodcarving masters here are skilled in creating natural yet vivid shapes based on the original shape of the wooden blocks.

3. 「龍騰斷橋」是台灣山線鐵路中最高的橋樑。

   Longteng Broken Bridge is the highest bridge along Taiwan Rail's mountain line.

4. 「龍騰斷橋」是用紅磚塊所搭建而成的拱形建築，民國24年因為大地震而斷毀。

   Longteng Broken Bridge is an arch of red brick once destroyed in an earthquake in 1935.

5. 「飛牛牧場」區內植物茂盛，還有一座種類眾多的蝴蝶園。

   Plants dot the Flying Cow Ranch, which also has a butterfly farm that houses a wide variety of butterflies.

6. 「勝興車站」建於民國五年，車站內設有一座標示海拔高度402公尺的紀念碑。

Inside the 1916-built Shengxing Railway Station is a monument attesting its height of 402 meters above sea level.

7. 「勝興車站」整棟以木頭建造，每根樑柱的銜接完全不用釘子。

Shengxing Railway Station is a structure made entirely out of wood. The points where beams connect use no nails at all.

8. 「勝興車站」雖然歷經多次大地震，卻屹立不搖。

Shengxing Railway Station remains standing strong despite having experienced numerous earthquakes.

9. 「泰安車站」有造型優美的外型及豐富的歷史，是台灣老式車站的典範。

With its elegant design and rich history, Taian Railway Station is a fine specimen of an old-fashioned Taiwanese railway station.

10. 「西湖渡假村」位於高速公路三義交流道旁邊，因為風景美麗，被取名為「西湖」。

West Lake Resortopia is located next to the Sanyi interchange. It is called "West Lake" because of the beauty of its scenery.

11.　「西湖渡假村」有歐式花園和遊樂設施，是適合全家的遊樂區。

West Lake Resortopia, with its European-style gardens and amusement facilities, is an ideal destination for family outings.

12.　「華陶窯」是一對陶藝家夫婦的工作室，整個園區依山而建。

Huataoyao, the workshop of a pottery-making couple, is built along the contours of a mountain.

CD
1-15

泰安溫泉和馬拉邦山
Taian Hot Springs and Mt. Malabang

Robert: Wow, this "hot spring sand bath" is better than the real hot spring!

Kitty: Well, Taian is the only place on the whole island where you can find a sand bath like this. The local hot spring **operators** have collected tiny **grains** of sand from along the **riverside** and placed them on top of the hot spring **pipeline**. The sand is heated by the hot spring and then **shoveled** to cover up your body.

Taike: Wow, it's only been a few minutes but I'm already sweating!

Kitty: It's said that the sand bath will not only speed up your blood **circulation** but also **beautify** your skin. Perfect for a pretty girl like me, ha!

Robert: That's right. Your face is as red as the Dahu strawberries that we just picked.

Taike: Dahu's strawberries are not only **appealing** to look at but delicious as well!

Robert: And I've heard that Mt. Malabang, where we'll be visiting tomorrow, is very beautiful too. It is **shrouded** in clouds and mists all year round, and in the fall and winter the **slopes** are covered with red maple leaves. Rumor has it that the view is even prettier than Kitty's pink **cheeks**! Ha!

Kitty: In addition to its colorful maple leaves, Mt. Malabang is known for the **impressive** sight of its **ever-changing** sea of clouds. Other **attractions** include the peach **blossoms** in spring, the green bamboo in summer, and the **plum** blossoms in winter.

Robert: God, this sand bath is getting too hot! I can't stand it.

Kitty: Then go ahead and switch to the hot spring. The temperature of the water here is about 47℃, and the water is **creamy** white in color and smooth to the touch. You will love it!

羅波：哇，這「溫泉沙浴」比泡真的溫泉還舒服！

高貴：嗯，這種沙浴全台只有泰安有喔！這裡的業者將河邊的小砂石採
　　　集，堆在溫泉管線上方，透過溫泉的熱氣讓砂石加熱，然後鏟到
　　　遊客身上。

邱克：哇，才做不到幾分鐘，我就已經開始流汗了。

高貴：據說沙浴會加速你的血液循環，還可以保養皮膚，最適合我這種
　　　美女了，嘻嘻。

羅波：對呀，妳的臉現在就有如我們剛剛採的大湖草莓一樣紅了。

邱克：大湖的草莓真的又漂亮又好吃！

羅波：嗯，聽說我們明天要去的馬拉邦山也很漂亮，終年雲霧裊繞，而
　　　且秋、冬時節滿徑楓紅，據說比高貴的蘋果臉更美呢！哈！

高貴：馬拉邦山除了色彩繽紛的楓葉很有名，它變化多端的雲海也很壯
　　　觀。除此之外，春天的桃花、夏天的綠竹、冬天的寒梅也很有特
　　　色呢！

羅波：哇，這沙浴太熱了，我受不了了！

高貴：那你換去泡溫泉好了。泰安溫泉的溫度大約攝氏47度，顏色乳
　　　白，水質滑潤，你會喜歡的！

單字

- ❖ **operator**（**n.**）經營者
- ❖ **grain**（**n.**）顆粒
- ❖ **riverside**（**n.**）河岸
- ❖ **pipeline**（**n.**）管線；導管
- ❖ **shovel**（**v.**）用鏟子鏟
- ❖ **circulation**（**n.**）循環
- ❖ **beautify**（**v.**）使美麗
- ❖ **appealing**（**adj.**）吸引人的
- ❖ **shroud**（**v.**）覆蓋；籠罩
- ❖ **slope**（**n.**）斜坡
- ❖ **cheek**（**n.**）臉頰
- ❖ **impressive**（**adj.**）令人印象深刻的
- ❖ **ever-changing**（**adj.**）不斷改變的
- ❖ **attraction**（**n.**）吸引人之事物
- ❖ **blossom**（**n.**）(果樹的)花
- ❖ **plum**（**n.**）梅子；李子
- ❖ **creamy**（**adj.**）奶油似的；乳白色的

片語與句型

❖ **speed up**：使加速

　⑩ Nutritious food and fresh air will speed up your recovery.（營養的食
　　物與新鮮的空氣將會加速你的復原。）

❖ **rumor has it that...**：據說……

　rumor (n.) 傳聞；謠言

　⑩ Rumor has it that he is bisexual.（據說他是個雙性戀者。）

❖ **in addition to...**：除了……之外

　⑩ In addition to strengthening your heart and helping maintain your
　　ideal weight, exercise may also strengthen your immune system.（除
　　了強化心臟、保持理想體重，運動還可以加強你的免疫力。）

❖ **cannot stand**：無法忍受

　⑩ I can't stand living with him anymore!（我再也無法忍受和他一起
　　住了！）

發音小技巧

Xue Mountain, the highest peak in Xueba National Park,
is also the second-highest mountain in Taiwan.

雪山是「雪霸國家公園」境內的最高峰，也是台灣第二高峰。

● 趴趴走好用句

1. 「泰安溫泉」於日據時代即已開發，為鹼性碳酸泉，溫度約47度。

The Taian Hot Springs were first developed during the Japanese colonial period. An alkali-based bicarbonate spring, its temperature hovers around 47 degrees Celsius.

2. 進入泰安溫泉區必須辦入山證。

A Class A mountain permit is required to gain access to the Taian Hot Springs.

3. 苗栗縣的大湖鄉有山有水，風景宜人，草莓是此地一大特產。

Miaoli County's Dahu Township, a breathtaking destination where mountains and seas converge, is famous for its strawberries.

4. 大湖地區的草莓園在每年二至四月時，總是吸引大批遊客前往採草莓。

Dahu's Strawberry Garden attracts throngs of strawberry-picking crowds every year between February and April.

5. 大湖除了盛產新鮮草莓，當地農夫也會在路旁銷售草莓醬及草莓酒。

Aside from producing strawberries in abundance, local Dahu farmers also peddle strawberry jam and strawberry wine by the roadside.

6. 「雪霸國家公園」位於台灣的中北部，是台灣積雪最厚的山區。

Xueba National Park, located in mid-northern Taiwan, is the mountainous region that accumulates the most snow in the country.

7. 「雪霸國家公園」內有許多稀有的動物，包括國寶級的魚類「櫻花鉤吻鮭」、台灣黑熊、帝雉、藍腹鷴、台灣山椒魚等。

Xueba National Park is home to many endangered animals, including the national treasure fish, the Formosan landlocked salmon, along with the Formosan black bear, the Mikado pheasant, Swinhoe's pheasant, and the Formosan salamander.

8. 「雪霸國家公園」內的「武陵遊憩區」四季各有迷人的景緻。

Wuling Recreation Area in Xueba National Park is home to marvelous scenery throughout the year.

9. 「馬那邦山」高1,406公尺，是原住民泰雅族瓦崗部落的所在地。

Rising to an altitude of 1,406 meters, Mt. Malabang is home to the Wakan tribe of the Atayal.

10. 「馬那邦山」盛產水果及花卉，也是國內最著名的賞楓景點之一。

Mt. Malabang is a huge supplier of fruits and flowers, and one of the most popular maple leaf-viewing spots in the country.

11. 「獅頭山」有許多古老的寺廟，是名聞全省的佛教聖地。

Lion's Head Mountain, home to many ancient temples, is known throughout Taiwan as a Buddhist mecca.

12. 「獅頭山」因為外形酷似獅子的頭而得名。

Lion's Head Mountain derives its name from its striking resemblance to the head of a lion.

CD
1-16

台中市
Taichung City

Robert:　Sitting outdoors by the **sidewalk** drinking coffee makes me feel right at home!

Taike:　Yeah, Jingming 1st Street's 100-meter-long **pedestrian** mall is lined with fashion **boutiques**, **galleries**, foreign restaurants, and so on. Better yet, here you can also **sample** the world-famous **pearl milk tea** at "Chun Shui Tang," the birthplace of pearl milk tea in Taiwan.

Kitty:　I prefer "Green **Parkway**," where we ate our lunch. Each restaurant and shop there has its own style with **elaborate decor**. It really suits my high-society style!

Taike:　Then do you have any idea where all the high-society people hang out? Let me tell you: at the National Museum of Natural Science and the National Taiwan Museum of Fine Arts!

Robert:　I've heard that the Museum of Natural Science **houses** several fantastic **exhibition** halls, such as Space Theater, China Science Hall, Life Science Hall, Earth Environment Hall, and so on.

Taike:　Yes; there's also a tropical **rainforest greenhouse**. The museum is the largest recreational and educational center, as well as the best **equipped** museum in Taiwan!

Robert:　And where should we spend our evening?

Taike:　Zhonghua Road Night Market, of course! We can taste a wide variety of local delicacies and shop around. The prices there are very **reasonable**, too.

Kitty:　Not the night market again! You two can call yourselves "the night market experts!" I'd rather go by the train station and buy Yixin **dried bean curd** and sun cakes for my dad!

羅波：在這人行道上的露天座椅喝咖啡，讓我有一種家的感覺！

邱克：嗯，「精明一街」一百公尺的徒步區兩旁有精品、畫廊可以逛，
　　　又有異國餐點可以吃，更可以喝到「珍珠奶茶」的發源地的「春
　　　水堂」奶茶！

高貴：我喜歡我們吃午飯的「綠園道」，那裡的每間餐廳和商店都有獨
　　　特的風味，且裝潢別緻，很符合我上流社會的風格呢！

邱克：那妳知道這裡上流社會的人都去哪裡逛嗎？「國立自然科學博物
　　　館」和「國立台灣美術館」！

羅波：我聽說那個博物館擁有好幾個很棒的展示館，像是太空劇場、中
　　　國科學廳、生命科學廳、地球環境廳等等。

邱克：對，還有一個熱帶雨林的溫室呢。這博物館是台灣最大、設備最
　　　好的娛樂教育中心！

羅波：那我們晚上要去哪裡逛？

邱克：那當然是中華路夜市囉！那裡除了可以吃到各式小吃，還可以買
　　　東西，價格都很公道。

高貴：又要逛夜市，你們兩個可以當「夜市達人」了！我寧願去車站附
　　　近買「一心豆乾」和太陽餅回去給我爸！

單字

❖ **sidewalk**（n.）人行道

❖ **pedestrian**（adj.）徒步的；行人的

❖ **boutique** [buˋtik]（n.）精品店

❖ **gallery**（n.）畫廊

❖ **sample**（v.）品嚐；嘗試

❖ **pearl milk tea** 珍珠奶茶

❖ **parkway**（n.）林蔭道；公園大道

❖ **elaborate**（adj.）精心的；巧緻的

❖ **decor**（n.）裝飾；室內裝潢

❖ **house**（v.）收藏；儲存

❖ **exhibition**（n.）展示

❖ **rainforest**（n.）雨林

❖ **greenhouse**（n.）溫室

❖ **equip**（v.）裝備；備置

❖ **reasonable**（adj.）合理的

❖ **dried bean curd** 豆乾

片語與句型

* **be lined with...**：沿路排列
    * 例 The parkway is lined with many tall trees.（這公園道沿途種了許多大樹。）
* **hang out**：常去（之處）；常聚集在一起（玩）
    * 例 My friends and I usually hang out on Saturday nights.（我和朋友星期六晚上通常會聚在一起玩）。

發音小技巧 🔊

The third largest city in Taiwan, Taichung is also known as the "Culture City."

台中市是台灣第三大城市，有「文化城」的美稱。

● 趴趴走好用句

1.　台中市四季氣候溫和、很少下雨，被公認是台灣最適於居住的城市。

Taichung enjoys moderate weather and minimal precipitation all year long. It is commonly considered to be Taiwan's most pleasant city to live in.

2.　台中市有豐富的藝術文化與教育資源，包括國立台灣美術館、自然科學博物館、台中市立文化中心、文英館、台中民俗公園等。

Taichung City is rich in art, cultural, and educational resources. These include the National Taiwan Museum of Fine Arts, the National Museum of Natural Science, Taichung Municipal Culture Center, Wenying Hall, and Taichung Folklore Park.

3.　「中山公園」是台中市重要的地標，也是當地人休閒運動的場所。

Zhongshan Park is an important landmark in Taichung City. It is also where the locals go for leisure and exercise.

4.　台中市有許多面積廣大、裝潢別緻的餐飲店，吸引許多台北人前往消費。

Taichung City boasts a multitude of spacious and elegantly decorated dining establishments that attract business from Taipei consumers.

5.　珍珠奶茶的創始店「春水堂」位於精明一街。

Chun Shui Tang, the birthplace of pearl milk tea in Taiwan, is located on Jingming 1st Street.

6. 精明一街是台中市第一條露天咖啡街兼行人徒步街。

Jingming 1st Street is the first outdoor café/pedestrian mall in Taichung City.

7. 「國立台灣美術館」與台中市文化局相鄰，北邊有「國立自然科學博物館」。

The National Taiwan Museum of Fine Arts and the Taichung Municipal Culture Center are located side by side. To its north lies the National Museum of Natural Science.

8. 「國立台灣美術館」前有寬敞的「綠園道」，道路兩側有許多別具特色的餐廳與咖啡館。

The spacious Green Parkway runs past the front of the National Taiwan Museum of Fine Arts, lined with distinctive restaurants and cafés on both sides.

9. 「東海大學」的校園廣闊，有「最美麗校園」的封號。

The vast Tunghai University grounds have been dubbed "the most beautiful campus."

10. 「東海大學」著名景觀為建築大師貝聿銘設計的「路思義教堂」。

I. M. Pei's Luce Memorial Chapel is a well-known attraction at Tunghai University.

11. 「東海藝術街坊」是一個集合人文藝術景觀和社區營造於一身的社區。

Tunghai Art Street is a neighborhood that combines art and cultural attractions with a community atmosphere.

12. 「逢甲夜市商圈」位於逢甲大學附近,是台中最熱鬧的夜市。

Fengchia Night Market and Shopping District, located near Fengchia University, is the busiest night market in Taichung City.

廬山溫泉和谷關溫泉
Lushan and Guguan Hot Springs

Robert: This Lushan Hot Spring is **phenomenal**. It's hard to imagine this place was once hit by the 921 **Earthquake**!

Taike: Yeah. Ren'ai **Township** in Nantou County was hit badly during the quake. Many roads and houses were destroyed. But thanks to the hard work of the town's Atayal **residents**, many areas have been **rebuilt**.

Kitty: To help the locals here, let's try our best to spend money! Why don't we buy some local **delicacies**, such as Sakura **mochi** and **millet** cakes, later?

Robert: No problem! Hey, I just ate several spring-boiled eggs, and my stomach feels a bit funny now. What should I do?

Kitty: Why don't you drink some of this spring water? The **bicarbonate** water here is clear and **odorless**, and it is said to help **mediate gastric** acid imbalances and cure **chronic** gastritis!

Robert: Is it that magical?

Taike: Sure. Taiwan's hot springs all have **curative** effects! Did you forget about the Guguan Hot Spring in Heping Township, Taichung County that cured your **athlete's foot**? Ha ha.

Robert: Yeah, right. And don't you forget it also cured your skin **ailments**. Ha ha.

Kitty: Stop attacking one another. Other than curing the "**unspeakable**" diseases you two have, Guguan Hot Spring's bicarbonate water is believed to be **effective** against **arthritis**, **neuralgia**, and **gastrointestinal** diseases.

Robert: And there you can also enjoy Lishan's main products, the **temperate-zone** fruits: peaches and apples. It's definitely memorable!

羅波：這廬山溫泉真棒，一點都看不出這裡曾經受到921大地震的侵襲
呢！

邱克：對啊，當時南投縣仁愛鄉受創嚴重，很多房屋跟道路全毀，不過
在泰雅族鄉民的努力下重建了許多。

高貴：為了幫助這裡的居民，我們一定要努力消費！等會兒多買些這裡
的特產櫻花米麻糬和小米糕吧！

羅波：沒問題！喂，我剛剛吃了許多溫泉煮的蛋，肚子有點不舒服，怎
麼辦？

高貴：那你喝點溫泉水好了。這裡的溫泉是碳酸泉，既清澈又無味，據
說可以調整胃酸、治療慢性胃炎呢！

羅波：真有這麼神奇啊？

邱克：是啊，台灣的溫泉都超有療效的。你忘了上次我們去泡台中縣和
平鄉的谷關溫泉，把你的香港腳都治好了呢！哈哈。

羅波：是喔，你別忘了它也治好你的皮膚病，嘿嘿。

高貴：你們兩個不要互揭瘡疤了啦。除了你們兩個不可告人的疾病，谷
關的碳酸泉對於關節炎、神經痛、腸胃病也很有效耶。

羅波：嗯，而且那裡還可以吃到梨山盛產的溫帶水果水蜜桃和蘋果，超
令人回味的！

單字

- ❖ **phenomenal**（**adj.**）非凡的
- ❖ **earthquake**（**n.**）地震
- ❖ **township**（**n.**）鄉鎮
- ❖ **resident**（**n.**）居民
- ❖ **rebuild**（**v.**）重建；改造
- ❖ **delicacy**（**n.**）珍饈；佳餚
- ❖ **mochi**（**n.**）麻糬
- ❖ **millet**（**n.**）黍類；小米
- ❖ **bicarbonate**（**n.**）碳酸
- ❖ **odorless**（**adj.**）無氣味的
- ❖ **mediate**（**v.**）調整
- ❖ **gastric**（**adj.**）胃的；胃部的
- ❖ **chronic**（**adj.**）慢性的
- ❖ **curative**（**adj.**）治療的
- ❖ **athlete's foot** 香港腳
- ❖ **ailment**（**n.**）（輕度的）疾病
- ❖ **unspeakable**（**adj.**）無法向外人說的
- ❖ **effective**（**adj.**）有效的
- ❖ **arthritis** [ɑrˋθraɪtɪs]（**n.**）關節炎
- ❖ **neuralgia** [njuˋrældʒə]（**n.**）神經痛
- ❖ **gastrointestinal**（**adj.**）胃與腸的
- ❖ **temperate-zone** 溫帶

片語與句型

❖ **thanks to...**：幸虧……、由於……
　⑩ Thanks to your help, we were able to finish the project on time.（由於你的幫忙，我們在預定時間內完成計畫。）

❖ **feel funny**：感到怪怪的
　funny (adj.) 稍有不適的；奇怪的
　⑩ After the surgery, her eyes felt a bit funny.（手術後，她的眼睛感到有些怪怪的。）

發音小技巧

Wuling Veterans' Farm abounds in fruits and vegetables and enjoys a very prosperous tourism industry.

「武陵農場」盛產蔬菜水果，觀光事業十分發達。

● 趴趴走好用句

1. 谷關隸屬台中縣和平鄉，以品質優良的溫泉揚名中外。

Guguan, under the jurisdiction of Heping Township in Taichung City, is renowned both in and beyond Taiwan for its quality hot springs.

2. 谷關是中橫公路的中途站，許多遊覽中橫的旅客都會在谷關住宿。

Guguan is a midway station along the Central Cross-Island Highway. Travelers taking the highway usually spend the night in Guguan.

3. 谷關溫泉是鹼性碳酸泉，溫度大約攝氏 48 度，無色無臭，可飲可浴。

Guguan Hot Springs are alkali-based bicarbonate acid springs with a temperature of about 48 degrees Celsius. The spring waters are colorless and odorless, and can be both drunk and bathed in.

4. 谷關溫泉因為含有硫化物及鹽分，據說對關節炎、神經痛、胃腸病、香港腳、皮膚病等均有療效。

Guguan Hot Springs is said to have curative effects against arthritis, neuralgia, gastrointestinal diseases, athlete's foot, and skin ailments because of its sulfide and salt content.

5. 「后里馬場」位於台中后里鄉，是台灣目前設備最完善的馬場。

Houli Horse Farm, located in Taichung's Houli Township, is currently the best-equipped horse farm in Taiwan.

6.　台中縣大甲鎮的「鎮瀾宮」有兩百多年的歷史，供奉的主神是媽祖。

Zhenlan Temple, located in Dajia Township in Taichung County, has more than two hundred years of history. The temple is chiefly dedicated to the goddess Matzu.

7.　民國95年9月，「鎮瀾宮」主持了史上最大的跨海進香團，到大陸的湄州舉行祈福大典。

In September 2006, Zhenlan Temple organized the largest-scale cross-strait pilgrimage in history to Meizhou in mainland China for a blessing ceremony.

8.　梨山位於台中縣和平鄉，高約二千公尺，盛產溫帶水果。

Lishan, located in Heping Township in Taichung County at an altitude of 2,000 meters, is a large supplier of temperate-zone fruits.

9.　梨山夏天可以避暑，冬天可以賞雪。

Lishan is a great place to escape from the summer heat and a great place to see snow in winter.

10.　「武陵農場」位於台中縣和平鄉，是台灣國寶魚「櫻花鉤吻鮭」的故鄉。

Wuling Veterans' Farm, located in Heping Township in Taichung County, is home to the national treasure fish, the Formosan landlocked salmon.

11.　「盧山溫泉」屬於碳酸泉，據說對關節炎、神經痛，以及糖尿病很有療效。

Lushan Hot Springs is bicarbonate and supposedly has curative effects against arthritis, neuralgia, and diabetes.

12.　盧山附近櫻花處處，附近的霧社有當年抗日事件的紀念碑。

Cherry blossoms grow in abundance in the area around Lushan, while nearby Wushe features a memorial to commemorate the Wushe Incident of yesteryear.

18

鹿港（一）
Lugang（I）

Robert: Whew! That **blast** was very **frightening**! I thought it was a **terrorist attack**, like a **suicide bombing** or something.

Taike: You're such a **chicken**. You **peed** your **pants** over a few **firecrackers exploding**?

Robert: Hey, I happened to be in Manhattan when 9-11 happened!

Kitty: Don't worry, this is nothing but firecrackers in front of Longshan Temple. The sound is nothing compared to the celebration of the Matzu's birthday, which is on the 23rd day of the 3rd **lunar** month. On that day there will be huge and exciting celebrations at the Tianhou Temple. The explosions then will be much **scarier**!

Robert: So you mean Osama bin Laden may try to bomb this place?

Taike: Come on, don't worry—no place is safer than Taiwan! But you... I'm not sure if you are "safe..."

Robert: What do you mean?

Taike: Well, we're **heading** toward the "Narrow **Lane**," **aka** "Touch **Breast** Lane," where the narrowest section of the alley is only 70 **centimeters** wide. As we walk through, you'd better behave yourself and not touch me!

Robert: Don't you even worry. I'm no Ennis, and you sure are no Jake!

Kitty: Well, don't you listen to Taike. The lanes there were built so narrow and **winding** only to prevent **thieves** from entering and avoid damage from the strong wind!

羅波：哇，剛剛那聲音真的好可怕！我還以為是恐怖攻擊，像是自殺炸彈之類咧。

邱克：你真是膽小鬼，一點鞭炮聲就嚇得屁滾尿流啊？

羅波：喂，九一一發生時我人剛好在曼哈頓耶！

高貴：別擔心，那不過是龍山寺放的鞭炮聲啦。這和媽祖誕辰的慶典比起來根本不算什麼。每年的農曆三月23日是媽祖誕辰，那天「天后宮」會舉行盛大的慶典活動，那時的鞭炮聲才嚇人呢！

羅波：你是說賓拉登可能會來炸？

邱克：唉唷，別擔心，台灣超安全的啦！倒是你，我不知道你安不安全……

羅波：什麼意思勒？

邱克：我們等會兒要去「窄巷」，又稱「摸乳巷」，那裡最窄的地方只有70公分，到時候你可不要亂摸我喔！

羅波：別擔心，我不是恩尼斯，你也不是傑克！*

高貴：唉呀，別聽邱克亂說。那些巷子之所以那麼窄和曲折，是為了要防止盜賊入侵及強風的侵襲啦！

* Ennis 與 Jake 是電影 Brokeback Mountain（斷背山）主角。

單字 🔊

✤ **blast**（**n.**）爆炸

✤ **frightening**（**adj.**）令人恐懼的

✤ **terrorist**（**n.**）恐怖份子

✤ **attack**（**n.**）攻擊

✤ **suicide bombing** 自殺炸彈（轟炸）

✤ **chicken**（**n.**）（俚語）膽小鬼

✤ **pee**（**v.**）小便；撒尿

✤ **pants**（**n.**）（複數）褲子

✤ **firecracker**（**n.**）鞭炮

✤ **explode**（**v.**）爆炸

✤ **lunar**（**adj.**）陰曆的

✤ **scary**（**adj.**）駭人的

✤ **head**（**v.**）朝某方向前進

✤ **lane**（**n.**）小巷

✤ **aka**（或 **a.k.a.**，即 **also known as**）又名⋯⋯

✤ **breast**（**n.**）乳房

✤ **centimeter**（**n.**）公分

✤ **winding**（**adj.**）曲折的

✤ **thief**（**n.**）小偷

片語 與 句型

* **happen to**：剛好；恰巧
  * 例 She happened to run into her ex last weekend.（她上週末恰巧遇見前男友。）
* **be nothing but...**：只不過是……
  * 例 Don't feel sorry for him; he is nothing but a bitter, cruel old man.（別為他感到難過；他不過是個尖酸苛刻的老人。）
* **come on**：（口語）拜託（又拼為 **C'mon**）
  * 例 C'mon, a little alcohol won't kill you!（拜託，喝點酒不會死啦！）
* **had better**：最好……
  * 例 Your mom called; you'd better go home.（你媽打電話來了；你最好回家。）

發音 小 技巧

Popular tourist attractions in Lugang include Nine Turns Lane, Old Market Street, and Wenkai Academy.

鹿港著名的遊覽景點包括「九曲巷」、「古市街」、「文開書院」。

● 趴趴走好用句

1. 「天后宮」建於明朝萬曆十九年，當初建立的目的是為了祈求航海安全。

   Tianhou Temple was built in the nineteenth year of the reign of Ming emperor Wanli. It was originally built to pray for safety on the seas.

2. 鹿港「天后宮」供奉媽祖，且神像遠從大陸福建省的湄洲媽祖廟而來。

   Lugang's Tianhou Temple is dedicated to Matzu. The idol in the temple was imported from the Matzu Temple in Meizhou, Fujian Province, China.

3. 「天后宮」的信徒遍佈於台灣各地，每年的農曆一月至三月間是進香旺季。

   Worshipers at the Tianhou Temple hail from all over Taiwan. Temple visits peak between January and March in the lunar calendar.

4. 「天后宮」的媽祖神像臉龐原本是粉紅色，但多年來受到香火的薰繞，因此呈現黑褐色。

   The face of the Matzu statue in Tianhou Temple was originally pink in color. Following years of exposure to incense fumes, however, it has turned brownish-black.

5. 「天后宮」建有「香客大樓」供信徒過夜，可供上千人住宿。

   The Pilgrims' Building at Tianhou Temple provides overnight accommodations for temple worshipers. The building can accommodate up to thousands of people at a time.

6. 鹿港「龍山寺」建於明朝永曆七年，是台灣三大古廟之一。

Longshan Temple in Lugang, constructed in the seventh year of Ming emperor Yongli's rule, is one of Taiwan's three greatest ancient temples.

7. 鹿港在每年農曆五月五日端午節會舉辦龍舟競賽和全國的民俗才藝活動。

Lugang hosts dragon boat races and National Folk Arts Festival events during the Dragon Boat Festival, which falls on the fifth day of the fifth month in the lunar calendar.

8. 鹿港的「摸乳巷」巷子狹窄，僅容一人穿過，若兩個人迎面走來，都會不小心碰到彼此。

Lugang's Narrow Lane is an alley barely wide enough to allow one person to pass through at a time. When two people come through in opposite directions, they will inevitably brush against one another.

9. 男生走過「摸乳巷」時，因為必須小心不碰觸迎面而來的女生的身體，因此又稱「君子巷」。

When men pass through Narrow Lane, they need to be careful not to bump into oncoming females. The lane is thus otherwise known as "Gentleman's Lane."

10. 鹿港的「半邊井」其實是完整的井，但被一道牆隔成兩半。

Lugang's half-sided well is, in fact, an intact well. It is, however, split in half by a wall.

11.　「半邊井」的用意為一半供自己人使用、一半供他人使用，可見過去當
　　地濃厚的人情味。

The logic behind the design of the half-sided well is for half of the well to be reserved for private use, and the other half for public, evidence of the rich spirit of camaderie that prevailed in the old days.

12.　「甕牆」位於鹿港小鎮的巷弄間，遊客必須仰望上方才可看到。

The urn wall is located among the lanes and alleys of Lugang. Visitors have to look up to locate the place.

CD
1-19

鹿港（二）
Lugang（II）

Robert: It's hard to imagine that an old-style town like Lugang still exists in modern Taiwan!

Kitty: You're right. But Lugang had its day. In the 17th **century**, Dutch **occupiers** used Lugang as an important **harbor** for **exports**, and it became the **gateway** to central Taiwan.

Robert: Really? Then what happened?

Kitty: In early 20th century, the **conservative** local **residents refused** to allow the North-South Railway and some major highways to pass through the town, and that was the beginning of Lugang's **decline**.

Taike: Yeah, and the harbor became choked up with **silt**, reducing Lugang from the second largest city in Taiwan to a small town.

Kitty: But it was the town's decline that allowed the **preservation** of traditional Lugang!

Robert: That's very true. So, what are we eating now?

Taike: It's **oyster omelet**. The seafood here is **fantastic**.

Robert: Well, it is quite different from the omelet that I usually have.

Kitty: Hurry up, you two. After we're done eating, we can **stroll** along Zhongshan Road, where you can find traditional **handicrafts**, including **woodworking**, **fan** making, **incense manufacturing** and **lantern** making.

Robert: It's **scorching** hot today. I could definitely use a paper fan!

羅波：真難想像在現代化的台灣，還有鹿港這種古老的風味！

高貴：是啊，不過鹿港也曾經繁華過。十七世紀時，荷蘭佔領者將鹿港當作重要的外銷港，結果它成為中台灣的主要門戶呢。

羅波：真的啊？那結果呢？

高貴：二十世紀初，這裡保守的居民因為拒絕讓南北縱貫鐵路及一些主要公路經過，這裡就開始沒落了。

邱克：嗯，還有就是港口淤泥，導致這裡從台灣的第二大城變成小鎮。

高貴：不過也正因為如此，鹿港的傳統風貌才得以保存啊！

羅波：說的也是。那我們現在吃的是什麼東東？

邱克：是蚵仔煎啦。這裡的海鮮超好吃的。

羅波：嗯，這跟我常吃的蛋餅很不一樣耶。

高貴：你們兩個快點吃啦，吃完我們可以沿著中山路逛逛，那裡有許多傳統工藝店，例如木工、製扇、製香、製燈籠等等。

羅波：今天好熱，我剛好可以去買把紙扇子！

單字

✤ **century**（n.）世紀

✤ **occupier**（n.）佔領者

✤ **harbor**（n.）港

✤ **export**（n.）輸出

✤ **gateway**（n.）出入口

✤ **conservative**（adj.）保守的

✤ **resident**（n.）居民

✤ **refuse**（v.）拒絕

✤ **decline**（n.）衰退

✤ **silt**（n.）粉砂

✤ **preservation**（n.）保存

✤ **oyster**（n.）牡蠣

✤ **omelet**〔ˋɑmlɪt〕（n.）蛋餅

✤ **fantastic**（adj.）極好的

✤ **stroll**（v.）閒逛；漫步

✤ **handicraft**（n.）手工藝品

✤ **woodworking**（n.）木工藝

✤ **fan**（n.）扇子

✤ **incense**（n.）香

✤ **manufacturing**（n.）製造（業）

✤ **lantern**（n.）燈籠

✤ **scorching**（adj.）灼熱的；燃燒般的

片語與句型

✤ **had its day**：曾經繁華輝煌過
　⑩ This singer had his day, but he is going downhill now.（這歌者曾經紅過，但現在走下坡了。）

✤ **choke up with...**：被……塞住
　choke (v.) 阻塞
　⑩ When the bomb went off, the street was choked up with people.（炸彈爆炸時，街上擠滿了人。）

✤ **be done V+ing...**：做完某事
　⑩ When you're done working, remember to turn off the light.（工作做完時，記得要關燈。）

發音小技巧 🔊

Aside from its seafood, Lugang's traditional pastries and cakes are also very popular.

鹿港除了海鮮聞名，各式各樣的傳統糕點也十分知名。

● 趴趴走好用句

1. 清朝乾隆、嘉慶期間是鹿港的黃金時期。

   The Qianlong and Jiaqing periods of the Qing Dynasty were the golden age of Lugang.

2. 鹿港的港口和街道結構上，都保有大陸泉州的風味，因此被稱為「小泉州」。

   The ports and streets of Lugang are laid out in the Quanzhou style; thus the town is also known as "Little Quanzhou."

3. 鹿港的中山路及兩旁的巷弄有各式各樣的寺廟、古蹟及商店。

   There are all kinds of temples, relics, and shops on Zhongshan Road and the lanes and alleys that branch off it.

4. 鹿港到處都是便宜美味的傳統小吃，處處也可見小型夜市及傳統市場。

   Delicious and affordable traditional snacks can be found everywhere in Lugang. Small-scale night markets and traditional markets are also ever present.

5. 鹿港的知名小吃包括肉包、麵線、魷魚羹、肉羹、蚵仔煎等。

   Famous Lugang specialties include pork buns, Mien Xian, squid stew, meat stew, and oyster omelets.

6.　「益源大厝」位於彰化縣秀水鄉，是彰化縣境內最大的古宅。

The Maxingchen Residence, located in Changhua County's Xiushui Township, is the largest ancient residence in the county.

7.　「八卦山風景區」北起大肚溪、南到濁水溪，長約33公里，橫跨十個鄉市鎮。

The Baguashan Scenic Area stretches from Dadu River in the north to Zhuoshui River in the south. Its 33-kilometer length spans ten cities and towns.

8.　八卦山的「大佛風景區」有一座巨大的佛像，是台灣八大名勝之一。

A giant statue of Buddha, one of Taiwan's Eight Famous Attractions, can be found in Baguashan's Great Buddha Scenic Area.

9.　「田尾公路花園」位於田尾鄉與永靖鄉附近的「一號省道」。

Tianwei Highway Garden is located near Provincial Route No. 1, which runs near the towns of Tianwei and Yongjing.

10.　「田尾公路花園」有許多專業栽培的園區，著名的植物有仙人掌、向日葵、菊花等。

Tianwei Highway Garden is home to numerous professionally tended gardens. Popular plants include cacti, sunflowers, and chrysanthemums.

11. 每年12月到隔年2月是「田尾公路花園」的觀光花季。

The flower season at Tianwei Highway Garden begins in December of each year and lasts until the following February.

12. 「鹿港民俗文物館」與「台灣民俗村」皆位於彰化縣,是瞭解台灣民俗風情的好去處。

Lugang Folk Arts Museum and Taiwan Folk Village, both located in Changhua County, are ideal places to learn more about Taiwanese folk customs.

埔里與奧萬大
Puli and Aowanda

Robert: Puli is so **breathtakingly** beautiful! I really don't get why the elderly Japanese couple didn't like it here!

Kitty: (Sigh) Well, they were high-class Japanese. They complained about the poor environmental **sanitation** of Puli, the **proliferation** of dog droppings, and the lack of **civism** among the local residents. Of course they didn't want to stay.

Robert: C'mon, what's not to like about Puli? It **boasts** sweet spring water, good wine, fresh flowers, and beautiful women. What is there to **criticize**?

Taike: Robert, I'm so **touched** that you'd stand up for Taiwan. But for you to say something like that means that you're becoming more and more like a Taiwanese. You don't even notice the litter on the ground anymore. Ha ha!

Kitty: Puli is actually still very beautiful. A typical **basin** town, it is **surrounded** by mountains on four sides and is known as a "mountain city." What's more, it is warm all year round and the water is clean and pure. There are even green hills and clear waters... I myself am itching to move here!

Taike: But since Puli's water quality is so good, the local girls are extremely beautiful. Aren't you afraid of being **outshined** by the **competition**? Ha ha!

Robert: It is said that because of the fine water quality they have in Puli, the wine **fermented** at the Puli **Winery** is especially **fragrant**.

Taike: You **drunkard**! Now you've turned back into being an American!

Kitty: I for one prefer to stay for a period of time in Aowanda! Before we come here next time, we should definitely book a **cabin** at the Aowanda Forest **Recreation** Area!

羅波：埔里真是美到不行！我真搞不懂為什麼那對日本老夫婦會不喜歡這裡！

高貴：唉，人家是高級的日本人嘛，嫌埔里環境衛生不好、狗屎超多、當地居民又沒公德心，當然不想住啦。

羅波：拜託，埔里有什麼不好？甘泉、美酒、鮮花、美人，樣樣不缺，有什麼好挑剔的？

邱克：羅波，你這樣力挺台灣讓我很感動。不過你會這麼說，表示你真的越來越像台灣人了，連地上的垃圾都可以視而不見，哈哈！

高貴：其實埔里還是很美的，它是個標準的盆地小鎮，四面環山，有「山城」之稱。而且四季溫和，水質甜美，山明水秀……，連我都很想搬到這裡住呢！

邱克：不過埔里的水質優良，當地的女生因此都超美的，妳不怕被比下去嗎？哈哈！

羅波：據說埔里的水好，連帶的「埔里酒場」釀出來的酒也特別香！

邱克：你這個酒鬼！這時候你又變得很像美國人了！

高貴：我倒想去附近的奧萬大住一陣子呢！我們下次來之前，一定要先在「奧萬大森林遊樂區」預訂小木屋！

單字

- ✤ **breathtakingly**（adv.）驚人地
- ✤ **sanitation**（n.）公共衛生
- ✤ **proliferation**（n.）增加；繁殖
- ✤ **civism**（n.）公德心
- ✤ **boast**（v.）擁有（可誇耀的事物）
- ✤ **criticize**（v.）批評
- ✤ **touch**（v.）感動
- ✤ **basin**（n.）盆地
- ✤ **surround**（v.）包圍；環繞
- ✤ **outshine**（v.）勝過……
- ✤ **competition**（n.）競爭
- ✤ **ferment**（v.）發酵
- ✤ **winery**（n.）釀酒場
- ✤ **fragrant**（n.）芳香的
- ✤ **drunkard**（n.）酒鬼
- ✤ **cabin**（n.）小屋
- ✤ **recreation**（n.）休閒；娛樂

片語與句型

✤ **do not get why...**：不瞭解為什麼……

　get (v.) 瞭解；學會

　例 Poor Judy, she doesn't get why her husband wants to divorce her.（可憐的 Judy，她不知道為何老公要和她離婚。）

✤ **be itching to...**：心癢難耐

　itching (adj.) 渴望的

　例 As a dot-comer, he is itching to meet venture capitalists.（身為網路創業家，他等不及要見創投家。）

發音小技巧 🔊

Puli has bred many well-known Taiwanese artists and creative people.

埔里孕育了很多台灣知名的藝術家與創作者。

● 趴趴走好用句

1. 風光明媚的埔里鎮，以四個W而聞名，即 water（水）、weather（天氣）、wine（酒）、與 women（美女）。

   Breathtaking Puli Township is known for its 4 W's: water, weather, wine, and women.

2. 「埔里酒廠」創設於日據時代，廠區內有典雅的日式建築。

   Puli Winery was first developed during the Japanese colonial era. The winery is dotted with elegant Japanese-style buildings.

3. 「埔里酒廠」以生產紹興酒為主，廠內也以紹興酒研發出各式食品，包括紹興冰棒、紹興米糕、紹興茶葉蛋等。

   Puli Winery mainly produces Shaoxing wine, but it has also developed various derivative foods that include Shaoxing wine as an ingredient, including Shaoxing popsicles, Shaoxing rice cakes, and Shaoxing tea eggs.

4. 由於埔里的水質好，「廣興紙寮」做出來的紙不會因時間或日曬而變黃。

   Due to the high quality of the water in Puli, paper products manufactured at the Guangxing Paper Factory do not yellow easily with time or exposure to the sun.

5. 「廣興紙寮」提供自己動手做的紙藝課程，讓遊客親自體驗造紙的過程。

   The Guangxing Paper Factory provides make-your-own-paper classes to give tourists a chance to experience the paper production process firsthand.

6.　「廣興紙寮」的手工紙最具特色，這種紙是以農產品的廢棄物再利用而
研製成的。

Among all Guangxing Paper Factory products, the handmade
paper is the most distinctive. This type of paper is made out of
recycled farm waste.

7.　「鯉魚潭風景區」距離埔里鎮市區約15分鐘車程，宛如鬧區中的世外桃
源。

The Carp Lake Scenic Area, a fifteen-minute drive from the Puli city
center, is a retreat away from the turmoil of the world.

8.　「鯉魚潭」面積約17公頃，據說因為地處台灣地理的中心處，因此風水
絕佳。

Carp Lake occupies an area of approximately 17 hectares. It is
said that because of its location in the center of Taiwan, it enjoys
excellent feng shui.

9.　奧萬大位於南投仁愛鄉，被稱為「楓葉故鄉」。

Aowanda is located in Nantou's Ren'ai Township and is otherwise
known as "the home of maples."

10.　奧萬大以山泉、瀑布與賞楓、賞鳥聞名。

Aowanda is best known for its mountain springs and waterfalls, as
well as maple-viewing and birdwatching.

11. 奧萬大最好的賞楓季節是在秋天變冬天時。

The best time to see the maple leaves at Aowanda is as the seasons change from fall to winter.

12. 「奧萬大森林遊樂區」可以賞楓、賞鳥、欣賞不同的自然生態。

You can enjoy the sight of the maples, birds, and other natural ecology at the Aowanda Forest Recreation Area.

合歡山
Hehuan Mountain

Robert: Oh, you must be kidding me! This is not snow; this is **slush**!

Taike: Hey, don't act up, okay? It took us a very long time to get up here!

Kitty: That's true. And anyway, this is my first **glimpse** of snow. Although I don't like big crowds, I'm still thrilled!

Robert: I'm sorry, but I just don't see what's so special about snow. Where I come from, people **fret** when they see snow. However, it is pretty amazing to see snow in a **subtropical** area like Taiwan!

Kitty: That's true. Hehuan Mountain is **situated** on the **border** of Hualien County and Nantou County. It is also known as "Snow Country" and **boasts** Taiwan's only **ski resort**.

Robert: There is so little snow here. Can it be skied on? It would hurt pretty badly if you were to fall!

Taike: It is **richly** green in Hehuan Mountain in the summer though!

Kitty: It's freezing here! We'd better check into one of the hotels at the Qingjing Farm while it's still early.

Robert: Right. I can't wait to see the wide open **pastures**, drink high-mountain tea, enjoy the high mountain flowers, and have a "beef **banquet**!"

Kitty: I'll have their special **temperate-zone** fruits for a better **complexion**!

Taike: Then I'd like to go to nearby Wushe. It is located at an **elevation** of 1,150 meters, and is **inhabited** largely by members of the Atayal **aborigine** tribe. Its cherry blossoms are said to be of **extraordinary** beauty!

羅波：啊，不會吧，這根本不是雪，而是爛泥嘛！

邰克：喂，你別這樣好不好，我們可是花了很久的時間才上來的耶！

高貴：對啊，不管怎樣，這是我第一次看到雪，雖然我不喜歡人擠人，還是很興奮的！

羅波：不好意思，我只是不知道下雪有什麼了不起的。在我老家，大家一看到雪就煩咧！不過能在亞熱帶的台灣看到雪，也算很新鮮啦！

高貴：是啊，合歡山位於花蓮縣和南投縣的交界，有「雪鄉」之稱，有台灣唯一的滑雪場呢。

羅波：這裡的雪那麼少，能滑雪嗎？如果跌倒應該會很痛吧！

邰克：不過夏天的合歡山可是綠意盎然喔！

高貴：這裡超冷的，我們還是趁早住進清境農場的旅館吧。

羅波：對啊，我等不及去看遼闊的牧場、喝高山茶、欣賞高山花卉、吃「全牛大餐」了！

高貴：我要吃那裡不同的溫帶水果，養顏美容！

邰克：那我要去附近的霧社，那裡海拔1,150公尺，居民大多是泰雅族原住民，據說櫻花美得不得了！

單字 ‥‥‥

✤ **slush**（**n.**）泥濘

✤ **glimpse**（**n.**）一瞥

✤ **fret**（**v.**）煩惱；鬱悶

✤ **subtropical**（**adj.**）亞熱帶的

✤ **situate**（**v.**）位於；處於

✤ **border**（**n.**）邊界

✤ **boast**（**v.**）擁有（可誇耀的事物）

✤ **ski resort** 滑雪勝地

✤ **richly**（**adv.**）充分地；富裕地

✤ **pasture**（**n.**）牧場

✤ **banquet** [`bæŋkwɪt]（**n.**）宴會

✤ **temperate-zone** 溫帶

✤ **complexion**（**n.**）氣色；膚色

✤ **elevation**（**n.**）高度；海拔

✤ **inhabit**（**v.**）居住

✤ **aborigine**（**n.**）原住民

✤ **extraordinary**（**adj.**）非常的；驚人的

片語與句型

❖ **be kidding someone**：開某人玩笑

　　kid (v.) 取笑；欺騙

　　例 They kid him about his paunch.（他們取笑他的大肚子。）

❖ **act up**：任性

　　例 For some reason, he has been acting up constantly in school.（不知為
　　　何，他最近在學校都一直任性調皮。）

❖ **be thrilled**：非常興奮的

　　thrilled (adj.) 極為激動的

　　例 She is thrilled that her brother got into the best college.（她弟弟上了
　　　最好的大學，讓她很興奮。）

發音小技巧 🔊

Qingjing Farm, occupying an area of 760 hectares, is one of
the hottest vacation spots in Taiwan.

「清境農場」面積有760公頃，是台灣熱門的度假地點。

1. 合歡山是大甲溪、濁水溪和立霧溪的分水嶺。

   Hehuan Mountain is the watershed of the Dajia, Zhuoshui, and Liwu Rivers.

2. 合歡山的主峰高達3,416 公尺,春天可賞花,夏天可避暑,秋天可踏青、冬天可玩雪。

   The main peak of Hehuan Mountain stands at 3,416 meters. You can enjoy the delightful sight of flowers in the spring, escape the heat in the summer, get close to nature in the fall, and have fun in the snow in the winter.

3. 到合歡山賞雪最好準備登山鞋、太陽眼鏡、熱水壺,以及防寒衣物。

   It's advisable to equip yourself with climbing boots, sunglasses, a thermos bottle, and warm clothing to keep out the cold when traveling to Hehuan Mountain to see the snow.

4. 每當冬天寒流來襲,合歡山的雪景總是吸引大批人潮,因此總會大塞車。

   Every time a cold front comes in the winter, Hehuan Mountain's snow scene attracts crowds of people, thus causing heavy traffic.

5. 合歡山山上常有高冷蔬菜,如白菜、高麗菜出售,十分清脆可口。

   The high mountain vegetables (such as Chinese cabbages and cabbages) often sold on Hehuan Mountain are crunchy and delicious.

6. 「清境農場」海拔介於1,600-2,100公尺之間，屬溫帶氣候。

Qingjing Farm is located between 1,600 and 2,100 meters above sea level, where the weather is usually moderate.

7. 「清境農場」最具代表性的農產品包括水蜜桃、蜜蘋果、世紀梨、奇異果、高山茶、香水百合等。

Characteristic produce of Qingjing Farm includes honey peaches, honey apples, century pears, kiwis, high mountain tea, and oriental lilies.

8. 921地震後，清境地區的觀光業一度重挫，但現在已經重現旅遊契機。

Tourism in the Qingjing area dropped post-921, but it has now recovered and is showing great promise.

9. 「惠蓀林場」是全台規模最大的原始森林。

Huisun Forest is the largest virgin forest in Taiwan in terms of scale.

10. 霧社因為終日雲霧繚繞，因而得名。

Wushe got its name because it is frequently shrouded in clouds and mist.

11. 每年冬、春交替之時，霧社山區內總是櫻花盛開，因此霧社又被稱為「櫻都」。

> Every year when winter turns to spring, cherry blossoms bloom in profusion all over the mountainous region of Wushe, thus earning it the name, "the capital of cherry blossoms."

12. 霧社的抗日紀念碑是紀念在日據時代，當地居民反抗日本殘暴統治的事件。

> The memorial to anti-Japanese resistance at Wushe commemorates the locals' struggle against brutal Japanese rule during the occupation period.

CD
1-22

集集與水里
Jiji and Shuili

Robert: Ah, you scared me! I thought we were coming here to eat **barbeque** snake!

Taike: You Americans are so **lame**! You jump every time you hear people say the word "snake!"

Kitty: Well, here we are at the **renowned** Shuili Snake **Kiln**. It is Taiwan's oldest, most traditional wood-burning kiln.

Taike: Yeah, and you're eating tasty Shuili **meat balls** and ice-on-a-**stick**. They have **absolutely** nothing to do with snakes, so take it easy!

Robert: But the meat balls have nothing to do with American meat balls—they almost **choked** me to death. This ice-on-a-stick is pretty interesting; it's similar to the corndogs I used to eat in America!

Taike: Your **comparison** is pretty **weird**! Hurry up; we need to rush on to Jiji.

Robert: Jiji? The name sounds funny.

Kitty: The Jiji Train Station is the oldest train station left in Taiwan. It was built **entirely** of red **cypress**. In addition, Jiji is not only a train station, but also a little town, which **features** the Mingxin **Academy** of Classical Learning, Green **Tunnel**, and a railway museum.

Taike: Jiji is also the name of a **branch** railway line. The line is filled with **enchanting** sights of farm country. It's fascinating!

Robert: Tell me about it! On our way here there were old red-brick houses and clear streams everywhere. It was **breathtaking**!

羅波：啊，剛剛真的嚇了我一大跳，我以為我們要來這裡吃烤過的蛇呢！

邱克：你們美國人實在太沒用了，每次聽到蛇就皮皮挫！

高貴：這裡是著名的「水里蛇窯」啦，是台灣現存最古老、最有傳統文化的柴燒窯。

邱克：是啊，而且你現在吃的是好吃的水里肉圓和枝仔冰，跟蛇一點關係也沒有，安啦！

羅波：不過這肉圓和美國的肉圓差很多耶，差點把我噎死。這枝仔冰倒很好玩，很像我在美國常吃的玉米熱狗！

邱克：你的比較很詭異耶！趕快吃啦，我們等會還要去集集呢。

羅波：集集？好怪的名字。

高貴：集集是台灣現存歷史最悠久的火車站，完全是用紅檜搭建的。而且集集不僅是車站，也是個小鎮，那裡有明新書院、綠色隧道、鐵路文物博覽館等等。

邱克：集集也是一條鐵路支線的名稱，沿線的田野風光很迷人！

羅波：對啊，我們來的時候到處都是紅瓦古厝和清澈的水道，真是美呆了！

單字

- ❖ **barbeque**（**n.**）烤肉
- ❖ **lame**（**adj.**）（口語）很遜的
- ❖ **renowned**（**adj.**）著名的
- ❖ **kiln**（**n.**）窯
- ❖ **meat ball** 肉圓；肉丸（台式肉圓又稱 **round dumplings/round dumplings with ground meat**）
- ❖ **stick**（**n.**）細棒；竿
- ❖ **absolutely**（**adv.**）絕對地
- ❖ **choke**（**v.**）窒息
- ❖ **comparison**（**n.**）比較
- ❖ **weird** [wɪrd]（**adj.**）怪異的
- ❖ **entirely**（**adv.**）全然地；完全地
- ❖ **cypress** [ˋsaɪprɪs]（**n.**）檜；柏
- ❖ **feature**（**v.**）以……為特色
- ❖ **academy**（**n.**）專科學校；學苑
- ❖ **tunnel**（**n.**）隧道
- ❖ **branch**（**n.**）支線
- ❖ **enchanting**（**adj.**）迷人的
- ❖ **breathtaking**（**adj.**）驚人的；令人透不過氣來的

片語與句型

❖ **have nothing to do with...**：與……無關

㊟ I have nothing to do with his breaking up with her.（他和她分手和我一點關係也沒有。）

❖ **Tell me about it!**：意為「我同意你的說法」、「還用你說嗎？我完全同意」

㊟ "I don't like him at all." "Tell me about it!"（「我一點都不喜歡他。」「那還用說嗎？」）

發音小技巧 🔊

The Sacred Tree in Xitou is over 2,800 years old; it is an active giant red cypress tree.

溪頭的神木年齡高達2,800年，是活的紅檜巨木。

● 趴趴走好用句

1. 集集支線位於彰化縣二水鄉至南投縣車埕間。

The Jiji Branch Railway Line runs between Ershui Township in Changhua County and Checheng in Nantou County.

2. 集集支線全長約三十公里，至今已有七十多年歷史，是台灣第一條觀光鐵路。

The Jiji Branch Railway Line is 30 kilometers long, has over 70 years of history, and is Taiwan's foremost tourist railway.

3. 「綠色隧道」位於名間與集集之間，有長達4.5公里的樟樹景觀。

Green Tunnel, tucked between the towns of Mingjian and Jiji, features a 4.5-kilometer-long view of camphors.

4. 「綠色隧道」沿途樹木茂密，又有小火車經過，是許多結婚新人攝影留念的景點。

Rows of trees line Green Tunnel and miniature trains pass through it, thus making it a favorite wedding photo shoot destination for newlyweds.

5. 「水里蛇窯」是順著山坡地形以土磚砌成，因為遠望的形狀像蛇，因而得名。

Shuili Snake Kiln, built with bricks against the contours of the mountainous terrain, got its name from its resemblance to a snake when seen from a distance.

6. 「水里蛇窯陶藝文化園區」是由原來的舊窯場改建而成。

The Shuili Snake Kiln Ceramics Park was reconstructed from what was previously a kiln.

7. 「溪頭森林遊樂區」因位於北勢溪的源頭而得名。

The Xitou ("River Head") Forest Recreation Park got its name from its location at the source of the Beishi River.

8. 溪頭位於海拔1,150公尺處，屬於台灣大學的實驗林場。

Xitou is located approximately 1,150 meters above sea level. It is affiliated with the Experimental Forest Station of National Taiwan University.

9. 溪頭三面環山，終年氣候涼爽。

Xitou is surrounded by mountains on three sides and thus enjoys cool weather year round.

10. 溪頭的主要景觀包括大學池、銀杏林、青年活動中心、紅檜林等。

The main attractions in Xitou include the university pond, the ginkgo forest, the youth activity center, and the Taiwan red cypress forest.

11.　溪頭的「921巨石」是因921地震而產生的巨石，重達2,400公噸。

The "921 Giant Rock" at Xitou is a huge rock that came into being with the 921 earthquake. It weighs 2,400 metric tons.

12.　「杉林溪森林遊樂區」位於南投縣竹山鎮，有原始的山林，全年花開不斷。

The Sun Link Sea Forest Recreation Area in Nantou County's Zhushan Township features native mountains and trees as well as flowers in bloom throughout the year.

CD
1-23

日月潭與九族文化村
Sun Moon Lake and
Formosan Aboriginal Culture Village

Robert: This Sun Moon Lake is **serene**! I can't believe there's a lake at an **elevation** of 748 meters above sea level in the middle of Taiwan! But what does it have to do with the sun and the moon?

Kitty: Because the northern part of the lake is shaped like a sun and the southern part like a new moon.

Taike: Hey, why did you buy so many **aboriginal handicrafts**? Want to open your own shop?

Robert: Of course not. I'm sending them back to the States for my parents. They love everything with an **ethnic** flavor.

Kitty: No way. You were buying all this junk because you like that Thao girl selling the stuff!

Robert: Well, she was **gorgeous**. She invited me to come back for the traditional **harvest** festival in the eighth lunar month, where I can dance with people from her tribe.

Taike: If you're so into aboriginal culture, we can visit the **Formosan** Aboriginal Culture Village tomorrow. There you will find the traditional houses and other buildings of original **inhabitants** of Taiwan, all nine tribes of them. There is also a Naruwan Theater where you can "**rehearse**" your aborigine-style singing and dancing first.

Kitty: But do you have any idea what the "nine tribes" are?

Robert: Of course I do—and **incidentally**, the number of tribes **officially identified** is thirteen, not nine; they are: Yami (Tao), Amis, Atayal, Saisiat, Bunun, Puyuma, Rukai, Paiwan, Tsou, Kavalan, Truku, Thao, and Sakizaya!

羅波：這日月潭真寧靜！沒想到台灣中間還有海拔748公尺的湖呢！只不
　　　過它跟日、月有何關係？

高貴：因為湖的北半部形狀像太陽，南半部形狀像新月啦。

邱克：喂，你買這麼多原住民的手工藝品幹嘛？要開店嗎？

羅波：不是啦，我是要寄回美國給我爸媽。他們超喜歡有民族風味的東
　　　西。

高貴：才不是呢，你是因為喜歡賣東西的那個邵族女生才大手筆的啦！

羅波：她真的超正。她還要我農曆八月再回來這裡耶，因為到時會有傳
　　　統年祭，可以和她的族人一起共舞。

邱克：你對原住民文化那麼有興趣，那明天我們可以去「九族文化
　　　村」，那裡以台灣原住民的原始部落建築為主，裡面的娜魯灣劇
　　　場還可以讓你先「排練」你的山地歌舞秀。

高貴：不過你可知道這「九族」是哪九族？

羅波：當然知道囉——而且官方認定的台灣原住民有十三族，並非九族
　　　——雅美、阿美、泰雅、賽夏、布農、卑南、魯凱、排灣、鄒
　　　族、噶瑪蘭族、太魯閣族、邵族和撒奇萊雅族！

單字

✤ **serene** [sə`rin]（**adj.**）寧靜的；安詳的

✤ **elevation**（**n.**）（海拔）高度

✤ **aboriginal**（**adj.**）原住民的

✤ **handicraft**（**n.**）手工藝品

✤ **ethnic**（**adj.**）民族的；族群的

✤ **gorgeous**（**adj.**）極好的；美妙的

✤ **harvest**（**n.**）收穫

✤ **Formosan**（**adj.**）台灣的

✤ **inhabitant**（**n.**）居民

✤ **rehearse**（**v.**）預演；彩排

✤ **incidentally**（**adv.**）附帶一提

✤ **officially**（**adv.**）官方地；正式地

✤ **identify**（**v.**）確認、驗明

片語與句型

✤ **have something to do with...**：和……有關
   例 Do you have something to do with the missing money?（你和不見的
   錢有什麼關係嗎？）
✤ **be into something**：對某事熱衷
   例 She's very into online games.（她對網路遊戲很是熱衷。）

發音小技巧

Sun Moon Lake is the most popular of Taiwan's reservoir
and lake scenic areas.

日月潭是台灣的水庫湖泊風景區中最受歡迎的。

● 趴趴走好用句

1.　「日月潭國家風景區」是全台灣最大的淡水湖泊。

Sun Moon Lake National Scenic Area is the largest freshwater lake in all of Taiwan.

2.　日月潭面積116平方公里，以「光華島」為界，將湖分為南北。

Sun Moon Lake has an area of 116 square kilometers, divided into northern and southern halves by Guanghua Island.

3.　日月潭的水主要用於發電，發電量佔台灣水力發電的56%。

The water in Sun Moon Lake is mainly used to generate power, a total of 56% of the hydropower in Taiwan.

4.　遊日月潭可選擇搭遊艇、健行、或騎自行車等方式。

You can explore Sun Moon Lake on a ferry, by hiking, or by bike.

5.　「日月潭國家風景區」近年因開放大陸地區人士觀光，成為熱門的觀光景點。

After Sun Moon Lake National Scenic Area was opened up for tourism to mainland Chinese tourists, the area became a major tourist destination.

6. 「日月潭國家風景區管理處」近年來規劃了幾條自行車路線，其中以「環湖公路」最佳，全長約33公里。

The Sun Moon Lake National Scenic Area Administration has developed bike paths in recent years, the best of which is the 33-kilometer round-the-lake highway.

7. 「九族文化村」是結合文化、遊憩及教育的多元化旅遊景點。

The Formosan Aboriginal Culture Village is a multifaceted tourist attraction that incorporates culture, travel, and education.

8. 日月潭岸的邵族是原住民族群中人最少的一族，人數約五百人。

Along the shore of Sun Moon Lake live the Thao, Taiwan's smallest aboriginal tribe, with a population of approximately 500.

9. 台灣原住民族屬於南島語系，人種上屬於馬來人。

Taiwanese aborigines belong to the Austronesian language family and are genetically related to the Malay.

10. 台灣原住民傳統以小米為主食，但近代由於受漢人影響，大都改以稻米為主食。

Millet has traditionally been the staple food of Taiwan aborigines. Due to influence from the Han, however, most have now switched to rice.

11.　邵族於民國九十年成為臺灣原住民族的第十族。

The Thao were officially recognized as Taiwan's tenth aboriginal tribe in 2001.

12.　泰雅族是台灣原住民第二大族，男女在成年後有黥面的習俗。

The Atayal is the second-largest aboriginal group in Taiwan. According to custom, men and women have their faces tattooed when they come of age.

雲林
Yunlin

Robert: Wow! Of all the festivities I've taken part in, this has got to be the **liveliest** and largest in **scale**!

Kitty: This is the Beigang Chaotian Temple's famous Matzu **pilgrimage**. During Matzu's birthday late in the third lunar month, numerous **grand** temple fairs, traditional Taiwanese Yi-Ge **mobile stage** performances, lantern performances, and **prayer** pilgrimages are held. These events always attract scores of international media to **capture** them on film!

Robert: What's a traditional Taiwanese Yi-Ge mobile stage performance?

Taike: Those were the electronic **floats** you were **gaping** at just now!

Robert: They were? Man, I'm so tired from walking! I've heard the coffee in Yunlin is on par with Colombian coffee. Where can we find it? I need a cup to **jolt** me awake!

Taike: You're referring to Gukeng coffee—that's a locally-produced **variety**. But to tell you the truth, there aren't many coffee trees in Gukeng. Everything you've heard is just **marketing hype**.

Kitty: However, Yunlin does have such local specialties as Beigang peanuts, Douliu **pomelos** and Xiluo rice.

Robert: Xiluo? Is that in any way related to the largest bridge in the Far East, Xiluo Bridge?

Kitty: Bingo. The bridge **stretches** across the Zhuoshui River. When it was built, it brought convenient transport and economic **prosperity** to Yunlin.

Taike: However, it was also because of the bridge that many of the local youngsters left, thus **draining** the area of its **productivity**. That's why the people of Xiluo have mixed feelings about the bridge!

羅波：哇，這是我參加過最熱鬧、規模最大的慶典了！

高貴：這就是知名的北港朝天宮「媽祖進香活動」了。每年在農曆三月
下旬媽祖誕辰的前後，這裡都會舉辦許多大型的廟會、藝閣、花
燈表演、繞境祈福活動，而且總是吸引許多外國媒體前來拍攝
呢！

羅波：什麼是「藝閣」？

邱克：就是你剛剛看得目不轉睛的「電子花車」啦！

羅波：是喔。唉，我走得好累喔！據說雲林有可以媲美哥倫比亞出產的
咖啡，在哪裡啊？我要喝一杯提神！

邱克：你說的是「古坑咖啡」啦，那是我們台灣的土產咖啡喔！不過老
實說，古坑那裡根本沒有多少咖啡樹，這都是人為炒作的啦！

高貴：不過雲林的特產還有北港的花生、斗六的文旦，以及西螺米。

羅波：「西螺」？是和「遠東第一大橋」的「西螺大橋」有關嗎？

高貴：沒錯。那座橋橫跨濁水溪，它曾經為雲林帶來便捷的交通和經濟
繁榮。

邱克：不過也因為那座橋，造成當地許多年輕人出走，生產力外流，所
以西螺人對它是又愛又恨的！

單字

- **lively** [ˈlaɪvlɪ] (**adj.**) 生氣勃勃的；熱鬧的
- **scale** (**n.**) 規模
- **pilgrimage** (**n.**) 朝聖；進香
- **grand** (**adj.**) 大的；壯觀的
- **mobile** (**adj.**) 可移動的
- **stage** (**n.**) 舞台
- **prayer** (**n.**) 祈福；祈禱
- **capture** (**v.**) 獲取；捕捉
- **float** (**n.**) 遊行車；花車
- **gape** (**v.**) 嘴巴合不攏地瞪視
- **jolt** (**v.**) 猛擊
- **variety** (**n.**) 種類
- **marketing** (**n.**) 行銷
- **hype** (**n.**) 噱頭
- **pomelo** [ˈpɑməlo] (**n.**) 柚子；文旦
- **stretch** (**v.**) 伸展
- **prosperity** (**n.**) 繁榮；成功
- **drain** (**v.**) 使耗盡
- **productivity** (**n.**) 生產力

片語與句型

✤ **of all the...**：在所有的……當中

Of all the children she has, she loves Mike the most.（在她所有的孩子中，她最愛的是 Mike。）

✤ **take part in...**：參加

例 Last year she took part in the overseas rescue mission.（她去年參與海外救援團的工作。）

✤ **be on par with...**：與……同等重要；與……齊名

例 As a writer he was on par with the great novelists.（他是與偉大小說家齊名的作家。）

發音小技巧 🔊

Beigang's Matzu pilgrimage is one of Taiwan's twelve biggest international folk custom tourism events.

北港的媽祖進香活動是台灣十二大國際民俗觀光節慶之一。

● 趴趴走好用句

1. 雲林縣北港鎮最熱鬧的地方是朝天宮一帶，這裡每年都會舉辦各式各樣的活動。

   The area surrounding Chaotian Temple is the busiest region in Beigang Township, Yunlin County. Every year, events of all kinds are held in the area.

2. 朝天宮每年農曆元月15日的元宵節有大型花燈展。

   Chaotian Temple holds a large-scale lantern display during the Lantern Festival, which falls on the fifteenth day of the first month in the lunar calendar.

3. 「西螺大橋」全長1,939公尺，曾經是台灣南北運輸的交通樞紐。

   Xiluo Bridge, with a total length of 1,939 meters, once served as a pivotal transportation junction between the island's northern and southern regions.

4. 「西螺大橋」橋身為紅色，橫跨濁水溪，但現因高速公路的出現而運輸量大減。

   The red Xiluo Bridge spans the Zhuoshui River, but it has lost a great deal of traffic with the advent of expressways.

5. 在鄉村地區十分流行的電子花車，是從傳統的「藝閣」得到靈感所演變而來的。

   Electronic floats, immensely popular in the countryside, are inspired modifications of the traditional Yi-Ge.

6. 雲林縣的斗六、北港等地區，在年節慶典時都會有藝閣的演出。

Yi-Ge performances can be seen in Chinese New Year celebration in such places as Douliu and Beigang in Yunlin.

7. 藝閣從大陸引進到台灣，至今約有三百年的歷史。

It has been approximately three hundred years since Yi-Ge performances first came to Taiwan from mainland China.

8. 「劍湖山世界」位於雲林縣古坑鄉，是台灣中南部最具規模的旅遊據點。

Janfusun Fancyworld, located in Yunlin County's Gukeng Township, is the largest tourist attraction in central Taiwan.

9. 「劍湖山世界」裡有摩天輪、雲霄飛車等遊樂設施，還有台灣民間最大的博物館。

Janfusun Fancyworld features such amusement facilities as Ferris wheels and roller coasters; it also boasts the largest non-government-operated museum in Taiwan.

10. 古坑鄉的「草嶺風景區」有瀑布、溪流、斷崖、山洞等自然奇觀。

Gukeng's Caoling Scenic Area boasts such natural wonders as waterfalls, streams, precipices, and caves.

11.　虎尾鎮的「虎尾糖廠」在日據時代糖產量居全台之冠。

During the Japanese colonial era, the Huwei Sugar Mill in Huwei Township was the largest sugar supplier in Taiwan.

12.　雲林縣的特產包括草嶺的苦茶油、北港的花生及麻油，以及西螺的醬油、西瓜、濁水米。

Yunlin County specialties include tea seed oil from Caoling, peanuts and sesame oil from Beigang, and soy sauce, watermelon, and Zhuoshui Rice from Xiluo.

CD
1-25

嘉義
Chiayi

Robert: This place sure is **spooky**! I was scared **witless** seeing all the trees lining the road where we came from, and the **cemetery** nearby!

Taike: Well, you were the one who suggested a trip to Minxiong's **haunted** house. So now you've scared yourself, huh?

Kitty: Look, you guys, that's the **well** the **maid** was pushed into!

Robert: That's enough for me. Let's get out of here! I'm ready to throw up the two **bowls** of chicken and rice I had for lunch!

Taike: You can't! The chicken and rice we had was from the grandfather of all chicken and rice stores located by the Central Fountain at the Chiayi Train Station!

Kitty: Plus, we've still got to try the famous local snacks: pork buns and goose meat!

Robert: When are we going to see the "**Koji pottery**?" Chiayi happens to be the place where Taiwan's Koji pottery **originated**!

Kitty: Right. Koji pottery used to be used as **decoration** for temples. However, due to its **kaleidoscopic** colors and **elegant** design, people now collect it as art.

Taike: I've heard that Chiayi hosts the Chiayi City International Band Festival at the end of each year. **Wind orchestras** from all over Taiwan and even some from abroad come here to take part in the event.

Robert: Also, I heard that there's a place in Chiayi City with a sign that says "**Tropic of Cancer**." Where's that?

Kitty: That's at the **intersection** of Boai Road and Shixian Road. We can go check it out when we get back. I'd also like to take the chance to buy my dad some of his favorite **cubic biscuits**!

羅波：這裡好陰森喔！剛剛我們來這裡的路上有好多樹，附近又有墓園，真是嚇死人了！

邱克：還不是你說要來民雄看鬼屋的？現在自己嚇自己了吧？

高貴：你們看，這就是當初婢女被推下去的那口井啦！

羅波：好了好了，我們走吧！我都快把中午吃的兩碗「雞肉飯」吐出來了！

邱克：千萬不行！我們吃的可是在嘉義火車站前、中央噴水池旁邊的那家創始店的雞肉飯耶！

高貴：而且我們現在還要去吃這裡的著名小吃「肉包」和「鵝肉」耶！

羅波：那我們什麼時候去看「交趾陶」？嘉義可是台灣交趾陶工藝的發源地呢！

高貴：對，交趾陶早期是應用在寺廟建築的裝飾，不過因為它的色彩千變萬化，造型優美，現在已變成了藝術的收藏品。

邱克：據說嘉義每年歲末時還會定期舉辦「嘉義市國際管樂節」，台灣各地、以及一些國外的管樂團都會來參加！

羅波：而且我聽說，嘉義市某個地方有「北回歸線」的標誌，那在哪裡啊？

高貴：就在博愛路與世賢路口。我們回去時可以去看看，順便買我爸喜歡吃的方塊酥！

單字

- ✤ **spooky** (**adj.**) 令人毛骨悚然的
- ✤ **witless** (**adj.**) 瘋的
- ✤ **cemetery** (**n.**) 墓地
- ✤ **haunted** (**adj.**) 鬧鬼的
- ✤ **well** (**n.**) 井
- ✤ **maid** (**n.**) 奴婢；女僕
- ✤ **bowl** [bol](**n.**) 碗
- ✤ **Koji pottery** 交趾陶
- ✤ **originate** (**v.**) 開始；發端
- ✤ **decoration** (**n.**) 裝飾
- ✤ **kaleidoscopic** (**adj.**) 千變萬化的
- ✤ **elegant** (**adj.**) 優雅的
- ✤ **wind orchestra** 管樂團
- ✤ **Tropic of Cancer** 北回歸線
- ✤ **intersection** (**n.**) 十字路口
- ✤ **cubic** (**adj.**) 方塊的
- ✤ **biscuit** [`bɪskɪt](**n.**) 餅乾

片語與句型

❖ **used to**：曾經；過去經常……

　　⑨ He used to smoke a lot, but not anymore.（他曾經是癮君子，但不再是了。）

❖ **check out...**：（口語）瞧瞧；看看

　　⑨ Come check out this cute puppy!（來瞧瞧這隻可愛的小狗！）

發音小技巧

Chiayi City is situated on the Northern Jia'nan Plain in Southwestern Taiwan.

嘉義市位於台灣西南部「嘉南平原」的北端。

● 趴趴走好用句

1. 嘉義市具有深厚的文化與歷史，擁有「畫都」的美譽。

Chiayi City has rich cultural and historical roots, and is thus known as the "City of Paintings."

2. 台灣的交趾陶早期多應用在寺廟建築的裝飾上，傳統題材以人物為主。

Taiwan's Koji pottery was originally used to decorate temple architecture. People were traditionally the theme of the decorations.

3. 交趾陶以往多安裝在廟宇的高處，現在已是民間蒐藏的珍品。

Koji pottery was once installed in unreachable places in temples. Those decorative pieces have now turned into priceless items collected by civilians.

4. 嘉義市每年定期舉辦管樂節活動，已成為全台灣管樂界的盛事。

Chiayi City hosts the annual Band Festival, which has become one of the most important events in Taiwan's band music industry.

5. 嘉義市聞名的美食包括雞肉飯、方塊酥、米糕等。

Famous Chiayi City delicacies include chicken rice, cubic biscuits, and rice cakes.

6.　　北回歸線經過嘉義市。

The Tropic of Cancer runs through Chiayi City.

7.　　「中華民俗村」是阿里山公路上的主題樂園，園區前身是「吳鳳紀念園」。

The China Folk Custom Village is a theme park located on Alishan Highway. It was previously known as Wufeng Memorial Park.

8.　　「曾文水庫」位於嘉義縣與台南縣的交界，是台灣最大的水庫。

Zengwen Reservoir, located on the border separating Chiayi County from Tainan County, is the largest reservoir in Taiwan.

9.　　臺灣第一座交趾陶館位於嘉義市文化局的地下室，館內有陶藝作品陳列及免費的陶藝課程。

Taiwan's foremost Koji museum is located in the basement of the Chaiyi City Cultural Affairs Bureau. The museum features pottery artwork displays and free pottery lessons.

10.　　嘉義縣溪口鄉的開元殿主要供奉民族英雄鄭成功，擁有號稱世界最高的鄭成功神像。

Kaiyuan Temple, in Xikou Township, Chiayi County, primarily worships the folk hero Koxinga. It is known to have the world's tallest Koxinga statue.

11.　嘉義縣布袋鎮有一座又一座的鹽山，布袋漁港則有新鮮的海產。

Chiayi County's Budai Township features mountains of salt; Budai Fishing Port, on the other hand, offers fresh seafood.

12.　東石鄉位於嘉義縣的極西處，居民半漁半農，民風十分純樸。

Dongshi Township is located in the westernmost section of Chiayi County. Its residents, half of whom are fishermen and the other half farmers, live very simple lives.

26

阿里山
Alishan

Robert: This is **surreal**! I've never seen such a beautiful sunrise in my entire life!

Taike: Me too... I'm **speechless**. Kitty, isn't this **breathtaking**?

Kitty: My head hurts like crazy. Don't talk to me!

Robert: Are you ticked off because we woke you up and **dragged** you up here in the middle of the night? Lack of beauty sleep?

Kitty: Sure. And I'm **surrounded** by you and a bunch of other crazy people making a big fuss about an ordinary, everyday sunrise.

Taike: But honestly, when experiencing the "Five **Wonders** of Alishan"—sunrises, seas of clouds, sunsets, forests, and mountain railways—normal people can't help but yell and shout!

Kitty: Are you calling me a **freak**? Anyway, Alishan is just not my cup of tea! It was burning hot at the foot of the mountain, and now I'm freezing to death. I'll get a cold for sure!

Robert: That's because Alishan is such a high mountain. It has incredibly diverse **forestry**, with **tropical**-, **subtropical**-, **temperate**-, and **frigid**-zone forests all in one scenic area. I've heard that the most precious trees of all are the old-growth **cypresses**.

Kitty: But the Japanese **colonizers** stole and **smuggled** most of them to Japan! Speaking of which, isn't that "**Sacred** Tree" already dead?

Taike: The original one is dead all right, but now several Sacred Trees have been **identified**. Hey, how about this, after we're done watching the sunrise, we'll go soak ourselves in **pythoncidere** in the Alishan National Scenic Area. That will sure **stimulate** your mind.

羅波：這真是太神奇了！我這輩子沒看過這麼美的日出！

邰克：我也是……真是說不話來了！高貴，妳說美不美？

高貴：我頭痛死了，不要跟我說話啦！

羅波：我們把妳半夜吵醒拖上山，打斷妳的美容覺，妳很不爽吧？

高貴：那當然，而且我身邊又跟著一堆瘋狂的人，連看個平常的日出都大驚小怪。

邰克：不過說真的，正常人在經歷「阿里山五奇」──「日出」、「雲海」、「晚霞」、「森林」、「高山鐵路」時，本來就會情不自禁的大喊大叫啊！

高貴：那你是說我不正常嗎？反正這阿里山跟我犯沖！本來山腳熱得要命，現在卻冷得要死，我一定會得感冒啦！

羅波：那是因為阿里山很高啊！它森林資源豐富，景色優美，橫跨熱帶林、暖帶林、溫帶林和寒帶林，而且聽說這裡的檜木很珍貴呢！

高貴：但殖民時代的日本人把大部分的檜木都盜到日本了。說到這個，阿里山的那棵神木不是死了嗎？

邰克：原來的是死了，不過現在又有幾棵被稱為神木。這樣好了，等會兒我們看完日出後，就去吸收阿里山森林遊樂區的芬多精，讓妳好好振奮一下！

單字

* **surreal**（adj.）超現實的；夢幻般的
* **speechless**（adj.）（因情緒激動而）說不出話來的
* **breathtaking**（adj.）驚人的
* **drag**（v.）拖拉
* **surround**（v.）環繞
* **wonder**（n.）令人驚奇的事物
* **freak**（n.）怪物
* **forestry**（n.）林業；森林學
* **tropical**（adj.）熱帶的
* **subtropical**（adj.）亞熱帶的
* **temperate**（adj.）溫和的
* **frigid**（adj.）嚴寒的
* **cypress**（n.）檜木
* **colonizer**（n.）殖民者
* **smuggle**（v.）走私
* **sacred**（adj.）神聖的
* **identify**（v.）指認；確認
* **pythoncidere**（n.）芬多精
* **stimulate**（v.）刺激

片語與句型

* **be ticked off**：為⋯⋯生氣、不爽
  例 He is ticked off about his friend's unwillingness to help.（他對朋友的不願相助很不爽。）

❖ **a bunch of...**：一群

　　例 I just gave away a bunch of clothes I've been meaning to give away for a long time.（我剛剛才將長久以來一直想要捐贈的一堆衣服捐贈出去。）

❖ **make a fuss about...**：對……大驚小怪

　　fuss (n.) 小題大作；大驚小怪

　　例 I only smoke one pack a day—please don't make a great fuss about nothing.（我一天才吸一包菸——請不要大驚小怪。）

❖ **cannot help but...**：忍不住；不得不……

　　例 I couldn't help but laugh at her stupidity.（我忍不住嘲笑她的愚蠢。）

❖ **be not one's cup of tea**：某人對某人事物不感興趣

　　例 Please don't try to set me up with him——he is not my cup of tea!（請不要將我和他湊對—我對他不感興趣！）

The Alishan Forest Railway was originally intended as a logging road, but has now become a tourist railway.

「阿里山森林鐵路」原先是用來運送木材的，現在則是觀光鐵路。

● 趴趴走好用句

1. 阿里山位於嘉義縣，是東南亞最高峰玉山的支脈。

   Alishan, located in Chiayi County, is a spur of Southeast Asia's tallest peak, Mt. Jade.

2. 「阿里山森林鐵路」已有九十多年的歷史，是世界上僅存的三條高山鐵路之一。

   The Alishan Forest Railway has over 90 years of history and is one of the three remaining mountain railways in the world.

3. 「阿里山森林鐵路」爬行時有幾次的螺旋環繞及Z字形爬升，十分特殊。

   A unique characteristic of the Alishan Forest Railway is that it travels through numerous spirals and switchbacks on its way up.

4. 阿里山日出的最佳觀賞季節為十月到二月之間，觀賞地點為祝山觀日台。

   October to February is the best time of year to see the sunrise from Alishan; the best place to do so is from the sunrise viewing area at Zhushan.

5. 旅客可坐祝山觀日火車前往觀賞祝山的日出，大約四十鐘分可抵達。

   Visitors can take the Zhushan Tourist Train to watch the sunrise from Zhushan. The trip takes about 40 minutes.

6. 　「阿里山森林鐵路」從海拔30公尺的嘉義開往海拔2,216公尺的阿里山。

The Alishan Forest Railway climbs from Chiayi, 30 meters above sea level, to Alishan, 2,216 meters above sea level.

7. 　阿里山的櫻花季在每年的三、四月。

The cherry blossom season on Alishan reaches its peak during March and April.

8. 　阿里山神木曾兩度遭雷擊、後因連日大雨而被撕裂、倒塌而死亡。

Alishan's Sacred Tree perished after being struck twice by lighting and enduring days of hard rain before splitting up and falling down.

9. 　阿里山有兩株老檜木，它們的樹幹與根相連成為一個大心型，是遊客拍照的熱門景點。

One of the hottest picture-taking spots at Alishan is the place where the trunks and roots of two old cypress trees form the shape of a heart.

10. 　阿里山是鄒族原住民聚集之處。

Alishan is inhabited by the Tsou tribe of aborigines.

11.　奮起湖是阿里山森林鐵道最大的中點站；「奮起湖便當」十分知名。

Fenqihu is the largest halfway station along the Alishan Forest Railway. The Fenqihu lunch boxes there are immensely popular.

12.　「奮起湖老街」坐落於海拔1,405公尺，是台灣最高的老街。

Fenqihu Old Street, situated 1,405 meters above sea level, is the highest old street in Taiwan.

27

CD
2-2

台南縣
Tainan County

Robert: The "Fire on Water" is so **bizarre**. Who would have thought that fire and water can **coexist**?

Taike: Yep. Even fire and water can coexist, but the pan-blue and pan-green parties in the Taiwan political **arena** can never coexist!

Kitty: Stop talking about **annoying** politics! This **phenomenon** is made possible because of the spring water and natural gas that **simultaneously ooze** from the **palisades**! This happens to be one of the two main attractions of the Guanzailing Scenic Area!

Robert: What's the other one? Snacks?

Kitty: No, hot springs! The Guanzailing hot springs are special hot **mud** springs. You could say they're the perfect natural **cosmetic**!

Robert: So you're planning to soak yourself in there the whole day? What are we supposed to do?

Taike: Don't worry. There are all kinds of fun places to go around here, like Baihe **Reservoir**, Daxian Temple, Biyun Temple and Hero **Slope**, as well as Jianshanpi Jiangnan Resort and Wushantou Reservoir Scenic Area a bit farther away from here.

Robert: So when are we going to Yanshui to see the **beehive firecrackers**?

Kitty: It's the wrong time of the year to see them! Those festivities are held by the local Yanshui people to celebrate the Lantern Festival and to give back to Guan Gong for his **blessings**.

Taike: Plus, you're so timid that you'd have to prepare all kinds of **protective gear**, from a helmet and raincoat to **goggles** and gloves!

Robert: If the Yanshui beehive firecrackers are so terrifying, are you sure Guan Gong won't be scared into hiding?

羅波：這「水火同源」實在太詭異了。誰能想到水和火可以同時並存呢？

邰克：對啊，水火都可以相容，台灣政壇的藍、綠對決卻永遠水火不容！

高貴：別談煩人的政治了！那是因為巖壁同時冒出泉水和天然氣的緣故啦！這可是「關仔嶺風景區」的兩大招牌之一喔！

羅波：另一個呢？小吃嗎？

高貴：溫泉啦！關仔嶺的溫泉是特殊的泥漿溫泉，可說是天然的美容聖品喔！

羅波：所以妳決定要在那裡泡一整天囉？那我們怎麼辦？

邰克：別擔心，這附近好玩的地方可多了，像是白河水庫、大仙寺、碧雲寺、好漢坡，還有遠一點的尖山埤江南渡假村和烏山頭水庫風景區。

羅波：那我們什麼時候去鹽水看蜂炮？

高貴：現在季節不對啦！那是鹽水人為了慶祝元宵節和回報關公的保佑所舉行的慶典啦。

邰克：而且你這麼膽小，大概所有的護身工具，像是安全帽、雨衣、護目鏡、手套……等都要準備吧！

羅波：如果鹽水蜂炮這麼可怕，你確定關公不會也嚇得躲起來嗎？

單字

✤ **bizarre** [bɪˋzɑr]（**adj.**）古怪的

✤ **coexist**（**v.**）共存；並存

✤ **arena**（**n.**）（政治）競爭的場所

✤ **annoying**（**adj.**）討厭的

✤ **phenomenon**（**n.**）現象

✤ **simultaneously** [ˌsaɪməlˋtenɪəslɪ]（**adv.**）同時地

✤ **ooze**（**v.**）滲出；漏出

✤ **palisades** [ˌpælɪˋsedz]（**n.**）（複數）峭壁；巖壁

✤ **mud**（**n.**）泥

✤ **cosmetic**（**n.**）化妝品

✤ **reservoir**（**n.**）水庫

✤ **slope**（**n.**）斜坡

✤ **beehive**（**n.**）蜂巢

✤ **firecracker**（**n.**）鞭炮；爆竹

✤ **blessing**（**n.**）祝福

✤ **protective**（**adj.**）防護的；保護的

✤ **gear**（**n.**）裝備

✤ **goggles**（**n.**）（複數）護目鏡

片語與句型

❖ **happen to...**：剛好
   ⑩ He happened to walk by there when the accident took place.（事件發生時，他剛好經過那兒。）
❖ **give back to...**：回報……
   ⑩ She established a foundation to give back to the community.（她成立一個基金會以回饋社區。）

發音小技巧 🔊

The Yanshui Fireworks Festival is a rare folk event that is deafeningly loud.

「鹽水蜂炮」現場震耳欲聾，是項難得一見的民俗活動。

● 趴趴走好用句

1.　「虎頭埤風景區」位於新化鎮，距台南市15公里。

> Hutoupi Scenic Area is located in Xinhua Township, which is 15 kilometers from Tainan City.

2.　每年的六月到八月是白河鎮蓮花盛開的季節。

> The lotuses are in full bloom between June and August in Baihe Township.

3.　「白河水庫」兼具灌溉、防洪、工業用水、自來水供給及觀光等多項用途。

> Baihe Reservoir has multiple functions, including irrigation, flood control, industrial water supply, tap water supply, and tourism.

4.　「關仔嶺風景區」位在台南縣白河鎮，是台南縣最熱門的風景區。

> Guanzailing Scenic Area, located in Tainan County's Baihe Township, is the most popular scenic area in Tainan County.

5.　關仔嶺溫泉與北投、陽明山、四重溪等溫泉並稱台灣四大溫泉。

> Guanzailing Hot Springs is one of the four greatest hot springs in Taiwan, along with the hot springs at Beitou, Yangmingshan, and Sichongxi.

6. 關仔嶺溫泉顏色灰黑，含有硫磺成分，是台灣特有的「濁泉」，或稱「泥巴溫泉」。

The water in Guanzailing Hot Springs is grayish-black in color and contains sulfur. It is one of Taiwan's rare muddy springs, otherwise known as mud springs.

7. 鹽水鎮因每年農曆正月15的元宵節放蜂炮習俗而聲名大噪。

Yanshui Township is known widely for its ritual beehive firecrackers event observed on the Lantern Festival, the fifteenth day of the first month in the lunar calendar.

8. 「大仙寺」是關仔嶺風景區的著名古寺。

Daxian Temple is a well-known ancient temple in the Guanzailing Scenic Area.

9. 官田鄉因總統陳水扁的故鄉在此，現已成為熱門的旅遊景點。

Guantian Township has become a popular tourist attraction due to the fact that it is President Chen Shui-bian's hometown.

10. 「尖山埤江南渡假村」位於台南縣柳營鄉，原是台糖公司糖廠的蓄水庫。

Jianshanpi Jiangnan Resort, located in Tainan County's Liuying Township, was originally a water reservoir belonging to Taiwan Sugar Corporation.

11.　「尖山埤江南渡假村」是關仔嶺與烏山頭水庫間的一個風景點，是休閒度假的好去處。

Jianshanpi Jiangnan Resort, a scenic spot squeezed between Guanzailing and Wushantou Reservoir, is an ideal vacation destination.

12.　台南縣以官田的菱角、麻豆的文旦、關廟的鳳梨等聞名。

Famous Tainan County specialties include water chestnuts from Guantian, pomelos from Madou, and pineapples from Guanmiao.

台南市（一）
Tainan City（I）

Robert: Hmm, people here are extremely **hospitable** and **friendly**, and the whole place is filled with **historical** sites and cultural **heritage**!

Kitty: Yes. Tainan was the first **developed** city in Taiwan and is now the island's fourth largest city. You can see **structures** with an air of the past everywhere you go.

Taike: And the best thing is that the local snacks here are super delicious and super cheap!

Robert: You bet they are. But people are eating danzai noodles and **mackerel*** stew first thing in the morning—isn't that a bit strange?

Kitty: People in southern Taiwan are usually a bit **odd**. I only drink **organic** vegetable juice for breakfast. It's very good for my health!

Taike: Hey Robert, do you know what you're eating now? **Coffin** toast!

Robert: Mama Mia! Are you kidding me? This is nothing but deep-fried bread **stuffed** with various **ingredients**, like chicken, seafood, beans and milk-based **sauces**. It's like the **chicken pot pie** that my mom used to make.

Taike: But your mom's chicken pot pie is round-shaped, and this one is coffin-shaped. It's more special!

Kitty: You two quit your **bickering**. We still have several sights to see. The first one is the **ruins** of Anping Fort. It was built in 1624 and was the first **fortress** built in Taiwan by the Dutch. It was originally called "Fort Zeelandia" and was the **administrative** center of the Dutch **regime** and a **hub** for international **trading**.

Robert: The Dutch again? They sure liked to build things in Taiwan!

羅波：嗯，這裡的人好熱情好友善，而且到處充滿了古蹟和文化！

高貴：是啊，台南是台灣最早開發的都市，現在是台灣第四大城市。這裡處處可以感受到過往的建築風味。

邱克：而且最棒的是這裡的小吃都超好吃、超便宜！

羅波：是啊，不過這裡的人一大早就吃擔仔麵和土魠魚羹，好奇怪喔！

高貴：他們南部人通常蠻奇怪的。像我，早餐都只喝有機蔬菜汁，超健康的。

邱克：羅波，那你知道你現在吃的是什麼嗎？棺材板耶。

羅波：媽呀，你別開玩笑了！這明明是炸麵包裡面放著各種材料——雞肉、海鮮、豆子和牛奶濃醬嘛。很像我媽以前常做的雞肉派。

邱克：可是你媽的雞肉派是圓的，我們這個是棺材形狀的啊，比較特殊嘛！

高貴：你們倆別吵了，我們等會兒還要去幾個地方呢！第一站是「安平古堡」，建於1624年，是荷蘭人在台灣建的第一個城堡，原名叫「熱蘭遮城」，曾是荷蘭人統治的中樞，也是對外貿易的樞紐。

羅波：又是荷蘭人？他們可真愛在台灣建東西！

* 土魠魚又稱 Spainish mackerel

單字

- ✤ **hospitable**（**adj.**）好客的
- ✤ **friendly**（**adj.**）友善的
- ✤ **historical**（**adj.**）具歷史性的
- ✤ **heritage**（**n.**）資產；傳統
- ✤ **developed**（**adj.**）發達的；已開發的
- ✤ **structure**（**n.**）建築物
- ✤ **mackerel**（**n.**）鯖魚；土魠魚
- ✤ **odd**（**adj.**）古怪的
- ✤ **organic**（**adj.**）有機的
- ✤ **coffin**（**n.**）棺材
- ✤ **stuff**（**v.**）填塞；裝填
- ✤ **ingredient**（**n.**）原料
- ✤ **sauce**（**n.**）醬汁
- ✤ **chicken pot pie** 雞肉餡餅派
- ✤ **bickering**（**n.**）爭吵
- ✤ **ruins**（**n.**）（複數）廢墟；殘骸
- ✤ **fortress**（**n.**）要塞
- ✤ **administrative**（**adj.**）行政上的
- ✤ **regime** [rɪˋʒim]（**n.**）政體；統治型態
- ✤ **hub**（**n.**）中樞；中心
- ✤ **trading**（**n.**）貿易；通商

片語與句型

✤ **an air of...**：有……的氛圍

air（n.）氣氛

⑨ The sky of this area is always gloomy, giving off an air of mystery.（這地區的天空總是陰陰暗暗的，使得這地方有股神祕的氣氛。）

✤ **You bet.**：當然。

bet（v.）斷言；確信

⑨ "Do you love her?" "You bet!"（「你愛她嗎？」「那當然！」）

發音小技巧 🔊

Tainan is located on 176 square kilometers of level land, making it the fourth-largest city in Taiwan.

台南市地勢平坦，面積176平方公里，是台灣第四大城市。

趴趴走好用句

1. 台南市舊名赤崁，位於台灣西南海岸，嘉南平原的南端。

Tainan City was originally known as Chikan. It is located on Taiwan's southwestern coast, at the southernmost tip of the Jia'nan Plain.

2. 台南市開發甚早，所謂「一府、二鹿、三艋舺」的「府」指的就是台南。

Tainan City was developed very early. The "Fu" in the saying, "One is Fu (Tainan), two is Lu (Lugang), and three is Manka," refers to Tainan.

3. 台南市是著名的歷史古城，明朝、清朝時為台灣的首府。

Tainan is famous as a historical city. It served as the capital of Taiwan during the Ming and Qing dynasties.

4. 台南市的西南區是古蹟匯集處，包括赤崁樓、孔廟、延平郡王祠等。

Taiwan's southwestern district is a cornucopia of relics, including Chikan Tower, the Confucian temple, and the Koxinga shrine.

5. 台南市的東區有成功大學、台南神學院等，是台南的文教重鎮。

National Cheng Kung University and Tainan Theological College and Seminary, both located in the east part of the city, are the centers of education in Tainan.

6. 台南市的西部郊區「安平區」深具古意，有安平老街、舊的聚落、古堡、炮臺、洋樓、漁港等。

Anping District in the eastern suburbs of Tainan has a very ancient feel to it. Here you will find Anping Old Street, ancient residences, old forts, redoubts, Western-style buildings, and harbors.

7. 「延平老街」有許多傳統的店鋪，如香燭店、麵粉廠、蜜餞行等。

Yanping Old Street features a plethora of traditional shops, such as incense shops, flour factories, and stores that sell preserved fruit.

8. 「安平古堡」是荷蘭佔據臺灣時期，為拓展遠東貿易所建的。

The Dutch built Anping Fort when they colonized Taiwan with the aim of promoting trade in the Far East.

9. 「安平古堡」建有鄭成功銅像及安平古堡紀念碑。

A bronze statue of Koxinga and the Anping memorial plaque can be found in Anping Fort.

10. 台南市的小吃種類豐富、價格便宜，包括棺材板、鱔魚意麵、碗粿等。

Tainan City snacks are plentiful and inexpensive. They include coffin toast, fried eel noodles, and salty rice pudding.

11. 台南著名的小吃店「周氏蝦捲」的招牌小吃包括蝦捲、擔仔麵、魚羹、魚丸、蝦丸湯。

Chou's Shrimp Rolls, a well-known snack shop in Tainan, is famed for its fried shrimp rolls, danzai noodles, fish stew, fish balls, and shrimp ball soup.

12. 台南美食處處可見，尤其集中在夜市、廟口、戲院、菜市場等地區。

Tainan delicacies can be enjoyed everywhere, especially in night markets, in front of temples, near theaters, and in fresh produce markets.

CD
2-4

台南市（二）
Tainan City（II）

Kitty: Our second stop is Chikan Tower. It was built by the Dutch in 1653 and was **originally** called "Provintia," meaning "**eternity**." It was also an **administrative** center during the Dutch **occupation** period. In front of Chikan Tower there is a row of nine **turtle-borne steles** with **inscriptions**.

Robert: Aren't turtles somewhat slow and **stupid**?

Taike: Turtles **symbolize longevity** in Chinese society!

Robert: I see. And then where will we be going?

Kitty: Then we'll visit "Eternal Fortress," the first modern Western-style fort to be built in Taiwan. There's a **moat** around the fort, and the fort is **fortified** with **cannons**.

Robert: It does sound pretty **invulnerable**! And then what?

Taike: And then we'll go to the Confucian temple. You've been in Taiwan for several months, but you know very little about Taiwanese **customs** and history. Maybe you will become smarter after you **worship** there!

Kitty: This Confucian temple is very special; it was the first one in Taiwan.

Robert: Then I definitely need to go. That way maybe I'll be able to get into a Taiwanese **graduate school** next year.

Taike: With your **talents**... worshipping is definitely not enough. Let's go eat some **Elite** Cake first so that you will be **blessed** to get into the graduate school with **stellar marks** on your **entrance exam**!

高貴：我們的第二站是「赤崁樓」，這是1653年荷蘭人建的，原名叫
　　　Provintia，意思是「永恆」。那裡在荷蘭人佔領時期也曾被當做
　　　行政中心。在赤崁樓前有九座石龜，背上馱著刻字的石碑。

羅波：烏龜不是又慢又笨嗎？

邱克：中國人認為烏龜象徵長壽嘛！

羅波：喔，那再來呢？

高貴：再來我們要去「億載金城」，這可是台灣第一個現代化的西式碉
　　　堡，四周有護城河，還有大炮呢！

羅波：聽起來刀槍不入呢！還有嗎？

邱克：再來是孔廟。你來台灣幾個月了，對台灣的習俗、歷史都不了
　　　解，帶你去孔廟拜一拜，看你會不會變聰明點！

高貴：這孔廟可大有來頭喔，它是台灣第一間孔廟呢。

羅波：那我肯定要去拜一拜，說不定明年就可以進台灣的研究所。

邱克：以你的資質拜孔廟肯定不夠啦，走！先帶你去吃狀元糕，保佑你
　　　明年碩士入學考考高分！

單字

- ❖ **originally**（adv.）原本地
- ❖ **eternity**（n.）永恆
- ❖ **administrative**（adj.）行政上的
- ❖ **occupation**（n.）佔領；佔據
- ❖ **turtle**（n.）烏龜
- ❖ **bear**（v.）負載；支撐
- ❖ **stele** [ˋstilɪ]（n.）石柱
- ❖ **inscription**（n.）碑文
- ❖ **stupid**（adj.）愚蠢的
- ❖ **symbolize**（v.）象徵
- ❖ **longevity** [lɑnˋdʒɛvətɪ]（n.）長壽
- ❖ **moat**（n.）護城河；壕溝
- ❖ **fortify**（v.）築防禦工事於……
- ❖ **cannon**（n.）大砲
- ❖ **invulnerable**（adj.）刀槍不入的
- ❖ **custom**（n.）風俗習慣
- ❖ **worship**（v.）崇敬；參拜
- ❖ **graduate school** 研究所
- ❖ **talent**（n.）天賦；才能
- ❖ **elite** [eˋlit]（n.）菁英
- ❖ **bless**（v.）賜福
- ❖ **stellar**（adj.）顯著的

❖ **mark**（**n.**）分數
❖ **entrance exam** 入學考試

片語與句型

❖ **a row of...**：一列⋯⋯
　row（n.）列；排
　⑲ He asked the gardener to plant a row of vegetables for his garden.（他
　　請園丁在他的菜園種一列的蔬菜。）

發音小技巧 🔊

The Confucian temple in Tainan was chiefly built to
commemorate the Great Sage, Confucius, and his 72
disciples.

台南「孔廟」以祭祀至聖先師孔子以及他的七十二位弟子為
主。

● 趴趴走好用句

1. 「赤崁樓」歷經荷蘭、清朝統治，具高度的歷史與文化價值。

   Having endured the Dutch colonization and the Qing Dynasty, Chikan Tower is a place of great historical and cultural value.

2. 「赤崁樓」是荷蘭人於西元1653年所建的，現為國家一級古蹟。

   Chikan Tower was built by the Dutch in 1653. It has now become one of the nation's Class I historical sites.

3. 「億載金城」當初是清朝為了加強海防所建的。

   The Eternal Fortress was built to strengthen coastal defenses during the Qing Dynasty.

4. 「億載金城」為西洋式紅磚建築，呈四方形，城外引海水為護城壕。

   The Eternal Fortress is a Western-style rectangular red brick building surrounded by a moat full of seawater.

5. 「億載金城」為一級古蹟，內有清朝大臣沈葆禎的紀念銅像。

   The Eternal Fortress is a Class I historical site. It houses a commemorative bronze statue of the Qing minister Shen Baozhen.

6.　「延平郡王祠」俗稱「鄭成功廟」，主要祭祀驅逐荷蘭人、光復台灣的鄭成功。

Koxinga Shrine, commonly known as Zheng Chenggong Temple, was built chiefly to commemorate Zheng Chenggong's successful venture in ridding Taiwan of the Dutch.

7.　「延平郡王祠」佔地廣闊，是台灣唯一的福州式廟宇建築。

Koxinga Shrine covers a vast expanse of land and is the only Fuzhou-style temple in Taiwan.

8.　「台南市民俗文物館」收藏許多台南文物，可以讓人了解前人的生活狀況。

The Tainan Folk Art Museum houses a multitude of local cultural relics, enabling people to better understand what life was like for people in the past.

9.　台南的孔廟建於明朝，有「全台首學」之稱，屬於國家一級古蹟。

Tainan's Confucian temple was built during the Ming Dynasty and is otherwise known as "the First School in Taiwan." It has been classified as a Class I historical site.

10.　台南孔廟裡面文物眾多，建築莊嚴宏偉，氣氛肅穆。

The Confucian Temple features an extensive display of cultural relics. The structure itself is grand and majestic and exudes an air of solemnity.

11.　「成功大學」以優良的學術風氣及造型優美的建築聞名。

National Cheng Kung University is known for its quality academic climate and brilliant architecture.

12.　「台南公園」園內有兒童遊樂區、噴水池、音樂台等,是市民休閒的好去處。

Tainan Park features a children's playground, a water fountain, and a music stage, making it an ideal place for locals to relax.

澄清湖與美濃
Chengqing Lake and Meinong

Robert: Wow! Chengqing Lake's "Bridge of Nine **Turnings**" really has nine turnings.

Taike: This Bridge of Nine Turnings is **modeled** after the Shanghai City God Temple's Bridge of Nine Turnings!

Kitty: Right you are. Chengqing Lake is located in Niaosong Township, Kaohsiung County. The largest lake in the Kaohsiung area, it is known as "Taiwan's West Lake." It was originally built as a **reservoir** for **industrial** purposes, and was later **transformed** into a beautiful forest park.

Taike: We should go climb the seven-**story** Zhongxing Tower up ahead.

Kitty: Wait. Take a picture of me holding a Meinong paper umbrella.

Robert: Kitty, you look so beautiful holding that paper umbrella. You look like a Japanese **geisha**!

Kitty: Give me a break. Paper umbrellas are the specialty of the **Hakka** town Meinong, and this paper umbrella **bears** a special meaning.

Robert: Oh, is that right?

Kitty: Paper umbrellas are round, which **symbolizes** the "**reunion**" of the family, a very important concept to the Hakka people. In addition, Hakka people place great **emphasis** on the education of their children. Therefore, Meinong has produced hundreds of masters and doctors.

Robert: Well, I really should move to Meinong, see if I could get a doctor's degree or something!

Taike: Not with your IQ! I for one really enjoyed the Meinong pig **knuckles** and **simmered white gourd** we ordered for lunch!

羅波：哇，這澄清湖的「九曲橋」真的有九個彎耶。

邱克：這九曲橋還是模仿上海城隍廟的九曲橋而建的呢！

高貴：嗯，澄清湖位於高雄縣的鳥松鄉，是高雄地區的第一大湖，被稱
　　　為「台灣西湖」。它本來是建造來當工業用的水庫，後來改造成
　　　了漂亮的森林公園。

邱克：我們應該去登前面那個七層樓的中興塔。

高貴：等等，你先幫我照張拿著美濃紙傘的照片啦。

羅波：高貴，妳拿著紙傘的姿勢真美，好像日本藝妓喔！

高貴：拜託，人家紙傘可是美濃這個客家小鎮的特產耶，而且這紙傘可
　　　是有特殊涵意的喔。

羅波：哦，真的嗎？

高貴：紙傘是圓的，象徵一家「團圓」，這是客家人十分注重的觀念。
　　　而且客家人十分重視孩子的教育，因此美濃當地已經出產好幾百
　　　個碩士、博士喔！

羅波：那我真該搬到美濃住，看能不能也拿個博士什麼的！

邱克：以你的智商是不可能的啦！我倒很喜歡我們吃午飯時點的「美濃
　　　豬腳」和「冬瓜封」呢！

單字 ·····

- ✦ **turning**（n.）轉彎
- ✦ **model**（v.）模擬
- ✦ **reservoir**（n.）水庫
- ✦ **industrial**（adj.）工業的
- ✦ **transform**（v.）改變
- ✦ **story**（n.）樓；層
- ✦ **geisha**（n.）藝妓
- ✦ **Hakka**（n.）客家
- ✦ **bear**（v.）具有（意義、性質等）
- ✦ **symbolize**（v.）象徵
- ✦ **reunion**（n.）團圓
- ✦ **emphasis**（n.）強調
- ✦ **knuckle**（n.）蹄；指關節
- ✦ **simmer**（v.）用文火慢煮
- ✦ **white gourd** 冬瓜

片語與句型

❖ **for... purposes**：因……目的
　⑩ It should be legitimate to use marijuana for medical purposes.（作為
　　醫療目的，大麻應被合法化。）

❖ **place emphasis on...**：將重點放在……；重視……
　emphasis（n.）強調
　⑩ This school places great emphasis on language study.（這所學校極重
　　視語言學習。）

發音小技巧 🔊

Chengqing Lake is at the same time a scenic area, a
reservoir, and a recreation area.

「澄清湖」包含風景區、水源地、遊憩區等三部分。

● 趴趴走好用句

1. 「澄清湖」原本是高雄地區的工業用水源地，整建後開放為風景區。

Chengqing ("Lucid") Lake was originally built as an industrial reservoir. It was later transformed into a scenic area.

1. 「澄清湖」闢有環湖公路，風景點則分散在公路的兩側。

There are scenic attractions on both sides of the highway around Chengqing Lake.

2. 「中興塔」是澄清湖中最高的建築，登上該塔便可飽覽湖區的全景。

Zhongxing Tower is the tallest structure in Chengqing Lake. A climb up the tower will afford you an all-encompassing view of the surrounding area.

3. 「澄清湖」的九曲橋長230公尺，是仿造上海城隍廟的九曲橋而建造的。

The Bridge of Nine Turnings in Chengqing Lake is 230 meters long and is modeled after the Shanghai City God Temple's Bridge of Nine Turnings.

4. 高雄縣旗山鎮早期因製糖業發達而帶動市街的繁榮，「旗山老街」尚可見到當初的舊式樓房。

The early development of Qishan Township's sugar industry resulted in the later prosperity of the town. Old-fashioned buildings from the town's early days can still be spotted today on Qishan Old Street.

5.　「寶來溫泉」位於南橫公路的西段，泉質清澈透明。

Baolai Hot Springs is located west of the South Cross-Island Highway. The spring water there is both clear and transparent.

6.　「荖濃溪」為台灣的第二大溪流，發源於秀姑巒山，是泛舟的熱門地點。

Laonong River is the second-largest river in Taiwan. Originating from Xiuguluan Mountain, it's a great place for whitewater rafting.

7.　美濃位於高雄縣東北處，是個民風純樸的客家小鎮。

Meinong, located in northeastern Kaohsiung, is a sleepy little Hakka town.

8.　「敬字亭」已有三百多年歷史，是美濃人重視教育文化的最好証明。

Jingzi Ting is over 300 years old. It serves as a testament to Meinong's emphasis on education and culture.

9.　「鍾理和紀念館」是為了紀念台灣鄉土文學的先驅、也是美濃客家作家的鍾理和。

The Chung Li-he Memorial Hall commemorates Chung Li-he, a Hakka author from Meinong and a pioneer in Taiwanese grassroots literature.

10. 「美濃民俗村」除了介紹客家文化、美食，還可看到當地傳統的手藝紙傘製作。

Aside from introducing Hakka culture and cuisine, Meinong Folk Village also affords the traveler a glimpse into the traditional local craft, paper umbrella making.

11. 「茂林國家風景區」有豐富的景觀資源，居民大多為魯凱族人。

Maolin National Scenic Area boasts an abundance of scenery. The local residents are predominantly members of the Rukai tribe.

CD
2-6

高雄市（一）
Kaohsiung City（I）

Robert: It's said that the Love River once had serious **pollution** problems. It's remarkable to see it this clean now!

Taike: Yep. Following years of **renovation**, along with the **proliferation** of coffee shops and restaurants that line the coast and the **street performers** that can be seen everywhere during the weekends, the Love River has become a favorite **leisure** spot for Kaohsiung citizens today!

Kitty: What I love seeing the most is the sight of lights being lit along the **riverbank** as **dusk** turns to night. It's so **romantic**!

Taike: It is. While **cruising** the river on board the "Love Boat" just now, the **enchanting** scenery almost made me fall in love with you!

Kitty: I, on the other hand, have fallen in love with the special art **districts**, film **archives**, music centers, and art **galleries** that line the riverbank!

Robert: I heard that there's an even more romantic place in Kaohsiung called the "**Urban Spotlight**." It's supposed to have been created by nine local Kaohsiung artists based on the theme of light.

Kitty: And they **decorated** the bus stops, **electrical** equipment boxes, and trash cans with multicolored lights!

Taike: Kaohsiung is Taiwan's largest **industrial** center, and the Kaohsiung **Harbor** is an important transportation **hub**. It's almost unimaginable that a **staid** and seriously polluted industrial city would one day become so **trendy**.

Robert: Hey, since Kaohsiung already has a Love River and even a Love Boat, maybe it should consider calling itself "The Love City!"

羅波：據說愛河曾經是條污染嚴重的河，沒想到現在竟然這麼乾淨！

邰克：是啊，愛河經過這幾年的整治，加上沿岸林立的咖啡廳和餐廳，再加上假日時隨處可見的街頭表演藝人，現在的愛河已是高雄人休閒時最愛去的地方了！

高貴：我最喜歡看愛河畔從黃昏進入黑夜，燈火四起的景象，真的很浪漫！

邰克：對啊，剛剛乘「愛之船」遊河時，我還因為景色太迷人而差點愛上妳呢！

高貴：我可是愛上了這沿岸的藝術特區、電影圖書館、音樂館、美術館呢！

羅波：我聽說高雄還有一個更浪漫的地方叫「城市光廊」，據說是九個高雄在地的藝術家以「光」為主題創作出的作品呢！

高貴：這些藝術家把公車亭、電器箱，以及垃圾桶都添了五彩的燈光！

邰克：高雄是台灣最大的工業重鎮，高雄港也是重要的運輸樞紐。沒想到原本一個硬梆梆的、污染嚴重的工業都市現在竟然也能如此時尚。

羅波：喂，高雄既然有愛河，又有「愛之船」，或許可以考慮稱自己是「愛之城」！

單字

- **pollution**（n.）污染
- **renovation**（n.）革新；翻修
- **proliferation**（n.）增長；繁殖
- **street performer** 街頭表演藝人
- **leisure**（n., adj.）空閒（的）
- **riverbank**（n.）河岸
- **dusk**（n.）傍晚
- **romantic**（adj.）有情調的；羅曼蒂克的
- **cruise**（v.）航行遊覽
- **enchanting**（adj.）迷人的；令人銷魂的
- **district**（n.）地區
- **archive** [ˈɑrkaɪv]（n.）檔案室
- **gallery**（n.）藝廊
- **urban**（adj.）都市的
- **spotlight**（n.）聚光燈
- **decorate**（v.）裝飾
- **electrical**（adj.）電的
- **industrial**（adj.）工業的
- **harbor**（n.）港口
- **hub**（n.）中樞
- **staid**（adj.）古板的；保守的
- **trendy**（adj.）時髦的；流行的

片語與句型

❖ **be supposed to...**：應該……；一般認為……

　⑩ He's supposed to return the DVD by eight o'clock.（他應該要在八點前還 DVD。）

❖ **It is unimaginable that...**：難以想像……

　unimaginable (adj.) 不可思議的；難以想像的

　⑩ It's unimaginable that your mother looks younger than you!（真難以相信你媽比妳長得還年輕！）

發音小技巧

Urban Spotlight artists decorated the bus stops, electrical equipment boxes, and trash cans with multicolored lights.
　　　　　　　　/ks/

「城市光廊」的藝術家們把人行道上的公車亭、電器箱，以及垃圾桶添加了五彩的燈光。

趴趴走好用句

1. 愛河早年扮演著運輸、交通等功能，現則多為遊憩、觀光的角色。

    The Love River was once used mainly for shipping and transportation. These days, however, it serves mostly as a destination for recreation and tourism.

2. 愛河沿岸有藝術特區、電影圖書館、市立音樂館、市立美術館等。

    Along the banks of the Love River can be found a special art district, along with the Kaohsiung Film Archives, Kaohsiung Music Center, and Kaohsiung Museum of Fine Arts.

3. 「城市光廊」除了燈光，還有別緻的咖啡座及現場音樂表演。

    The Urban Spotlight is not only about lights; it also features an elegant café and live musical performances.

4. 「城市光廊」現已成為高雄市的新地標及新的休閒景點。

    The Urban Spotlight has become a new landmark as well as a whole new place to kick back and relax in Kaohsiung.

5. 「高雄市中正文化中心」是高雄市舉辦表演及展覽的主要場所。

    The Kaohsiung Chiang Kai-shek Cultural Center is the foremost performance and exhibition venue in Kaohsiung City.

6.　「高雄市中正文化中心」的戶外綠地面積廣大，是市民玩直排輪、放風箏的熱門地點。

The expansive grounds of the Kaohsiung Chiang Kai-shek Cultural Center include areas for rollerblading and kite-flying, quite popular among local residents.

7.　「玫瑰聖母堂」建於清朝，為三級古蹟，是台灣第一座天主教堂。

The Kaohsiung Rose Basilica, built during the Qing Dynasty, is a Class III historical site as well as the first Catholic church in Taiwan.

8.　「玫瑰聖母堂」的外觀混合哥德式與羅馬式風格。

The exterior of the Kaohsiung Rose Basilica is an elaborate mix of Gothic and Romanesque architecture.

9.　「高雄市立歷史博物館」原為市政府的辦公大樓，建築融合中國及日本特色。

The Kaohsiung Museum of History began its life as the administrative building of the city hall. Its architecture is a fusion of Chinese and Japanese styles.

10.　「高雄市音樂館」位於愛河畔，除了室內的音樂廳，還有露天音樂表演台。

The Kaohsiung Music Center is located on the bank of the Love River. It features an indoor music hall as well as an outdoor music stage.

11.　「高雄市音樂館」的戶外廣場設有咖啡座，面對著愛河，景觀優美。

The café in the square outside the Kaohsiung Music Center boasts a beautiful direct view of the Love River.

12.　「國立科學工藝博物館」是台灣第一座應用科學博物館。

The National Science and Technology Museum is Taiwan's foremost applied science museum.

高雄市（二）
Kaohsiung City（II）

Robert: This NT$200 **steak** is a really good buy. It's delicious and **affordable**, and it even comes with salad, drinks, bread, and soup. If I were to have this meal in the United States, it'd **definitely** cost me at least NT$2,000!

Taike: Yep. This whole street of "**fair-priced** steak houses" is **characteristic** of the Liuhe Night Market.

Kitty: C'mon, a steak this cheap cannot possibly be actual beef. It could be rabbit or horse meat!

Taike: That can't be. At worst, it could be American beef with **mad cow disease**! Haha!

Robert: But this night market is really **awesome**. There are mountain **gourmet** shops, seafood shops, and ice treat shops everywhere... Hey, what are those people holding in their hands?

Kitty: That's **papaya** milk. "Kaohsiung Milk King" is known throughout Taiwan.

Robert: Papaya mixed with milk. Only you Taiwanese would think of something as **novel** as that.

Taike: Yeah, unlike you Americans, who don't even have papayas!

Kitty: I would like to try the **lamb** in **shacha sauce** and the rice cakes.

Taike: The seafood **porridge** and salt-steamed shrimp in this night market are very well known. Why don't we take a **ferry** over to Qijin Old Street tomorrow and have some seafood? The seafood there is fresh and **scrumptious**, and most importantly, the price is extremely fair.

Robert: Taiwan really is a **treasure island**! In the United States, having a meal with live seafood would cost quite a lot of money!

羅波：這兩百元的牛排真划算，又好吃又便宜，還有配沙拉、飲料、麵包和湯。這一餐如果在美國吃起來，肯定要兩千塊台幣以上！

邱克：是啊，這滿街的「平價牛排屋」可是六合夜市的特色喔。

高貴：拜託，這麼便宜的牛排，肯定不是真的牛肉，可能是兔肉或馬肉喔！

邱克：不會吧，頂多是得了狂牛病的美國牛肉吧！哈哈。

羅波：不過這夜市超讚的，到處都是山產店、海產店、冰店，不過這些人手上拿的是什麼啊？

高貴：是木瓜牛奶啦，「高雄牛乳大王」可是名震全台喔。

羅波：木瓜加牛奶，這種有創意的東東只有你們台灣人想得出來！

邱克：對呀，哪像你們美國連木瓜都沒得賣呢！

高貴：我倒是想試試這裡的沙茶羊肉和米糕。

邱克：這夜市的海產粥和鹽蒸蝦也很有名。我們明天乾脆坐渡輪去旗津老街吃海鮮，那裡的海鮮既新鮮又美味，最重要的是價錢還很公道呢！

羅波：台灣真是寶島！在美國，吃一頓這種活跳跳的海鮮餐，可是要花不少錢呢！

單字

- ❖ **steak**（**n.**）牛排
- ❖ **affordable**（**adj.**）負擔得起的
- ❖ **definitely**（**adv.**）絕對地
- ❖ **fair-priced**（**adj.**）價格合理的
- ❖ **characteristic**（**adj.**）特有的；有特色的
- ❖ **mad cow disease** 狂牛病
- ❖ **awesome**（**adj.**）超棒的；令人敬畏的
- ❖ **gourmet** [ˋɡʊrme] [ɡʊrˋme]（**n.**）美食；美饌
- ❖ **papaya**（**n.**）木瓜
- ❖ **novel**（**adj.**）新奇的
- ❖ **lamb**（**n.**）羊肉
- ❖ **shacha sauce** 沙茶醬（或稱 **satay sauce**）
- ❖ **porridge/congee**（**n.**）稀飯
- ❖ **ferry**（**n.**）渡船
- ❖ **scrumptious**（**adj.**）（口語）美味的
- ❖ **treasure island** 寶島

片語與句型

❖ **a good buy**：物美價廉

　⑩ This dress is definitely a good buy—it's from Japan and is only $300!（這洋裝絕對物美價廉——它是日本製的，且只有三百元！）

❖ **at worst**：大不了……

　⑩ He won't die—at worst, he will lose both his legs.（他不會死——頂多失去兩條腿。）

發音小技巧 🔊

Couples flock to Qijin Beach for a stroll when the sun goes down at dusk.

「旗津海水浴場」每到傍晚夕陽西下時，總有許多情侶來此散步。

● 趴趴走好用句

1.　「六合夜市」距高雄火車站約十多分鐘路程，沿中山路右轉至六合路即可到達。

　　Liuhe Night Market is approximately 10 minutes away from the Kaohsiung train station. Going straight along Zhongshan Road and making a right on Liuhe Road will take you there.

2.　「六合夜市」的小吃種類眾多，價格便宜。

　　The snacks at Liuhe Night Market are widely varied and can be enjoyed at a low cost.

3.　「六合夜市」以小吃、娛樂為主，衣服攤及雜貨攤等較少。

　　Snacks and entertainment are the main attractions in Liuhe Night Market. Clothes and grocery stalls are in the minority.

4.　「新堀江商圈」以休閒、購物、飲食為主，是高雄最受年輕人歡迎的地區。

　　The Xinkujiang Business Cluster is a prime destination for leisure, shopping, and dining. It is especially popular among the younger crowd of Kaohsiung.

5.　「柴山」又稱「壽山」，是高雄市的天然屏障，屬於保護管制區。

　　Chaishan, also called Shoushan, is Kaohsiung's natural barrier and is considered to be a protected area.

6. 「柴山」是高雄都會區的一塊綠地，有豐沛自然景觀及生態資源。

Chaishan provides a glimpse of green in metropolitan Kaohsiung. It features an abundant mix of natural attractions and ecological resources.

7. 「高雄中學」是高雄歷史最悠久的公立中學，其紅樓十分知名。

Kaohsiung Senior High School is Kaohsiung's most venerable public high school. Its Red Hall is quite famous.

8. 旗津老街位於渡輪碼頭至旗津海水浴場的路上，以新鮮海產聞名。

Qijin Old Street, located between the ferry dock and Qijin Beach, is known widely for its fresh seafood.

9. 「旗津天后宮」是高雄市第一座媽祖廟，亦為三級古蹟。

Qijin's Tianhou Temple, the first Matzu temple in Kaohsiung, is a Class III historical site.

10. 「旗津海水浴場」沙質細軟，海水清澈，很適合水上活動。

With its fine, soft sand and clear water, Qijin Beach is an ideal destination for water activities.

11.　「西子灣風景區」距高雄市中心約二十分鐘，以海水浴場及天然珊瑚礁聞名。

The Xizaiwan Scenic Area is approximately 20 minutes away from downtown Kaohsiung. It is known for its beaches and natural coral reefs.

12.　「西子灣」以夕陽美景聞名，著名的「中山大學」便位於此。

Xizaiwan is known for its beautiful sunsets and for being the home of National Sun Yat-sen University.

屏東
Pingtung

Robert: This fish is **squishy**, and it tastes like pork fat!

Taike: Give me a break. This fish is fresh and sweet, and it **melts** in your mouth. This is high-quality raw fish, and it costs several hundred dollars for a **bite**. It really is a waste to let someone who can't tell good from bad enjoy such a treat.

Kitty: That's right. Donggang is the largest fishing **port** in Southern Taiwan, and the most expensive fish they **catch** is none other than the **bluefin tuna**! The bluefin tuna is only **plentiful** between April and June of each year. There is even an event here called the Pingtung Bluefin Tuna Cultural Festival.

Taike: That's why bluefin tuna, **banded** coral shrimp and **mullet roe** are known as the "three **treasures** of Donggang!"

Kitty: Yep. Banded coral shrimp can only be found in the waters of Japan and Taiwan's Donggang and Fangliao. It is indeed extremely precious!

Robert: Even though we're still in Pingtung County, there are so many kinds of seafood here that are different from those we saw in Wutai Township a few days ago!

Kitty: There are numerous aboriginal Rukai tribes in Wutai Township, and thus **hints** of the Rukai culture can be seen all over the place. Remember the **slate** houses, the woodcarving art and the hundred-pace snake **totem**?

Taike: Plus, you could see yam and millet fields everywhere. It was **stunningly** beautiful.

Robert: But I felt a bit **intimidated**, because the people there seemed to really love snakes.

Kitty: You Americans are so afraid of snakes! The hundred-pace snake is a **symbol** of the Rukai's ancestral **spirit**, which is why its image can be found in their carvings!

羅波：這魚軟軟的，吃起來好像肥豬肉喔！

邱克：拜託，這魚肉質鮮美、入口即化，是頂級的生魚片，吃一口就要好幾百塊耶，給你這種不識貨的人吃真浪費！

高貴：對啊，東港是南台灣最大的漁港，漁獲中就屬黑鮪魚最珍貴呢！每年的四到六月是黑鮪魚盛產的季節，這裡還會舉辦「屏東黑鮪魚文化觀光季」。

邱克：這是為什麼黑鮪魚和櫻花蝦、油魚子被稱為「東港三寶」！

高貴：對，那櫻花蝦全世界只有日本和台灣的東港、枋寮才有，十分罕見珍貴呢！

羅波：同樣是屏東縣，這裡好多海產，和我們前幾天去的霧台鄉很不同！

高貴：霧台鄉有許多原住民魯凱族的村落，因此處處顯現魯凱族的文化特色，記不記得石板屋、木刻藝術和百步蛇圖騰？

邱克：而且到處可以看到山芋和小米田，很是漂亮。

羅波：不過我有點害怕，因為那裡的人好像很愛蛇！

高貴：你們美國人真的很怕蛇耶！百步蛇是魯凱族祖靈的象徵，因此在他們的雕刻作品中都會出現百步蛇的蹤跡啦！

單字

✤ **squishy**（**adj.**）濕軟的；黏糊糊的

✤ **melt**（**v.**）融化

✤ **bite**（**n.**）一口

✤ **port**（**n.**）港埠

✤ **catch**（**v.**）捕獲

✤ **bluefin tuna** 黑鮪魚

✤ **plentiful**（**adj.**）豐富的

✤ **banded**（**adj.**）有條紋的

✤ **mullet roe** 油魚子

✤ **treasure**（**n.**）寶物

✤ **hint**（**n.**）少許；微量

✤ **slate**（**n.**）石板

✤ **totem**（**n.**）圖騰

✤ **stunningly**（**adv.**）絕妙地；令人目瞪口呆地

✤ **intimidated**（**adj.**）害怕的；受驚的

✤ **symbol**（**n.**）象徵

✤ **spirit**（**n.**）靈魂

片語與句型

❖ **tell good from bad**：分辨好壞
> ⑩ Lisa has very refined tastes—she sure can tell good things from bad ones.（Lisa 有很高雅的品味——她完全知道如何分辨東西的好壞。）

❖ **none other than...**：（用於強調）正是⋯⋯
> ⑩ The new arrival was none other than the President!（剛剛抵達的不是別人，正是總統！）

發音小技巧

Dapeng Bay, located along the southwestern shores of Taiwan, is characterized by its unique natural lagoon.

「大鵬灣」位於台灣西南沿岸，以獨特的天然潟湖景觀為特色。

● 趴趴走好用句

1.　霧台是屏東縣東北處的一個山地鄉，是屏東最大的魯凱族聚落。

Wutai is a mountainous town in the northeast part of Pingtung County. It is home to the largest aboriginal tribe in Pingtung, the Rukai.

2.　魯凱族原住民在八月會舉行傳統的豐年祭，祭典包括歌舞、鞦韆大賽、拋物比賽等。

The Rukai people celebrate their traditional Harvest Festival in August with singing and dancing, a swing competition, and a throwing contest.

3.　霧台地區保留了許多代表魯凱族的文物，包括陶壺、木刻、刺繡等。

Scores of relics that represent Rukai culture are preserved in Wutai. These include pottery, woodcarvings, and embroidery.

4.　「台灣原住民文化園區」是國內規模最大、保存原住民文物最豐富的野外博物館。

The Taiwan Aboriginal Culture Park is an outdoor museum with the largest and most varied collection of aboriginal artifacts in the entire country.

5.　「台灣原住民文化園區」包括原住民的傳統建築和聚落展示區、歌舞表演場、文物陳列館等。

The Taiwan Aboriginal Culture Park features a display area showcasing traditional aboriginal architecture as well as a song-and-dance performance stage and an exhibition hall.

6. 東港是個充滿獨特景緻的漁村，這裡的日落、海景、蚵田、魚塭等都令人著迷。

Donggang is a fishing village filled with unique sights. Its sunset, ocean view, oyster farms, and fish farms are nothing short of captivating.

7. 「小琉球」位於東港外海，是台灣眾多離島中，唯一的珊瑚礁島嶼。

Xiao Liuqiu is located offshore of Donggang. It is the only coral reef island among Taiwan's many outlying islands.

8. 「小琉球」隸屬於屏東縣琉球鄉，有碧海、藍天、珊瑚礁。

Xiao Liuqiu is under the jurisdiction of Pingtung County's Liuqiu Township. The area features aquamarine seas, blue skies, and coral reefs.

9. 「四重溪溫泉」與陽明山、北投、關仔嶺溫泉並稱「四大溫泉」。

The Sichong Creek Hot Spring, along with the springs at Yangmingshan, Beitou, and Guanzailing, is one of Taiwan's "four great hot springs."

10. 「旭海大草原」瀕臨太平洋，海拔300多公尺，終年綠草如茵。

Xuhai Plain, located more than 300 meters above sea level near the shores of the Pacific, is a beautiful field of green throughout the year.

11.　東港的東隆宮每三年在農曆九月上旬會舉行「王船祭」。

Donggang's Donglong Temple holds the Boat Burning Ceremony once every three years on the first half of the ninth month in the lunar calendar.

12.　屏東縣萬巒鄉有聞名全台、以小火慢滷3小時以上的「萬巒豬腳」。

Wanluan Township in Pingtung County is home to the famous Wanluan Pig's Knuckle, prepared by three hours of stewing over a slow fire.

CD
2-9

墾丁
Kenting

Robert: That **boatman** was a lot of fun. He kept playing games with me by continually turning left and right.

Kitty: You **doofus**! Do you or do you not know what the game rules to "banana boating" are? He kept turning left and right so as to force us off the boat. You were keeping him from knocking us off the boat, which is why we are so **dizzy** now.

Taike: Right. I'm never going to let you sit in front again! Stay away from me when we go **snorkeling** later!

Robert: Okay, okay! But I have to say, Kenting really is a lot of fun. Aside from **skin diving**, we can also go swimming, **surfing**, sailing, **jetskiing**, **motorboating** and **parasailing**!

Taike: Yep. The best places to skin dive here are none other than South Bay and Little Bay. But I think it would be best if we went and grabbed a bite to eat first. The seafood restaurants here are all pretty good.

Robert: Are we still going to Kenting National Park?

Kitty: Of course we are. It's a **coral reef** park located in the **southernmost** tip of Taiwan, the Hengchun **Peninsula**. Due to its low **altitude** and its location in the tropics, it offers such varied scenery as lakes, **swamps**, **sand dunes**, forests and mountains.

Taike: Yep. It's also an ideal place for birdwatching, especially in the fall and winter months when birds **migrate** south from **frigid Siberia**, Japan, and China for the winter.

羅波：那個船老大好好玩，一直左轉右彎的跟我玩遊戲！

高貴：笨蛋，你到底會不會玩「香蕉船」啦？他一直轉彎就是要把我們摔下水，你一直不讓他摔，才會搞得我們七暈八素的。

邱克：對啊，以後不讓你坐第一個了啦！等會兒浮潛時離我遠一點！

羅波：好啦好啦！不過這墾丁真棒，除了潛水，還可以游泳、衝浪、玩帆船、水上摩托車、摩托船、拖曳傘！

邱克：對，這附近最好的潛水地方在南灣及小灣。不過我們最好先去吃點東西。這邊海鮮餐廳都很不錯。

羅波：那我們還要不要去「墾丁國家公園」呢？

高貴：當然要囉。它是個珊瑚礁型的公園，位於台灣最南端的恆春半島上。因為海拔低、位於熱帶，所以有湖泊、沼澤、砂丘、森林、山峰等不同的景觀。

邱克：嗯，那裡也是賞鳥的好地方，尤其在秋、冬季節；鳥兒們會從寒冷的西伯利亞、日本及大陸向南遷徙、避冬。

單字

❖ **boatman**（**n.**）船夫；船老大

❖ **doofus**（**n.**）愚蠢的人

❖ **dizzy**（**adj.**）眩暈的

❖ **snorkeling**（**n.**）浮潛

❖ **skin diving** 潛水

❖ **surfing**（**n.**）衝浪

❖ **jetskiing**（**n.**）(玩)水上摩托車

❖ **motorboating**（**n.**）(玩)摩托船

❖ **parasailing**（**n.**）(玩)拖曳傘

❖ **coral reef** 珊瑚礁

❖ **southernmost**（**adj.**）最南端的

❖ **peninsula** [pəˋnɪnsələ]（**n.**）半島

❖ **altitude**（**n.**）高度

❖ **swamp**（**n.**）沼澤

❖ **sand dune** 砂丘

❖ **migrate**（**v.**）遷移；移居

❖ **frigid**（**adj.**）嚴寒的

❖ **Siberia** [saɪˋbɪrɪə]（**n.**）西伯利亞

片語與句型

- ❖ **knock off**：打掉；碰掉
  - 例 He just knocked my books off the table.（他剛剛把我的書從桌上碰掉。）
- ❖ **stay away from...**：與……保持距離；不打擾……
  - 例 Tell your brother to stay away from me!（叫你哥哥離我遠一點！）
- ❖ **grab a bite**：(口語)裹腹；吃東西
  - bite (n.) 一口
  - 例 Let's grab a bite before watching the movie!（我們看電影前先吃點東西吧！）

發音小技巧

Kenting National Park was established in 1982, becoming the first national park in Taiwan.

「墾丁國家公園」成立於民國七十一年，是台灣第一座國家公園。

● 趴趴走好用句

1. 「墾丁國家公園」三面臨海，東邊是太平洋，西邊是台灣海峽，南邊是巴士海峽。

   Kenting National Park faces the sea on three sides, with the Pacific to its east, the Taiwan Strait to its west, and the Bashi Channel to the south.

2. 「墾丁國家公園」總面積共三萬多公頃，是生態與地形研究的重要區域。

   Kenting National Park occupies an area of more than 30,000 hectares and serves as an important region in the fields of ecological and topographical research.

3. 「墾丁森林遊樂區」是台灣第一座熱帶植物林，也是世界八大實驗林場之一。

   The Kenting Forest Recreation Area is Taiwan's foremost tropical forest. It is also one of the eight largest experimental forests in the world.

4. 夏日在墾丁，可以在南灣、小灣等地方玩水上活動，也可以到白沙灣撿貝殼。

   Water games can be enjoyed in both South Bay and Little Bay during the Kenting summer. Another option would be to collect shells along Baisha Bay.

5. 墾丁當地有許多租借水上活動設備的商店以及提供專業指導的教練。

   Kenting has many stores where one can rent equipment for water-based activities; many also provide training by professional coaches.

6. 「萬佛寺」位於墾丁半島，主殿內有一尊「千手千眼觀音菩薩」像。

Wanfo Temple is located on the Kenting Peninsula and houses a thousand-hand, thousand-eye Guan Yin in its main hall.

7. 「佳樂水」位在恆春半島東側的海岸上，風景區內有一條石板步道，直通瀑布。

Jialeshui is located on the eastern shore of the Hengchun Peninsula. The scenic area boasts a stone walkway that leads directly to the waterfalls.

8. 「大灣」即「墾丁海水浴場」，面臨巴士海峽，背向大尖石山。

Big Bay is otherwise known as Kenting Beach. It faces the Bashi Channel with Dajianshi Mountain at its back.

9. 「大灣」擁有全臺灣最美麗的海水浴場，並設有汽車旅館、海濱餐廳等。

Big Bay boasts the most beautiful beach in all of Taiwan; it also has motels and restaurants by the sea.

10. 「小灣海水浴場」可從事水上摩托車、香蕉船、拖曳傘等水上活動。

One can engage in water activities like jetskiing, banana boating, and paragliding in Little Bay Beach.

11.　「小灣海水浴場」有景色迷人的海岸線，很有異國風情。

Little Bay Beach offers a breathtaking coastline view that feels very exotic.

12.　墾丁白天雖然陽光炙熱，入夜後卻展現截然不同的風情，是與家人、朋友或情人出遊的浪漫地點。

Kenting may be scorching during the day, but it transforms completely when night falls, becoming a romantic haven for families, friends and lovers.

CD
2-10

鵝鑾鼻和貓鼻頭
Eluanbi and Maobitou

Robert: I can't believe that we've just been to the **southernmost** tip of Taiwan, Eluanbi. I feel very **accomplished**!

Taike: What's to feel accomplished about by reaching the southern end of Taiwan?

Robert: There's something you're missing here. The United States is very large, and it is not easy to reach the four ends of the country. I am now standing on the southernmost tip of Taiwan and facing a vast **expanse** of **seawater**. Isn't that enough reason to feel accomplished?

Taike: Yes, yes. Taiwan is "small yet beautiful" and the United States is "big yet **inappropriate**."

Kitty: The Eluanbi **Lighthouse** is so cool. It is said to have been built to **prevent** the aborigines from causing trouble to the foreign ships. It is the only **armed** lighthouse in the world and is currently the lighthouse with the strongest light power in all of Taiwan.

Robert: Where are we now?

Taike: We're on the border that separates the Taiwan **Strait** and Bashi **Channel**. It's called "Maobitou."

Robert: But I don't see any cat's nose!

Taike: Give me a break. It was named after a **protruding coral reef** rock that looks like a **squatting** cat.

Kitty: You two stop talking about boring rocks. I hate southern Taiwan. The sun's too bright here. I'm on the verge of turning black.

Robert: I just don't get you Taiwanese girls! At the **slightest exposure** to the sunlight, you complain. In the United States, everyone's **scrambling** to get a **tan**! And haven't you heard? "Black is beautiful!"*

羅波：真難想像我們剛剛去了台灣的最南端「鵝鑾鼻」。我超有成就
　　　感！

邱克：你到台灣南端有啥成就感？

羅波：這你有所不知。美國很大，要到達國土的東西南北端很難耶，而
　　　我現在踏在台灣最南端的土地上，還面對著壯闊的海水，能沒有
　　　成就感嗎？

邱克：是啦，是啦，我們台灣就是「小而美」，你們美國就是「大而無
　　　當」嘛！

高貴：「鵝鑾鼻燈塔」真酷，據說當時是為了防衛這裡的原住民侵擾外
　　　國船隻而建造的，是世界上唯一的武裝燈塔，而且是台灣地區目
　　　前光力最強的燈塔。

羅波：那我們現在在哪？

邱克：在台灣海峽和巴士海峽的交界處，叫「貓鼻頭」。

羅波：可是我沒看到貓鼻子啊！

邱克：拜託，它的名稱是來自一塊突出來的珊瑚礁岩，長得像一隻蹲坐
　　　的貓啦。

高貴：好了，你們兩個別在那裡研究無聊的石頭啦。我討厭南台灣，這
　　　裡的太陽超大，我都快變成黑人啦。

羅波：真搞不懂妳們台灣女生耶，曬點太陽就哇哇叫。在美國，大家都
　　　恨不得將自己曬黑呢！而且妳們沒聽過嗎，「黑才是美」耶！

* "Black is beautiful" 是美國六、七零年代人權運動時，由黑人提出的口號，用
　來表達對自己膚色的自豪。

單字

- ❖ **southernmost** (**adj.**) 最南端的
- ❖ **accomplished** (**adj.**) 有成就感的
- ❖ **expanse** (**n.**) 廣大的區域
- ❖ **seawater** (**n.**) 海水
- ❖ **inappropriate** (**adj.**) 不適當的
- ❖ **lighthouse** (**n.**) 燈塔
- ❖ **prevent** (**v.**) 預防；防止
- ❖ **armed** (**adj.**) 武裝的；有防禦力的
- ❖ **strait** (**n.**) 海峽
- ❖ **channel** (**n.**) 海峽
- ❖ **protruding** (**adj.**) 突出的
- ❖ **coral reef** 珊瑚礁
- ❖ **squat** (**v.**) 蹲下
- ❖ **slight** (**adj.**) 輕微的；少量的
- ❖ **exposure** (**n.**) 暴露
- ❖ **scramble** (**v.**) 爭奪；爭先恐後取得
- ❖ **tan** (**n.**) 曬成棕褐色膚色

片語與句型

✤ **prevent... from...**：防止……
　㊋ Water can prevent fire from spreading.（水可以防止火的蔓延。）

✤ **give someone a break**：（口語）拜託；真是夠了
　㊋ Would you give me a break? You are driving me crazy.（拜託好不好？你快把我逼瘋了。）

✤ **be named after...**：以……命名；因……而得名
　㊋ Scott Johnson Jr. is named after his father.（Scott Johnson 二世是以父親的名字命名的。）

✤ **on the verge of...**：在……的邊緣
　verge (n.) 邊緣
　㊋ Don't bug him; he is on the verge of a nervous breakdown.（別煩他；他正在瀕臨崩潰的邊緣。）

發音小技巧 🔊

Eluanbi features a forest bath, a coastal footpath, and prehistorical cultural relics.

鵝鑾鼻有森林浴、濱海步道，以及史前文化遺址。

● 趴趴走好用句

1.　「貓鼻頭」位於恆春半島的西南方，與「鵝鑾鼻」形成臺灣最南的兩端。

Maobitou is located on the southwestern side of the Hengchun Peninsula. Together with Eluanbi, it forms one of the two southern tips of Taiwan.

2.　貓鼻頭半島地勢西邊高、東邊低，以隆起的珊瑚礁海岸為主。

The Maobitou Peninsula terrain is higher to the west and lower to the east and has a protruding coral reef shore.

3.　「鵝鑾鼻公園」的地標為燈塔，其有「東亞之光」之稱。

The lighthouse is the landmark of the Eluanbi Park and is otherwise known as the Glory of East Asia.

4.　鵝鑾鼻燈塔是世界少有的武裝燈塔，塔身全白，為圓柱形。

Eluanbi Lighthouse is one of the world's rare armed lighthouses. The structure is entirely white and cylindrical in shape.

5.　每年9月，來自西伯利亞、大陸的紅尾伯勞會大批過境，「鵝鑾鼻公園」是極佳的觀賞地點。

Every September, droves of brown shrikes migrating south from Siberia and China pass through. Eluanbi Park is an ideal place to witness this rare sight.

6.　恆春位於台灣的南端，氣候四季如春，因此名為「恆春」。

Hengchun is located at the southern tip of Taiwan, where it feels like spring all year round; hence the name, "Hengchun (Eternal Spring)."

7.　「恆春三寶」是洋蔥、瓊麻、港口茶。

The "three treasures of Hengchun" are onions, sisal, and portside tea.

8.　每年3、4月是恆春半島的洋蔥產季。

Every March and April, it's onion season on the Hengchun Peninsula.

9.　瓊麻自從日據時代開始便是漁網和繩索的原料。

Since the Japanese colonial period, sisal has been used as a raw material in producing fishnets and ropes.

10.　恆春半島是台灣唯一產冬季西瓜的地方。

Hengchun Peninsula is the only place in Taiwan where watermelon is grown in the winter.

11. 「恆春搶孤」是恆春中元節傳統的民俗活動。

The Hengchun Ghost Grappling Contest is a traditional folk event held during Hengchun's Ghost Festival.

12. 恆春鎮現存的東、西、南、北四座古城門，是台灣唯一保留最完整的城門古蹟。

The surviving ancient city gates on the north, east, west, and south sides of Hengchun Township are the only such gates in Taiwan that remain well preserved.

知本溫泉與初鹿牧場
Zhiben Hot Springs and Chulu Pasturage

Robert: Ah... the hot springs, the beautiful scenery, and Kitty the beautiful **maiden**—what more could a guy ask for?

Taike: Are you blind? Don't you see that group of your **gorgeous** blonde **compatriots** over there?

Kitty: I'll have you know that Robert has good **judgment**. Zhiben Hot Springs is known as the "**foremost** attraction in eastern Taiwan." The five-star hot springs resorts built there recently have attracted a lot of foreign visitors.

Taike: Plus, the Zhiben Forest Recreation Area is right around the corner. It boasts camping areas, picnic areas, a **botanical garden**, waterfalls and hiking trails, as well as different types of **insects** and butterflies. It's truly a great place to enjoy Mother Nature!

Robert: Kitty, that **lumpy** tennis ball you have there on your hands looks **hideous**!

Kitty: Doofus! This is Taitung's local specialty, a **custard apple**. They're so sweet and delicious! Other local **specialties** include pineapples and **Roselles**.

Taike: This is also the local gathering place of the aborigines, which is the reason why aboriginal delicacies and mountain-grown vegetables and **game** are readily found here.

Robert: What I'm **yearning** for is some more of the fresh milk we had at Chulu **Ranch** yesterday. It was sweet, **rich** and all-around fantastic.

Taike: I liked their dairy-made fresh milk **steamed buns** and fresh milk soft ice cream!

Kitty: Yep. Due to its mild climate and **ample precipitation**, the ranch has an **abundant** supply of fresh **pasturage**. What's more, it was so **astonishingly** beautiful that I felt as if I were in Europe!

羅波：啊，溫泉、美景、加上高貴這位美女，人生夫復何求！

邱克：你瞎了眼嗎？那裡有好幾個你的同胞，都是金髮美女耶！

高貴：人家羅波眼光才好呢。知本溫泉有「東台第一景」的美名，而且
　　　自從有五星級溫泉觀光飯店進駐後，吸引了很多外國的觀光客。

邱克：而且這裡又靠近知本森林遊樂區，裡面有露營區、野餐區、植物
　　　園、瀑布、登山步道，還有許多昆蟲、蝴蝶，是觀賞自然生態的
　　　好地方！

羅波：高貴，妳手上拿的那顆長瘤的網球好恐怖喔！

高貴：神經！這是台東的名產釋迦啦，超甜超香的咧！這裡的名產還有
　　　鳳梨和洛神花。

邱克：這裡也是原住民的聚集地，所以有很多原住民美食及山菜野味。

羅波：我比較懷念昨天在初鹿牧場喝的鮮奶，又香又濃，超讚的。

邱克：我喜歡那裡用鮮奶做成的「鮮奶饅頭」以及「鮮奶雙淇淋」！

高貴：嗯，因為那裡的氣候溫和，雨量也充足，所以一年到頭都有新鮮
　　　的牧草。而且初鹿牧場漂亮得不像話，讓我感覺置身歐洲！

單字

- ✤ **maiden**（n.）少女
- ✤ **gorgeous**（adj.）極好的；美妙的
- ✤ **compatriot**（n.）同胞；國人
- ✤ **judgment**（n.）判斷力
- ✤ **foremost**（adj.）最佳的；首要的
- ✤ **botanical gardem** 植物園
- ✤ **insect**（n.）昆蟲
- ✤ **lumpy**（adj.）多腫塊的；多塊狀的
- ✤ **hideous**（adj.）恐怖的；毛骨悚然的
- ✤ **custard apple** 釋迦
- ✤ **specialty**（n.）招牌商品；特產
- ✤ **Roselle** 洛神花
- ✤ **game**（n.）獵物；野味
- ✤ **yearn**（v.）渴望
- ✤ **ranch**（n.）大牧場
- ✤ **rich**（adj.）（味道）濃稠的
- ✤ **steamed bun** 饅頭
- ✤ **ample**（adj.）充足的
- ✤ **precipitation**（n.）降雨
- ✤ **abundant**（adj.）豐富的；很多的
- ✤ **pasturage**（n.）牧草
- ✤ **astonishingly**（adv.）令人驚奇地

片語與句型

❖ **right around**（**the corner**）：就在（轉角）

　例 Your parents are waiting for you right around the corner.（你父母就在轉角處等你。）

❖ **yearn for...**：渴望……

　例 After being abroad for years, he yearns for his home and family.（出國多年後，他渴望故國家園。）

❖ **...-made**：以……製造的（文中的 **dairy-made** 為「用牛乳製造的」）

　例 This hand-made bag is very expensive!（這個手工做的袋子好貴！）

發音小技巧 🔊

Taiwan's Hongye Hot Springs has two locations: Hualien and Taitung.

台灣的「紅葉溫泉」有兩處，一處在花蓮，一處在台東。

● 趴趴走好用句

1.　「知本溪」把知本溫泉分成了內、外溫泉區。

Zhiben Creek divides Zhiben Hot Springs into inner and outer areas.

2.　知本因溫泉而崛起，成為台東地區最有名的遊覽勝地。

Zhiben's reputation grew from its hot springs, enabling it to become the best-known travel destination in the Taitung area.

3.　知本地區是魯凱族、排灣族等原住民的聚集地，當地處處可見原住民美食。

Zhiben is home to the Rukai and Paiwan tribes of aborigines, whose cuisine can be found everywhere.

4.　「知本溫泉」的水質屬於鹼性碳酸泉，無色無味，水溫可高達百度以上。

The waters of Zhiben Hot Springs are colorless and odorless alkaline bicarbonate spring waters that can get as hot as 100 degrees.

5.　知本溫泉可以促進血液循環、鬆弛肌肉，對皮膚病、關節炎、神經痛等皆有療效。

The water of Zhiben Hot Springs increases blood circulation, relaxes the muscles, and has curative effects against skin diseases, arthritis, and neuralgia.

6. 「知本森林遊樂區」內的好漢坡步道，共有792個階梯，因坡度陡峻而
得名。

Zhiben National Forest Recreation Area's Haohan ("Hero") Hill, so
called because of its steepness, has 792 steps.

7. 台東的「紅葉溫泉」因為滿山的楓樹而得名。

Taitung's Hongye ("Red Leaf") Hot Springs got their name from
the scores of maple trees that cover the entire mountain.

8. 「紅葉少棒紀念館」是為了紀念紅葉國小的少棒選手對台灣棒球的貢獻
所興建的。

The Maple Leaf Baseball Team Memorial Hall was built to
commemorate the Hongye Primary School little leaguers'
contributions to Taiwanese baseball.

9. 「初鹿牧場」是台灣土地銀行經營的牧場，乳牛是主要的經營目標。

Chulu Pasturage is managed by the Land Bank of Taiwan. Milking
cows is the main focus of the operation.

10. 「池上牧野渡假村」為台糖所經營，牧場面積達140公頃。

Chishang Pastoral Farm Resort is under the management of the
Taiwan Sugar Company. The farm is approximately 140 hectares in
area.

11. 「池上牧野渡假村」除了牧場之外，尚有親子活動區、營火活動場、露營烤肉區等。

In addition to pasturage, Chishang Pastoral Farm Resort also has a family area, bonfire grounds, and places to camp and barbeque.

12. 花東地區的特產包括台東的池上米、太麻里的金針、花蓮的花蓮薯與花蓮芋等。

Hualien/Taitung-area specialties include Chishang rice from Taitung, daylilies from Taimali, and sweet potatoes and taro cakes from Hualien.

37

花東地區（一）
The Hualien/Taitung Area（I）

Robert: I just can't wrap my mind around the fact that it's so lively here during the summer! **Harvest** Festivals are being held in Amis tribes all along the east coast!

Kitty: Yep. There are many **aborigines** living in the Hualien/ Taitung area, mainly from six tribes: the Amis, Yami, Bunun, Puyuma, Rukai, and Paiwan.

Taike: Yes, and although there are practically no differences between their **lifestyles** and those of the Han people, each tribe still **preserves** its own traditions, cultures, and customs. Plus, the tribes hold their own traditional festivals, such as the Harvest Festival of the Amis tribe every July and August and the Bamboo Pole **Ceremony** of the Paiwan tribe every five years.

Robert: The aborigines here are kind and **diligent**, completely **opposite** to the **rumors** I've heard about aborigines being **indolent** and heavy drinkers.

Taike: Those are all **stereotypes**! In fact, we are usually the reason why aborigines cannot find work.

Kitty: That's right. When our **ancestors** first came to Taiwan, they took over the finest lands and pushed the aborigines to the **desolate** mountain areas.

Robert: I beg to differ. I think this place is a much more **suitable** place to live in! Look around you. Both Taroko and Jade Mountain National Parks are here, as well as the **East Rift Valley** and East Coast National Scenic Areas and the Chinan, Fuyuan, and Zhiben Forest Recreation Areas. This place is practically heaven on earth. Who would want to rub **elbows** with people on the **flat** lands after coming here?

羅波：我真不敢相信這裡的夏天竟是如此熱鬧！東部海岸沿線都有阿美族的部落在舉行豐年祭！

高貴：是啊，花東地區有許多原住民，主要有阿美、雅美、布農、卑南、魯凱、排灣族六個。

邱克：嗯，雖然他們的生活習慣和漢人已經沒有很大差別，但還是各自保有特殊的傳統文化與風俗。而且不同的族群都會舉行自己的傳統祭典，像是每年七、八月的阿美族「豐年祭」和五年一次的排灣族「竹竿祭」。

羅波：這裡的原住民既和善又勤奮，和我來台灣之前聽到的，原住民不愛工作又愛喝酒的傳言完全不一樣。

邱克：那些都是刻板印象啦！其實原住民會找不到工作，很多都還是我們害的咧。

高貴：沒錯，我們的祖先遷移到台灣時，把好的平地都佔據了，把許多原住民趕到鳥不生蛋的山區裡。

羅波：住在這裡才好呢！你看這附近，又有太魯閣及玉山國家公園，又有花東縱谷和東部海岸這兩個國家風景區，還有池南、富源、知本三個森林遊樂區，簡直像人間仙境，誰還要去平地人擠人呢？

單字

- ✦ **harvest**（n.）收穫
- ✦ **aborigine**（n.）原住民
- ✦ **lifestyle**（n.）生活方式
- ✦ **preserve**（v.）保存
- ✦ **ceremony**（n.）儀式；典禮
- ✦ **diligent**（adj.）勤勞的
- ✦ **opposite**（prep.）相反
- ✦ **rumor**（n.）謠言
- ✦ **indolent** [`ɪndələnt]（adj.）怠惰的
- ✦ **stereotype**（n.）刻板印象
- ✦ **ancestor**（n.）祖先
- ✦ **desolate**（adj.）荒廢的；無人居住的
- ✦ **suitable**（adj.）適合的
- ✦ **East Rift Valley** 花東縱谷
- ✦ **elbow**（n.）肘
- ✦ **flat**（adj.）平的

片語與句型

❖ **take over**：控制；接收

⑩ The party has been taken over by extremists.（這政黨已被極端份子所控制。）

❖ **I beg to differ.**（用以表達意見與某人不同）恕無法認同

⑩ "She's clearly the best candidate for this job." "I beg to differ."（「她顯然是這職位最適合的候選人了。」「恕我不能認同。」）

發音小技巧

Sanxiantai is a special scenic area composed of small outlying islands and coral reef shores.

「三仙台」是由離岸小島和珊瑚礁海岸構成的特殊景觀區。

● 趴趴走好用句

1.　每年的七、八月，阿美族會舉行傳統的「豐年祭」。

The Amis tribe holds the traditional Harvest Festival every July and August.

2.　每年四、五月，布農族會舉行「打耳祭」。

The Bunun tribe holds the Manah Tainga (Ear-shooting Ritual) every April and May.

3.　「打耳祭」是布農族人在一年中最盛大的祭典，部落的成年男子必須去打獵，婦女必須釀製小米酒。

The Ear-shooting Ritual is the Bunun's grandest ceremony of the year. Adult males are required to hunt, while it is the duty of females to ferment kadavus.

4.　排灣族的裝飾工藝頗為發達，尤其長於木雕；百步蛇是排灣族的代表圖案。

The Paiwan tribe's decorative crafts are considerably well developed, especially woodcarving. The hundred-pace snake is the tribe's representative insignia.

5.　排灣族每五年會舉行一次「竹竿祭」。

The Paiwan tribe holds the Bamboo Pole Ceremony once every five years.

6. 每年十二月到一月，卑南族會舉行「猴祭」和「大獵祭」。

The Puyuma tribe holds the Vasivas (Monkey Ritual) and the Mangayau (Great Hunting Ritual) every December and January.

7. 蘭嶼的達悟族在三月上旬會舉辦「飛魚祭」，六月時會舉行「船祭」。

Orchid Island Tao tribe celebrates the Flying Fish Festival in early March and the Boat Ceremony in June.

8. 「三仙台」是東海岸最具知名度的風景點，島上有一座跨海人行步道橋。

Sanxiantai is the most famous scenic spot on the east coast. A footbridge leads over the ocean to the island.

9. 「富源森林遊樂區」位於花蓮縣瑞穗鄉，面積235公頃，是台灣最大的樟樹林森林遊樂區。

The Fuyuan Forest Recreation Area, located in Hualien County's Ruisui Township, covers an area of 235 hectares, making it the largest camphor tree forest recreation area in Taiwan.

10. 「富源森林遊樂區」的主要景觀為蝴蝶谷、富源瀑布、樟樹林、溫泉等。

The main attractions at the Fuyuan Forest Recreation Area include the butterfly valley, Fuyuan Falls, the camphor forest, and the hot springs.

11.　「富源森林遊樂區」的蝴蝶種類多達四十餘種，每年四至七月是最佳賞蝶季節。

There are more than 40 butterfly species at the Fuyuan Forest Recreation Area. The best time of year to see the butterflies is between April and July.

12.　「池南森林遊樂區」內有種類眾多的蝴蝶，冬季還可欣賞各種水鳥。

Different kinds of butterflies can be seen at the Chinan Forest Recreation Area. During the winter, waterfowl can also be seen.

CD
2-13

花東地區（二）
The Hualien/Taitung Area（Ⅱ）

Robert: Hey, did you feel that? That felt like another earthquake.

Taike: Come on, it's all in your head. Ever since we told you that the East Rift Valley is located on the border of the Philippine Sea Plate and the Eurasian Plate, you've gotten all **jumpy**.

Robert: Well, we only have **tornadoes** back home—no earthquakes. That's why I'm so afraid of them!

Kitty: Don't be! But it is true that the area's location on a **fault** zone, combined with the **erosion** caused by several rivers, created several diverse and **breathtaking** natural attractions.

Taike: That's true. The East Rift Valley is a green **corridor** with a length of 158 kilometers. It boasts **orchards**, tea **plantations**, rice **paddies** and **pastures**. Pretty much like... like what you **Christians** call "a land flowing with milk and honey!"

Robert: It definitely is! But why is it that we've been living like rabbits these past few days, feeding only on large amounts of vegetables?

Kitty: Give me a break—herbs and vegetables are the **essence** of Hualien/Taitung **cuisine**! And the aborigines keep their dishes simple, since that's the only way to **preserve** the "natural flavor" of the **ingredients**!

Robert: So that's how it is. I've also heard that **remnants** of the mid- and late-**Neolithic Age** and **megalithic culture** can be found here!

Kitty: You're right. What's more, Eight Immortals Cave is precisely the location of the **Paleolithic Period prehistoric** culture **archeological** site. It happens to be Taiwan's earliest prehistoric culture archeological site!

羅波：喂，感覺到了嗎？好像又有地震耶！

邰克：唉，這是你的心理作用啦。自從我們告訴你花東縱谷位於菲律賓海板塊和歐亞板塊的交界處，你就一直緊張兮兮的。

羅波：唉，我的老家只有龍捲風，沒有地震，所以我很害怕啦！

高貴：別怕！不過就因為這地方地處斷層帶，又有幾條河川的沖蝕，因此造就了多變又美麗的自然景觀。

邰克：沒錯，花東縱谷是一條長達一五八公里的綠色走廊，有果園、茶園、稻田、牧場，就像……就像是你們基督徒常說的「流奶與蜜之地」啦！

羅波：的確是！可是我們這幾天為什麼都像兔子一樣，只吃到一大堆蔬菜咧？

高貴：拜託，花東美食的精神就是花果野菜啊！而且原住民的烹調方式都很簡單，因為這樣才可以享受到「原味」啊！

羅波：原來是這樣。不過據說這裡也有新石器時代中、晚期及巨石文化的遺跡呢！

高貴：沒錯，而且「八仙洞」正是舊石器時代史前文化遺址的所在地，是台灣考古學上最早的史前文化遺址呢！

單字

- ❖ **jumpy**（adj.）神經質的
- ❖ **tornado**（n.）龍捲風
- ❖ **fault**（n.）斷層
- ❖ **erosion**（n.）腐蝕；侵蝕
- ❖ **breathtaking**（adj.）驚人的
- ❖ **corridor**（n.）走廊地帶
- ❖ **orchard**（n.）果園
- ❖ **plantation**（n.）農園；種植地
- ❖ **paddy**（n.）稻田
- ❖ **pasture**（n.）牧場
- ❖ **Christian**（n.）基督徒
- ❖ **essence**（n.）本質；精髓
- ❖ **cuisine** [kwɪˋzin]（n.）菜餚；烹飪風格
- ❖ **preserve**（v.）保存
- ❖ **ingredient**（n.）原料
- ❖ **remnant**（n.）遺跡；痕跡
- ❖ **Neolithic Age** 新石器時代
- ❖ **megalithic culture** 巨石文化
- ❖ **Paleolithic Period** 舊石器時代
- ❖ **prehistoric**（adj.）史前的
- ❖ **archeological**（adj.）考古學的

片語與句型

❖ **combine with...**：和……合併；加上……
　　⑩ Hydrogen combines with oxygen to form water.（氫與氧結合成水。）

❖ **what is more**：更有甚者；此外
　　⑩ She is very good-looking, and what's more, she is extremely wealthy!（她很好看，此外她還超有錢呢！）

發音小技巧 🔊

The East Rift Valley produces large quantities of rice, pomelos, tea leaves, and custard apples.

「花東縱谷」盛產稻米、文旦、茶葉和釋迦等。

● 趴趴走好用句

1. 花東地區的自然景觀多變，包括瀑布、溫泉、溪流、沖積平原、河床、沼澤等。

   The natural scenery at the Hualien/Taitung Area is widely varied, ranging from waterfalls and hot springs to streams, alluvial plains, riverbeds, and swamps.

2. 花東地區有許多天然美食，包括藤心、檳榔花、山苦瓜、過貓、山蘇等。

   Natural delicacies abound in the Hualien/Taitung Area, including rattans, areca flowers, wild bitter gourds, vegetable ferns, and bird's nest ferns.

3. 「卑南文化公園」是三級古蹟，緊鄰的月形石柱區是一級古蹟。

   Beinan Cultural Park is a Class III historical site, while the neighboring area that houses moon-shaped stone pillars is a Class I historical site.

4. 「卑南文化公園」的特色是從事考古發掘，並有遺址保存館對外展示。

   The Beinan Cultural Park is characterized by its archaeological pursuits and a relics preservation display that is open to the public.

5. 卑南遺址為全台規模最大，地下文物最豐富的遺址，也是東南亞地區最大的墓葬群遺址。

   The archeological site at Beinan is the largest and richest in Taiwan, not to mention the largest complex of ancient tombs in all of Southeast Asia.

6.　「國立台灣史前文化博物館」是一座以史前和原住民文化為主題的博物館。

The National Museum of Prehistory features prehistoric and aboriginal culture as its themes.

7.　「國立台灣史前文化博物館」是台灣第一座集合了博物館、考古遺址和自然生態公園的博物館。

The National Museum of Prehistory is the first museum in Taiwan to combine a museum, an archaeological site, and a natural ecology park.

8.　台東太麻里鄉在夏季到處是黃澄澄的金針花。

Dazzling yellow daylilies abound in Taitung's Taimali Township in the summer.

9.　「花蓮海洋公園」位於花蓮縣壽豐鄉，園內有三大主題區。

Hualien Ocean Park, situated in Hualien County's Shoufeng Township, features three themed areas.

10.　阿美族社會的母系倫理、年齡階級、巫師、及長老是部落自治最重要的力量。

The most important forces behind the autonomy of the Amis tribe society include tainaan, selar, sikawasay, and kalas.

11.　「花東縱谷」由花蓮溪、秀姑巒溪和卑南溪等三大水系所構成。

The East Rift Valley is comprised of three major river drainage systems: Hualien River, Xiuguluan River, and Beinan River.

12.　「惡地」是指地表遭受強烈侵蝕,而無法成為農業土地利用的地區。

Badlands are heavily eroded land surfaces that cannot be farmed.

CD
2-14

秀姑巒溪及瑞穗溫泉
Xiuguluan River and Ruisui Hot Springs

Robert: Oh my gosh, I almost **drowned** back there! What a **mean** guide—why did he **tip** over our boat on purpose?

Taike: That's the fun of **whitewater rafting**. Tipping the boats over is practically the **climax** of the whole event!

Kitty: Xiuguluan River is the largest river in the east, and it's extremely **circuitous**.

Taike: That's right. This is Taiwan's very own whitewater rafting **mecca**. You can go whitewater rafting any time of year, although the most ideal season is between May and October.

Robert: I think I hurt my **ribs** when I took a **dip** in the water back there.

Taike: Don't worry. We're going to Ruisui Township tomorrow to take a dip in the hot springs. That'll fix you up as good as new. Kitty needs to take a serious dip there too!

Kitty: And why is that?

Taike: Didn't you know that the hot springs there are carbonate **chloride** springs? It is said that frequent dips in this type of spring water will **boost** your chances of giving birth to a male **infant**!

Kitty: You're such a male **supremacist**! What's wrong with giving birth to a baby girl? What a **chauvinist**!

Robert: She's right. And I only heard about the spring water there being rich with iron, tasting of salt and rust, and looking **murky**.

Kitty: Actually, that's caused by the **salt crystals** on the water's surface. It's actually very effective towards treating sensitive skin and **arthritis** as well!

羅波：哇，我剛剛差點溺死了！那教練好卑鄙喔，為什麼故意翻我們的船？

邰克：這就是泛舟好玩的地方啊，翻船可是高潮所在呢！

高貴：秀姑巒溪是東部第一大河，河道非常迂迴呢。

邰克：對啊，這裡是全台灣最熱門的泛舟勝地，全年都可以泛舟，不過最好的季節是五月到十月。

羅波：我剛剛落水時，好像傷到肋骨了！

邰克：反正我們明天就要去瑞穗鄉泡溫泉了，你就可以好好修養了。其實高貴也要好好泡一下那瑞穗溫泉！

高貴：為什麼？

邰克：妳不知道嗎？那裡的溫泉是氯化物碳酸鹽泉，據說常浸泡在這種泉水裡，生男生的機率比較高呢！

高貴：你很重男輕女耶，生女生有什麼不好？真是大男人主義！

羅波：對啊，我只聽說那裡的泉水含豐富的鐵質，帶有鹹味和鐵鏽味，看起來髒髒的。

高貴：其實那是因為水的表面浮著結晶鹽，對治療過敏性皮膚病和關節炎很有效呢！！

單字

❖ **drown**（**v.**）溺死

❖ **mean**（**adj.**）（口語）卑鄙下流的

❖ **tip**（**v.**）使傾斜；打翻

❖ **whitewater rafting**（在激流處）泛舟

❖ **climax**（**n.**）高潮

❖ **circuitous** [sɚˋkjuɪtəs]（**adj.**）迂迴的

❖ **mecca**（**n.**）聖地；嚮往之地

❖ **rib**（**n.**）肋骨

❖ **dip**（**n.**）（口語）浸、泡

❖ **chloride**（**n.**）氯化物

❖ **boost**（**v.**）提高

❖ **infant**（**n.**）嬰兒

❖ **supremacist**（**n.**）至上主義者

❖ （**male**）**chauvinist** [ˋʃovɪnɪst]大男人主義者

❖ **murky**（**adj.**）暗的；深濃的

❖ **salt crystal** 結晶鹽

❖ **arthritis** [ɑrˋθraɪtɪs]（**n.**）關節炎

片語與句型

❖ **tip over**：翻轉；傾覆
　　例 Careful! You'll tip the boat over.（小心！你會把船弄翻。）

❖ **take a dip**：（口語）短時間的游泳或浸泡（也可說成 **have a dip** 或 **go for a dip**）
　　例 Let's take a dip in the river!（我們去河裡泡一泡！）

❖ **be rich with/in...**：盛產……；富含……
　　例 Oranges are rich in vitamin C.（柑橘富含維他命 C。）

發音小技巧

Hualien is the most densely populated region and the most important city in eastern Taiwan.

花蓮市是台灣東部地區人口最稠密的地方，也是台灣東部最重要的城市。

● 趴趴走好用句

1. 秀姑巒溪泛舟活動始於1982年，每到假日，瑞穗街上都是前來泛舟的遊客。

   Whitewater rafting in the Xiuguluan River began in 1982. On weekends and holidays, Ruisui Street is filled with travelers who come to raft.

2. 秀姑巒溪的河床落差有65公尺，其中有二十多個大、小激流。

   The Xiuguluan riverbed drops 65 meters and has more than 20 rapids of varying degrees of intensity.

3. 秀姑巒溪泛舟從瑞穗大橋出發到長虹橋的終點站，總共要三、四個小時。

   A rafting trip down the Xiuguluan River begins at Ruisui Bridge and ends at Changhong Bridge, a journey of three to four hours.

4. 花蓮市位於花蓮縣的中北部，地處花東縱谷北端，東臨太平洋。

   Hualien City is located in the mid-northern section of Hualien County, on the northern end of the East Rift Valley, with a view of the Pacific to the east.

5. 礦業是花蓮市的主要產業，尤以大理石、石灰石儲量最豐富。

   Mining is Hualien's main industry; the area is especially abundant in marble and limestone.

6. 「瑞穗溫泉」、「紅葉溫泉」及「安通溫泉」號稱花東縱谷的三大溫泉。

Ruisui Hot Springs, Hongye Hot Springs, and Antong Hot Springs are known as the three greatest hot springs in the East Rift Valley region.

7. 「瑞穗溫泉」因含豐富的鐵、鋇等礦質，水質呈現鏽黃或鏽紅色。

The water of Ruisui Hot Springs appears rusty yellow or red in color because of its rich concentration of iron, barium, and other minerals.

8. 花蓮的「紅葉溫泉」在日據時代即已聲名遠播，泉水是鹼性的碳酸泉。

Hualien's Hongye Hot Spring has been known far and near since the Japanese colonial era. The hot springs there are alkaline bicarbonate springs.

9. 「花東海岸公路」北起花蓮市，南至台東市，緊臨太平洋，沿途風光迷人。

The Hualien-Taitung Coastal Highway begins in Hualien City to the north and ends in Taitung City to the south. It runs through lovely scenery along the coast of the Pacific.

10. 「瑞穗牧場」是指瑞穗鄉所有牧場的統稱，瑞穗鄉為花蓮縣最大的乳牛養殖區。

Ruisui Farm is a blanket term referring to all of the farms in Ruisui Township. Ruisui Township is the largest dairy cow breeding area in Hualien County.

11. 「瑞穗牧場」草原豐富，水源潔淨，空氣新鮮，因此所生產的牛乳品質特佳。

Ruisui Farm enjoys plentiful grass, clear water, and fresh air; thus the milk it produces is especially high-quality.

12. 「舞鶴村」是天鶴茶的故鄉，也是著名的茶葉產地；當地有許多觀光茶園。

Wuhe Village, home of Tianhe Tea, is a renowned producer of tea leaves. Tourist tea gardens abound in the region.

CD
2-15

玉山
Yushan/Jade Mountain

Taike: Wow, I feel like we're standing on top of the world!

Kitty: Yep. Although Jade Mountain is not the highest peak in the world, at an **elevation** of 3,952 meters, its **pinnacle** is the highest peak in all of East Asia. It is also known as "the **Ridge** of Taiwan!"

Robert: Whoa, I feel **dizzy**; I feel like the room is **spinning**, and I'm having trouble breathing! I think I must be suffering from **altitude sickness**.

Taike: Shame on you! You're big and tall, but you're so useless!

Kitty: Alas, there are only flat corn fields and no high mountains in Robert's home of Ohio. You can't blame him for that!

Robert: She's right, you know. Which is why people there have never seen anything like Jade Mountain's **precious cypress** forests, Taiwan **hemlocks**, Jade Mountain **rhododendrons**, and high-mountain **junipers**!

Kitty: Poor Robert, you're turning blue. Are you sure you can go on?

Robert: Climbing Jade Mountain was one of my reasons for coming to Taiwan! I have to get to the top!

Kitty: But there is a "wind **gap**" before we reach the top. There will be **fierce** winds, and the air will become thin. You sure you can make it?

Robert: Well, we've already gotten our Class A mountain **permit**, and we'll have the assistance of professional **aboriginal trekkers**. I believe that we'll make it through in one piece.

Taike: Don't get any wild ideas about the trekkers. They'll serve as our **guides**, but they're not going to carry you up the mountain!

Robert: Sounds like it would be best to **double back** to the Tataka Recreation Area by the **New Central Cross-Island Highway**!

邱克：哇，感覺我們正站在全世界的屋頂呢。

高貴：嗯，雖然玉山不是世界第一高峰，但是它的主峰標高3,952公尺，
　　　是東亞第一高峰，被稱為「台灣的屋脊」呢！

羅波：唉喲，我頭暈、目眩、呼吸困難啦！我想我得了「高山症」。

邱克：虧你長得人高馬大，真的很沒用耶！

高貴：唉，羅波的家鄉俄亥俄州到處都是平坦的玉米田，沒有高山，不
　　　能怪他啦！

羅波：是啊，所以我們那裡也看不到像玉山這裡珍貴的檜木林、台灣鐵
　　　杉、玉山杜鵑和高山圓柏呢！

高貴：可憐的羅波，看你臉色發青，你確定還能繼續嗎？

羅波：可是攀登玉山是我來台灣的目的之一耶！我一定要登頂啦！

高貴：可是登頂前的「風口」風超強，空氣稀薄，你行嗎？

羅波：反正我們已辦入山證，又有山青們幫忙，應該沒問題吧。

邱克：拜託，你別打山青的主意，他們是我們的嚮導，可不負責背你上
　　　山喔！

羅波：看來我們還是折回去新中橫的「塔塔加遊憩區」好了！！

單字

- ❖ **elevation**（n.）高度；海拔
- ❖ **pinnacle**（n.）頂點；尖峰
- ❖ **ridge**（n.）山脊
- ❖ **dizzy**（adj.）頭暈的；眩暈的
- ❖ **spinning**（adj.）旋轉的
- ❖ **altitude sickness** 高山症
- ❖ **precious**（adj.）珍貴的
- ❖ **cypress**（n.）檜；柏
- ❖ **hemlock**（n.）鐵杉
- ❖ **rhododendron** [ˌrodəˋdɛndrən]（n.）杜鵑花
- ❖ **juniper**（n.）圓柏
- ❖ **gap**（n.）裂口
- ❖ **fierce**（adj.）強勁的
- ❖ **permit**（n.）許可證
- ❖ **aboriginal**（adj.）原住民的
- ❖ **trekker**（n.）登山者
- ❖ **guide**（n.）嚮導
- ❖ **double back** 順原路折返
- ❖ **New Central Cross-Island Highway** 新中橫

片語與句型

✤ **have trouble V+ing**：有困難……；無法……

　⑩ I'm having trouble hearing what people are saying.（我無法聽清楚人們在說些什麼。）

✤ **suffer from...**：吃苦；為……所苦；患有……

　⑩ He's suffering from memory loss.（他患有遺忘症。）

✤ **shame on...**：……對所做的事或所說的話應感到羞恥

　⑩ How could you treat them so badly? Shame on you!（你怎能待他們這麼壞？真可恥啊！）

✤ **blame someone for something**：因某事責怪某人

　⑩ He blamed me for not waking him up this morning.（他怪我今早沒叫醒他。）

✤ **in one piece**：（人）平安脫險；無恙

　⑩ They were very lucky to get back in one piece.（他們很幸運地平安回來。）

發音小技巧 🔊

Yushan National Park is located in Taiwan's central region and is the country's largest national park.

「玉山國家公園」位於台灣的中央地帶，是我國面積最大的國家公園。

趴趴走好用句

1.　「玉山國家公園」有許多高山，「台灣百岳」當中就有高三十多座在此。

There are numerous high peaks in Yushan National Park. More than thirty of the "hundred mountains of Taiwan" can be found there.

2.　「玉山國家公園」橫跨南投、嘉義、花蓮及高雄四縣，總面積約十萬公頃。

Yushan National Park straddles the four counties of Nantou, Chiayi, Hualien, and Kaohsiung, covering a total area of approximately 100,000 hectares.

3.　「玉山國家公園」有許多珍貴稀有的生物，包括台灣彌猴、台灣長鬃山羊、帝雉、酒紅朱雀、藍腹鷳、山椒魚。

Yushan National Park is a habitat for a number of rare species, including the Formosan rock monkey, Formosan serow, Mikado pheasant, vinaceous rose finch, Swinhoe's pheasant, and salamander.

4.　「玉山國家公園」是典型的亞熱帶高山的地質，地形以高山及河谷為主。

As is typical with subtropical alpine areas, the terrain of Yushan National Park consists mainly of high mountains and river valleys.

5.　在每年的夏季遊客可到八通關草原一帶欣賞杜鵑花及菊花。

Every summer, tourists can behold the sight of rhododendrons and chrysanthemums in the area around the Batongguan grasslands.

6.　每年的十月底到十一月中是到新中橫公路的「塔塔加」路段觀賞楓葉、芒花的好時機。

The best time to see the maple leaves and miscanthus along the New Central Cross-Island Highway's Tataka route is between late October and mid-November.

7.　「八通關古道」是遊客登山健行的熱門古道之一。

Batongguan Historic Trail is a favorite mountain-climbing and hiking destination among tourists.

8.　「玉山國家公園」有三個遊客中心：塔塔加、梅山、南安。

There are three tourist centers in Yushan National Park: Tataka, Meishan, and Nanan.

9.　登山可強化心、肺功能，增進個人的體力及耐力。

Mountain climbing can strengthen a person's cardiac and respiratory functions and improve personal strength and endurance.

10.　根據國外的研究報告指出，超過3,000公尺以上的高山常會使登山客發生急性高山症。

According to international research, peaks with an altitude of more than 3,000 meters often cause altitude sickness in mountain climbers.

11. 要預防高山症，登山者須緩慢爬升，讓身體有足夠時間適應高度的變化。

To avoid altitude sickness, mountain climbers should ascend slowly to allow their bodies to have ample time adjust to the difference in elevation.

12. 「急性高山病」的症狀包括頭痛、噁心、嘔吐、水腫、呼吸困難等。

Symptoms of acute altitude sickness include headache, nausea, vomiting, bloating, and trouble breathing.

太魯閣國家公園
Taroko National Park

Robert: Taroko **Gorge** is so impressive! I wonder if **the Grand Canyon** back in the States is anything like this.

Taike: Get real; it's not even close! Aside from the gorges, there are also waterfalls, **broadleaf** forests and tropical **monsoon** rainforest plants here. Plus, all kinds of animals can be seen here, including the Formosan rock monkey, Formosan red-bellied tree **squirrel**, and Formosan wild **boar**. This place is also ideal for bird- and butterfly-watching. You just can't compete with it!

Kitty: Well, I don't think the Grand Canyon is all that bad. But our Taroko National Park is known for its massive **marble cliffs**, deep gorges and **winding** tunnels.

Robert: Why is it so amazing?

Kitty: Four million years ago, the Central Range was formed by the **clashing** of **continental plates**. Afterwards, the **weathering** and **erosion** on the **surface** of the mountains made the **underlying** marble visible…

Taike: … And that marble was eroded by the Liwu River until it formed the almost **vertical** gorge you are looking at now.

Robert: That's such a **coincidence**—the Grand Canyon in the United States was also formed by river erosion!

Taike: Oh? But do you have such **magnificent** sights as Changchun **Shrine**, **Swallow** Grotto, Eight **Immortals** Cave, Tunnel of Nine Turns, or Qingshui Cliffs?

Kitty: Stop it, you guys! We're here to admire the view, not to **bicker**!

羅波：這太魯閣峽谷真是太壯觀了！真不知我們美國的大峽谷是不是也如這般？

邰克：拜託，你們那個差我們這個可遠了！我們除了峽谷，還有瀑布、闊葉林和熱帶季風雨林植物，而且還能看到各種動物，像是台灣彌猴、赤腹松鼠、台灣山豬，而且還可以賞鳥、賞蝶，不能比啦！

高貴：嗯，我想人家的大峽谷也很不賴啦。不過我們的「太魯閣國家公園」以壯闊的大理石斷崖、深邃的峽谷、以及曲折的山洞隧道聞名。

羅波：怎麼會那麼神奇呢？

高貴：四百萬年前，大陸板塊的碰撞形成了中央山脈，然後山上的表層岩層長期受到風化作用而被侵蝕，大理岩因而露出地表……

邰克：……而這些大理岩因為受到立霧溪長期的侵蝕下切作用，形成了這幾乎垂直的峽谷。

羅波：真巧，我們美國的大峽谷也是被河流侵蝕才形成的耶！

邰克：可是你們有美到不行的長春祠、燕子口、八仙洞、九曲洞、清水斷崖嗎？

高貴：好了，我們是來欣賞風景的，不是來鬥嘴的！

單字

- **gorge**（n.）峽谷
- **the Grand Canyon** [ˋkænjən]（美國科羅拉多州）大峽谷
- **broadleaf**（n.）闊葉樹
- **monsoon**（n.）季風
- **squirrel**（n.）松鼠
- **boar**（n.）野豬
- **marble**（n.）大理石
- **cliff**（n.）峭壁；斷崖
- **winding**（adj.）蜿蜒的；迂迴的
- **clash**（v.）碰撞
- **continental plate** 大陸板塊
- **weathering**（n.）風化
- **erosion**（n.）腐蝕；侵蝕
- **surface**（n.）表面
- **underlying**（adj.）在下面的
- **vertical**（adj.）垂直的
- **coincidence**（n.）巧合
- **magnificent**（adj.）壯麗的；宏大的
- **shrine**（n.）祠堂；神廟
- **swallow**（n.）燕子
- **immortal**（n.）不朽的人物；仙人
- **bicker**（v.）爭論

片語與句型

❖ **get real**：(口語)(暗示對方很傻或沒道理)醒醒吧！

　　例 Get real—she's not going to marry you.(別傻了，她是不可能嫁給你的。)

❖ **it is not even close**：簡直無法比；相差太大

　　例 His house is huge; yours is not even close.(他的房子超大；你的根本差太多了。)

❖ **aside from...**：除了……以外(也可用 **apart from...**)；還有……

　　例 Aside from the injuries to her face, she broke her left leg.(除了臉上的傷之外，她的左腳也斷了。)

發音小技巧 🔊

Taroko National Park is known for its majestic and almost vertical marble gorge scenery.

「太魯閣國家公園」以雄偉壯麗、幾近垂直的大理岩峽谷景觀聞名。

1.　「太魯閣國家公園」成立於1986年，是台灣面積第二大的國家公園。

Taroko National Park, established in 1986, is the second-largest national park in Taiwan.

2.　瀑布是「太魯閣國家公園」重要的景觀，包括白楊瀑布、銀帶瀑布等。

Waterfalls are an important part of the scenery at Taroko National Park. They include Baiyang Waterfall and Silver Ribbon Falls.

3.　「太魯閣國家公園」以高山、峽谷及大理石岩層最為著名。

Taroko National Park is best known for its high peaks, gorges, and marble terrain.

4.　「太魯閣牌樓」是個中國味十足的牌樓，是旅客照相紀念的熱門景點。

The Taroko Memorial Arch is a distinctively Chinese archway. It is a favorite picture-taking spot among tourists.

5.　「長春祠」的興建是為了紀念因開築「中部橫貫公路」而殉職的兩百多位人員。

Changchun Shrine was built to commemorate the more than 200 workers killed in accidents while building the Central Cross-Island Highway.

6. 車輛行駛於「九曲洞」之間時，有時一片漆黑，有時馬上又有陽光射入。

Cars driving through the Tunnel of Nine Turns will be blanketed in darkness one moment and bathed in bright light the next.

7. 「九曲洞」是人工與自然的結合。

The Tunnel of Nine Turns is a combination of both man-made and natural elements.

8. 「燕子口」的小岩洞曾有許多燕子在上面築巢，不過現在因遊客過多，燕子都被嚇走了。

The small holes on the stone walls of Swallow Grotto once served as nests for many swallows. The swallows have since fled, however, driven away by the crowds of tourists that now throng the area.

9. 「清水斷崖」指的是「蘇花公路」和平至清水之間長達二十多公里的路段。

Qingshui Cliffs refers to the twenty-plus-kilometer route from Heping to Qingshui along the Su-Hua Highway.

10. 「清水斷崖」蜿蜒曲折，是蘇花公路最驚險壯麗的景觀。

Qingshui Cliffs, with its serpentine windings, is the most thrilling and majestic sight on the Su-Hua Highway.

11.　「天祥」位在太魯閣峽谷西端，是泰雅族原住民長久以來的居住地。

Tianxiang is located on the western edge of Taroko Gorge. It has long been the residence of Atayal aborigines.

12.　「天祥」是為了紀念文天祥而改名，是中橫公路沿線非常熱門的風景區。

Tianxiang was renamed as such to commemorate Wen Tianxiang. It is a very popular scenic area along the Central Cross-Island Highway.

CD
2-17

蘇澳及礁溪溫泉
Suao and Jiaoxi Hot Springs

Robert: Jeez, this water is **freezing**! Aren't we supposed to **soak** ourselves in a hot spring?

Kitty: Well, this is Suao's low-**temperature** spa! Although it's only 22 degrees Celsius, after a while you'll start feeling warm all over, and pretty **alert**, too!

Robert: Humm, this water is **colorless**, **odorless** and clear. I feel like drinking it!

Taike: Go ahead and drink it! The cold spring here is **drinkable**.

Kitty: Yeah. Suao's **specialties**, red bean **jelly** and **marble** soda, are made from cold spring water!

Robert: But isn't there a **ground**-level hot spring nearby?

Kitty: That's right, the Jiaoxi Hot Spring. It's 58 degrees **Celsius**, and it's my favorite. After bathing, it leaves your skin feeling **smooth** and **velvety** without being **sticky** or **greasy** at all. It is also believed to **benefit** the skin and relieve **tension**, so it has become known as the "hot spring among hot springs!"

Robert: Hmm, no wonder people say that "**Beauties** are local specialties of Yilan!"

Taike: Well, you sure know a lot about Taiwanese beauties!

Kitty: Hum, I'm not from Yilan, but I sure am a beauty!

Taike: All right, all right. After our dip, let's go enjoy the hot spring vegetables that the local residents grow using the **mineral** water. Maybe we'll all turn out better-looking after the **feast**!

羅波：哇，這水真冷！不是說我們要來泡溫泉的咩？

高貴：啊，這是蘇澳的「低溫礦泉」啦，溫度雖只有攝氏22度，不過泡
　　　一下子後你就會覺得全身都暖和起來，而且精神振奮了！

羅波：嗯，這水無色無臭，水質清澈，好想喝喔！

邰克：你儘管喝呀！這裡的冷泉是可以喝的。

高貴：對呀，蘇澳的名產「羊羹」和「彈珠汽水」就是用這種冷泉調製
　　　的呢！

羅波：不過這附近不是聽說有平地溫泉嗎？

高貴：沒錯，「礁溪溫泉」。它的溫度是攝氏58度，是我最喜歡的溫
　　　泉。那裡的溫泉洗後光滑但不黏膩，具有養顏美容及鎮定神經的
　　　功效，所以被稱為「溫泉中的溫泉」！

羅波：嗯，難怪有人說「宜蘭出美女」！

邰克：咦，你對台灣美女倒很有研究嘛！

高貴：哼，我不是宜蘭人，還不是美女一個！

邰克：好啦好啦，等會兒泡完我們去吃礁溪居民用礦泉水種植的溫泉蔬
　　　菜，吃完看看我們會不會都變成俊男美女啦！

單字

✤ **freezing** (**adj.**) 酷寒的；冰凍的

✤ **soak** (**v.**) 浸泡

✤ **temperature** (**n.**) 溫度

✤ **alert** (**adj.**) 警覺的；機敏的

✤ **colorless** (**adj.**) 無色的

✤ **odorless** (**adj.**) 無味的

✤ **drinkable** (**adj.**) 適於飲用的

✤ **specialty** (**n.**) 招牌商品；特產

✤ **jelly** (**n.**) 軟凍；膠狀物

✤ **marble** (**n.**) 玻璃彈珠

✤ **ground** (**n.**) 地面；地表

✤ **Celsius** (**n.**) 攝氏

✤ **smooth** (**adj.**) 光滑的、平坦的

✤ **velvety** (**adj.**) 柔軟的

✤ **sticky** (**adj.**) 黏的

✤ **greasy** (**adj.**) 油膩的；滑膩的

✤ **benefit** (**v.**) 有益於……

✤ **tension** (**n.**) 緊張

✤ **beauty** (**n.**) 美人

✤ **mineral** [ˋmɪnərəl] (**n.**) 礦物

✤ **feast** (**n.**) 盛宴

片語與句型

❖ **go ahead...**：儘管……

　　例 Go ahead and do it—I don't care!（儘管去做吧——我才不在乎
　　呢！）

❖ **no wonder**：難怪

　　例 She's been eating like a pig—no wonder she's gained weight.（她這
　　陣子吃得超多——難怪她胖了。）

❖ **turn out**：變成；結果是

　　例 Their marriage turned out to be a big disaster.（他們的婚姻後來變成
　　個大災難。）

發音小技巧

Jiaoxi's hot spring area has nearly one hundred hotels and
baths.

礁溪的溫泉區有近百家的旅館及浴池。

趴趴走好用句

1.　「礁溪溫泉會館·遊客中心」位在礁溪火車站北方500公尺處。

The Tourist Information Center of Jiaoxi is located approximately 500 meters north of the Jiaoxi train station.

2.　「礁溪溫泉」沒有刺鼻的硫磺味，洗後皮膚感到光滑柔細。

The waters of Jiaoxi Hot Spring do not have a stinging sulfuric smell, and soaking in them leaves one's skin feeling smooth and velvety.

3.　旅客到礁溪除了可在旅館享受溫泉，還可到幾個公共澡堂免費泡湯。

In addition to taking a dip in the hot springs at a hotel, visitors to Jiaoxi can also enjoy a free dip in one of the public baths.

4.　宜蘭的「五峰旗風景區」是由五座山峰排列而成，遠看有如旗幟一般，因而得名。

Yilan's Wufengqi Scenic Area is comprised of a string of five peaks that look like a flag when viewed from a distance; hence its name, "Five-Peak Flag."

5.　「五峰旗瀑布」全長約100公尺，共分為三層，是礁溪鄉著名的風景區。

Wufengqi Falls, dropping 100 meters in three stages, is one of the more famous sights in Jiaoxi.

6. 沿著「五峰旗風景區」的步道可到達上方的「聖母山莊」，這裡可以讓遊客休息、住宿。

Walking up the Wufengqi Scenic Area footpath will lead you to St. Mary's Villa at the top, where travelers can rest their weary feet or spend the night.

7. 「跑馬古道」位於台北縣與宜蘭縣的界線上，原本是用來搬運木材。

Paoma Historic Trail is located at the conjunction of Taipei County and Yilan County. It was originally used to transport timber.

8. 「蘇澳冷泉」富含大量的二氧化碳，因只有攝氏22度，因此是冷泉。

Suao Cold Spring is rich in carbon dioxide. It is known as a cold spring because of its low temperature of 22 degrees Celsius.

9. 「蘇澳冷泉」據說浸泡可治皮膚病，飲用可治腸胃病。

A soak in Suao Cold Spring is said to have curative effects against skin diseases, while a drink of its water can be effective in treating gastrointestinal diseases.

10. 全世界有冷泉的國家只有義大利與台灣，台灣的冷泉以「蘇澳冷泉」最著名。

Italy and Taiwan are the only two countries with cold springs. Suao Cold Spring is the best-known of Taiwan's cold springs.

11.　「南方澳」是台灣東部最大的陸連島，與蘇澳港相通。

Nanfangao is the largest land-tied island in eastern Taiwan. It connects to Suao Harbor.

12.　「武荖坑風景區」面積有400公頃，可溯溪、玩水、釣魚、野餐、露營等。

Wulaokeng Scenic Area covers an area of 400 hectares and is a prime spot for stream tracing, playing in the water, fishing, picnicking, and camping.

CD
2-18

宜蘭與冬山河
Yilan and Dongshan River

Robert: Wow, the Dongshan River is beautiful! Look, lots of people are **cycling** just like we are!

Kitty: (Groaning) They're probably riding the bikes offered by their **bed-and-breakfasts** too! How **unoriginal**!

Robert: But seriously, Yilan is located in the **choicest** area of the Lanyang Plain, where numerous rivers and streams not only provide plenty of water for **irrigation**, but also add to its beautiful natural **vistas**.

Taike: Yes, and the Dongshan River Water Park's **multipurpose** riverside **recreation** area provides sports, leisure, and recreation activities suitable for everyone!

Kitty: That's right; the annual Dragon Boat races, International **Collegiate** Invitational **Regatta**, and International Children's **Folklore** & Folkgame Festival are all held here. If we keep on riding, we can even reach the National Center for Traditional Arts!

Taike: OK, we've been working hard—why don't we take a break and enjoy the local delicacies that we just bought? Here are **jujube** cakes, candied plums, duck **jerky**, and the newly popularized tea-smoked eggs and hand-made tea rice.

Kitty: I want the ox-**tongue** cookies!

Robert: Ox what? How disgusting! Don't tell me you Taiwanese eat everything, even ox tongue!

Taike: Don't you worry. They're named not for their **ingredients** but for their shape! And you Westerners eat **foie gras** and **calf's** liver all the time. What gives you the right to **criticize** us?

Robert: Come to think of it… you're right. But Americans only eat calf's liver. The **pretentious**, **snobby** French are the ones who eat the foie gras!

羅波：哇，這冬山河真美！你們看，有好多人跟我們一樣也在騎腳踏車耶！

高貴：哼，大家都應該是騎民宿免費提供的腳踏車的吧！真沒創意。

羅波：不過說真的，宜蘭位於蘭陽平原的精華地區，河川縱橫，除了提供豐富的灌溉資源，也讓這裡的景觀增色不少呢！

邰克：是啊，而且冬山河沿岸的「親水公園」這多用途的河濱遊憩區可以運動、休閒與玩樂，真是老少咸宜！

高貴：嗯，而且宜蘭一年一度的龍舟賽、國際名校划船邀請賽、國際童玩節也都在這裡舉行呢！如果我們一直騎下去，還可以騎到「國立傳藝中心」呢！

邰克：騎了這麼久，大家休息一下，吃吃剛剛買的宜蘭名產吧！這裡有棗餅、蜜李、鴨賞，還有這幾年才興起的茶燻蛋和手工茶粿。

高貴：我要吃牛舌餅！

羅波：牛什麼？好噁心啊！別告訴我你們台灣人什麼都吃，連牛的舌頭也不放過！

邰克：安啦，那不過是一種形狀長得像牛舌的餅乾啦！再說你們西方人不也常吃什麼鵝肝、牛肝之類的東東嗎？有什麼資格批評我們？

羅波：嗯，說的也是。不過我們美國人只吃牛肝，吃鵝肝的是做作又勢利眼的法國人啦！

單字

- ✤ **cycle**（**v.**）騎腳踏車
- ✤ **bed-and-breakfast**（**n.**）民宿
- ✤ **unoriginal**（**adj.**）無創造性的
- ✤ **choice**（**adj.**）精華的；精選的
- ✤ **irrigation**（**n.**）灌溉
- ✤ **vista**（**n.**）景色，風景
- ✤ **multipurpose**（**adj.**）多用途的
- ✤ **recreation**（**n.**）娛樂
- ✤ **collegiate** [kəˋlidʒɪɪt]（**adj.**）大學的
- ✤ **regatta**（**n.**）賽舟；划船比賽
- ✤ **folklore**（**n.**）民俗
- ✤ **jujube**（**n.**）棗子
- ✤ **jerky**（**n.**）肉乾
- ✤ **tongue**（**n.**）舌頭
- ✤ **ingredient**（**n.**）成分；原料
- ✤ **foie gras** [ˌfwaˋgra]鵝肝
- ✤ **calf** [kæf]（**n.**）小牛
- ✤ **criticize**（**v.**）批評
- ✤ **pretentious** [prɪˋtɛnʃəs]（**adj.**）自命不凡的
- ✤ **snobby**（**adj.**）勢利的

片語與句型

❖ **keep on V+ing**：持續（做某事）

  例 Don't worry about the guy; just keep on walking.（別管那傢伙；繼續往前走就是了。）

❖ **take a break**：休息；偷閒

  例 Let's take a ten-minute break and have some coffee.（我們休息十分鐘，喝杯咖啡。）

❖ **come to think of it**：那麼說來；仔細想想

  例 Come to think of it, she is not as nice as she appeared to be.（仔細想想，她不像她之前表現出來的那樣和善。）

發音小技巧

Yilan holds its International Children's Folklore and Folkgame Festival during the first weekend of July.

宜蘭「國際童玩藝術節」在七月的第一個週末舉行。

趴趴走好用句

1. 冬山河縱貫宜蘭冬山鄉至五結鄉，全長約24公里。

   Yilan's Dongshan River runs through Dongshan Township and Wujie Township for a total of 24 kilometers.

2. 冬山河的中游有著名的「冬山河親水公園」，是為了實踐人類「親近水」的理念而建。

   The Dongshan River Water Park, located midway down the Dongshan River, was built with the idea that people should be close to water.

3. 「冬山河親水公園」是著名的賞鳥勝地，也是生態保育區。

   The Dongshan River Water Park is a well-known birdwatching mecca as well as an ecological preservation area.

4. 冬山河的「國際名校划船邀請賽」常有來自世界各地的大學船隊互相競技。

   College rowing teams from all over the world compete in the International Collegiate Invitational Regatta, held in the Dongshan River.

5. 冬山河「國際名校划船邀請賽」提昇了台灣在國際上體育、觀光、文化的聲譽。

   The Dongshan River International Collegiate Invitational Regatta boosts Taiwan's reputation on the international stage in such areas as sports, tourism, and culture.

6.　　「羅東運動公園」位在羅東市區西北方，園區佔地47公頃，是當地民眾最佳的休閒去處。

Luodong Recreation Park, northwest of downtown Luodong, covers 47 hectares and is a favorite leisure getaway among the locals.

7.　　「羅東運動公園」有人工湖及遼闊的景觀，是集運動、休閒、遊憩功能於一身的公園。

Luodong Recreation Park has a man-made lake and an expansive landscape. The park integrates sports, leisure, and recreational functions.

8.　　「羅東夜市」周圍商店林立，販賣各種傳統風味的小吃。

Stores selling all kinds of traditional snacks abound in the vicinity of Luodong Night Market.

9.　　「國立傳統藝術中心」位於冬山河的下游，適合全家一起造訪。

The National Center for Traditional Arts, farther down Dongshan River, is a suitable destination for the whole family.

10.　　「國立傳統藝術中心」園區有許多傳統的景觀建築，並有露天舞台、戲劇館、傳統小吃坊等。

Traditional landscape architecture covers the grounds of the National Center for Traditional Arts. There is also an outdoor stage, a theater, and traditional snack stalls.

11. 「頭城老街」在清代時，一度是蘭陽平原最重要的經濟中心。

During the Qing Dynasty, Toucheng Old Street was the most important economic center in the Lanyang Plain.

12. 「頭城老街」有古老的建築、石雕，漫步其中可以想像當年頭城的繁華景象。

Strolling among the ancient structures and stone carvings of Toucheng Old Street, one can imagine what the town looked like in its glory days.

東北角海岸
The Northeast Coast

Robert: Wow! The beach, the music, the fireworks, the **starry** sky, the beautiful women, the beer… The Ho-Hai-Yan Rock Festival definitely lives up to its **reputation**!

Taike: It sure does. This annual summer music festival is held to **encourage** Taiwan's local creative bands, to promote interaction between **domestic** and foreign bands, and to **propagate** the concept "Music Knows No **Bounds**!"

Robert: Plus, holding it at Fulong Beach brings business to the **proprietors**, stalls, and hotel operators in the **vicinity**. It is said to bring in at least 200 million dollars a year!

Kitty: Yep. The music festivals of late have also **incorporated** anti-**nuke** messages, bringing the public's attention to the importance of **ecological** protection. Too bad many people still don't cherish this beautiful beach—just look at the mountain of trash over there!

Taike: That's why people are **initiating** the "Save Fulong Beach" **movement**!

Kitty: That's right! Truth be told, the charm of Taiwan's Northeast Coast does not end with its gorgeous beaches. There are also several **enchanting** hiking **trails**, including the Caoling Historic Trail, which is one of the most famous trails in northern Taiwan.

Taike: Yeah, I've hiked that trail before. It extends about ten **kilometers**, from Taipei County's Gongliao Township to Yilan County's Toucheng Township.

Robert: Whoa! That was so scary. Someone tried to sell me some **Ecstasy** just now! I really do think that the music festival should start promoting a "Say No to Drugs" movement!

羅波：哇，沙灘、音樂、煙火、星空、美女、啤酒……，這「貢寮國際海洋音樂祭」果真名不虛傳！

邱克：是啊，這一年一度在夏天舉行的音樂祭，為的是鼓勵台灣本土的創作樂團，讓國內、外的樂團相互交流，闡揚「音樂無國界」的理念！

羅波：而且在福隆沙灘舉行，帶給這附近商家、攤販和旅館業者無限的商機，據說一年至少2億元呢！

高貴：嗯，這幾年的音樂祭還加入了反核的聲音，讓大家更注意到生態保護的重要性。可惜很多人還是不愛惜這美麗的沙灘，你們看看這些堆積如山的垃圾！

邱克：這也是為什麼現在有人發起「搶救福隆沙灘」的運動了！

高貴：沒錯！其實台灣的東北角除了美麗的沙灘，還有許多迷人的登山路線，像是「草嶺古道」，那是北台灣十分著名的登山健行路線。

邱克：對，這我走過，它是從台北縣的貢寮鄉到宜蘭縣的頭城鎮，全長約十公里。

羅波：唉唷，好恐怖，剛剛竟然有人向我推銷搖頭丸！我覺得「音樂祭」真的該發起「拒絕毒品」的運動了！

單字

- **starry** [`stɑrɪ] (**adj.**) 多星的
- **reputation** (**n.**) 名聲；聲望
- **encourage** (**v.**) 鼓勵
- **domestic** (**adj.**) 國內的
- **propagate** (**v.**) 傳播；散佈
- **bound** (**n.**) 邊界；疆域
- **proprietor** [prə`praɪətə] (**n.**) 業主；經營者
- **vicinity** (**n.**) 附近；周圍
- **incorporate** (**v.**) 結合
- **nuke** (**n.**) 核子武器；核能發電廠
- **ecological** (**adj.**) 生態的
- **initiate** (**v.**) 發起
- **movement** (**n.**) 運動
- **enchanting** (**adj.**) 迷人的
- **trail** (**n.**) 小徑
- **kilometer** (**n.**) 公里
- **Ecstasy** (**n.**) 搖頭丸

片語與句型

✤ **live up to...**：符合……的標準；達到……的期待
⑩ She failed to live up to her parents' expectations.（她辜負了父母的
期待。）

發音小技巧

The Northeast Coast National Scenic Area, located in northeastern
Taiwan, encompasses 66 kilometers of coastline.

位於台灣東北方的「東北角海岸風景區」共有全長約66公里的
海岸線。

● 趴趴走好用句

1.　「東北角海岸風景區」有各式的奇岩海岸地形，是北台灣最受歡迎的旅遊景點。

The Northeast Coast National Scenic Area has all kinds of rock formations and coastal terrain. It is the most popular tourist attraction in northern Taiwan.

2.　「草嶺古道」歷史悠久，是清代宜蘭對外交通的唯一通道。

The Caoling Historic Trail has a venerable history. Back in the Qing dynasty, it was the only trail connecting Yilan to the outside world.

3.　遊客行走在「草嶺古道」上可欣賞起伏的山勢，還能目睹太平洋的壯闊。

While strolling along the Caoling Historic Trail, travelers can enjoy the rise and fall of the mountainous terrain and witness the vast grandeur of the Pacific Ocean.

4.　「草嶺古道」秋冬時節是觀賞芒草的熱門景點，屆時山頭會呈現一片白浪搖曳的景象。

The Caoling Historic Trail is a popular place to see silvergrass during the fall and winter months, when the mountaintops are covered in a blanket of white.

5.　「貢寮海洋音樂祭」已成為台灣一年一度搖滾樂團的朝聖祭典。

The Ho-Hai-Yan Rock Festival has now become Taiwan's annual rock band pilgrimage.

6. 蘭陽平原過去受雪山山脈阻隔，對外聯絡相當不便，「北宜公路」與「雪山隧道」通車後，大大改善此一情況。

The Lanyang Plain used to be isolated by the Xueshan Range, which made it difficult to communicate with the outside world. The situation improved when the Taipei-Yilan Highway and the Xueshan Tunnel were opened.

7. 「北宜公路」是台北通往宜蘭的重要管道，全長約82公里，行車時間約兩小時。

The Taipei-Yilan Highway is an important passageway that connects Taipei to Yilan. 82 kilometers long, the highway can be traveled in about two hours.

8. 「北宜公路」沿途景致優美，但因彎道過多，常造成交通事故。

The Taipei-Yilan Highway runs through lovely scenery, but its many windings make for frequent traffic accidents.

9. 2006年六月「雪山隧道」通車後，台北到宜蘭開車只需三十多分鐘。

After the Xueshan Tunnel opened to vehicular traffic in June 2006, the driving time from Taipei to Yilan was shortened to a mere thirty minutes.

10. 「雪山隧道」施工長達十五年，總長度12.9公里，是台灣和東南亞地區第一長的公路隧道。

It took fifteen years to build the Xueshan Tunnel. At 12.9 kilometers, it is the longest highway tunnel anywhere in Taiwan or Southeast Asia.

11.　「三貂嶺」十分高聳，旅客可以於山嶺上欣賞日出、日落或雲海的奇景。

San Diego is a towering peak where a hiker can view spectacular sunrises, sunsets, and seas of clouds.

12.　「十分瀑布」有「台灣的尼加拉瀑布」之稱，瀑布上常會有彩虹形成。

Shifen Falls is known as Taiwan's Niagara Falls. Rainbows can often be seen in the falling water.

北海岸
The North Coast

Taike:　The sea breeze at Yehliu sure feels comfortable! Robert, let's see how good your **imagination** is. What do these rocks look like to you?

Robert:　Hmm… I think this one looks like an **anorexic** Kitty, that one looks like my **stool**, and that one looks like the **sandals** on your feet.

Taike:　You really are **devoid** of artistic talent! This is Queen's Head Rock, and those two are **Candlestick** Rock and Fairy Shoe!

Kitty:　That's right. Yehliu is a **cape protruding** above sea level. This **spectacular**, internationally-known landscape was formed by wave **erosion**, **weathering** and **crustal** movement.

Robert:　Right. I've heard things about the sea-eroded **trenches**, mushroom rocks, bean curd rocks, **beehive** rocks, **potholes** and **dissolved basins** here.

Kitty:　Yep. What's more, Heping Island, Badouzi and Keelung **Islet** are right around the corner. These are all **geological** landscapes formed by **volcanic sedimentary rocks**. They are also very much worth visiting!

Taike:　Which reminds me, there's an "Ocean World" here in Yehliu. It's the foremost **marine** ecology center in the country. It even has an **underwater** tunnel! Do you want to go and take a look?

Kitty:　Sure. I'm very much looking forward to seeing **dolphins** and sea lions perform!

Robert:　What about dinner?

Taike:　Why don't we go to the Old Street in Jinshan for some duck? There used to be a snack stall selling duck near the temple there. Their business got so good that they rented the whole street to sell duck!

邱克：野柳的海風真舒服！羅波，考考你的想像力——這幾塊石頭長得像什麼？

羅波：嗯，我覺得這個像得了厭食症的高貴、那個像我的大便、那個則像你腳上的拖鞋！

邱克：你真沒藝術天分耶！這個是女王頭、那兩個是燭台石和仙女鞋啦！

高貴：對呀，野柳是個突出海面的岬角，因為海浪侵蝕、岩石風化及地殼運動的作用才造成了這些聞名國際的壯麗景色。

羅波：對對，我有聽過這裡的海蝕洞溝、蕈狀石、豆腐石、蜂窩石、壺穴和溶蝕盤。

高貴：嗯，而且這附近還有和平島、八斗子和基隆嶼，這些都是火山沈積岩構成的地質景觀，也很值得一遊！

邱克：對了，野柳這裡還有個「海洋世界」，它是全國第一個海洋生態育樂館，還有海底景觀隧道呢！要不要去看看呀？

高貴：好，我超想看海豚和海獅表演呢！

羅波：那今天的晚餐呢？

邱克：去金山的老街吃鴨肉好了。那裡廟口本來有一家賣鴨肉的小吃攤，因為生意超好，現在整條街都被他們租來賣鴨肉了！

單字

- **imagination**（n.）想像力
- **anorexic** [ænəˋrɛksɪk]（adj.）患厭食症的
- **stool**（n.）排泄物；大便
- **sandal**（n.）涼鞋
- **devoid**（adj.）缺乏的
- **candlestick**（n.）燭台
- **cape**（n.）岬角
- **protrude**（v.）突出
- **spectacular**（adj.）壯觀的
- **erosion**（n.）侵蝕
- **weathering**（n.）風化（作用）
- **crustal**（adj.）地殼的
- **trench**（n.）壕溝；深溝
- **beehive**（n.）蜂窩
- **pothole**（n.）壺穴
- **dissolved basin** 溶蝕盤
- **islet** [ˋaɪlɪt]（n.）小島
- **geological**（adj.）地質（學）的
- **volcanic**（adj.）火山的；由於火山作用的
- **sedimentary rock** 沈積岩
- **marine**（adj.）海的
- **underwater**（adj.）水面下的
- **dolphin**（n.）海豚

片語與句型

✤ **be devoid of...**：沒有……；毫無……
  例 This murderer is devoid of conscience.（這謀殺者喪盡天良。）

✤ **take a look**：瞧一瞧；看一看
  例 Let's take a look at this letter.（我們來看一看這封信。）

發音小技巧

Yehliu Ocean World boasts the only dolphin
performance stage in the country.

「野柳海洋世界」有國內唯一的海豚表演館。

● 趴趴走好用句

1. 北海岸風景線景色優美，包含野柳、金山、石門、三芝等風景區。

   The view on the North Coast is strikingly beautiful. The area includes such scenic areas as Yehliu, Jinshan, Shimen, and Sanzhi.

2. 北海岸風景線以海蝕洞、溫泉、風稜石、海洋生態等為主要的景觀。

   The main attractions on the North Coast include the sea-eroded trenches, the hot springs, the ventifacts, and the sea life.

3. 「野柳風景區」分三大區：第一區為女王頭、仙女鞋等，第二區為豆腐岩、龍頭石等，第三區為海蝕壺穴、海狗石等。

   The Yehliu Scenic Area is divided into three main areas: the first includes Queen's Head Rock and Fairy Shoe; the second, the bean curd rocks and dragonite; and the third, sea-eroded caves and seal rocks.

4. 「野柳海洋世界」有長約100公尺的海底隧道水族館，展示近200種的稀有魚類及海洋生物。

   There is an 100-meter undersea tunnel aquarium in Yehliu Ocean World where nearly 200 rare fish species and sea creatures are housed.

5. 「翡翠灣」介於金山與基隆間，是北海岸規劃最完整的遊憩區。

   Emerald Bay, located between Jinshan and Keelung, is the best-planned recreation area on the North Coast.

6. 「翡翠灣」可玩風浪板、衝浪、水上摩托車、拖曳傘、滑翔翼、飛行傘等。

At Emerald Bay, you can go windsurfing, surfing, jetskiing, paragliding, hanggliding, and parasailing.

7. 「朱銘美術館」位於金山鄉，進入金山市區後，約十分鐘車程即可抵達。

The Juming Museum is located in Jinshan Township, a mere ten-minute drive from downtown Jinshan.

8. 「朱銘美術館」的戶外展覽區以大型雕刻作品為主。

Juming Museum's outdoor exhibition area is dominated by largescale sculptures.

9. 「金山青年活動中心」是青年旅遊、家庭度假、團體會議研習的好地點。

The Jinshan Youth Activity Center is an ideal destination for youth outings, family vacations, and group meetings and seminars.

10. 「十八王公廟」位於北海岸線上，香火鼎盛。

The Eighteen Gods Temple is located on the North Coast. Its incense burns continually throughout the year.

11.　「富貴角」是台灣地理位置最北端；「富貴角燈塔」是台灣海岸線的最北點。

> Fugui Cape is the northernmost point in Taiwan, while the Fugui Lighthouse stands on the northernmost tip of the coast.

12.　遊客在「富基漁港」購買新鮮的海產後，可以交給當地的店家烹煮。

> In Fuji Fishing Port, visitors can leave the cooking up to the restaurant owners after they have made their fresh seafood purchases.

46

CD 2-21

金門（一）
Kinmen（I）

Robert: Taike, although I **tease** you a whole lot, I don't think that it's necessary for you to keep waving a kitchen knife on my face!

Taike: This happens to be one of the "Three Treasures of Kinmen"—the **artillery shell** knife! Back in the days of the August 23 Artillery Battle, the Chinese Communist Party fired more than 400 thousand shells at Kinmen in a mere 40 days. The locals were very smart. They used these shells to make kitchen knives, which later became the local specialty!

Robert: I see! But that was a long time ago. They must have already used up all the shells?

Kitty: Yep. But, some people do say that artillery shells still **abound** in Little Kinmen. Thus, Kinmen **blacksmiths** nowadays go to Little Kinmen to purchase them.

Taike: The Chinese Communist Party back then not only failed to **defeat** Taiwan but also handed out many kitchen knives to Kinmen for free. They must sorely **regret** doing such a thing!

Robert: What are the other two treasures of Kinmen?

Kitty: They're peanut **tribute** candy and kaoliang **spirits**. In addition to these, the local Kinmen thin noodles and Yitiaogen **medicinal** herbs are also local specialties!

Taike: That's right. The Kinmen County Ceramics Factory is Taiwan's only "official **kiln**." Kinmen's kaoliang is bottled in **porcelain** made there. Many foreigners **prize** the bottles enough to collect them!

Robert: Yep. The **aged special-grade** kaoliang sure is strong and sweet. Let me send a **crate** to Taipei by **express delivery**!

Kitty: I'll buy some Yitiaogen medicinal herbs then. The herbs only grow in the unique water, soil, and weather conditions that Kinmen provides. They are said to help **nourish qi** and blood.

羅波：邰克，雖然我常開你玩笑，不過你也不需一直拿著菜刀向我比劃吧！

邰克：這可是「金門三寶」中的一寶——砲彈鋼刀耶！當年的「八二三砲戰」，中共在短短的四十幾天內，就向金門發射了四十多萬發的砲彈。當地人很聰明，就利用這些砲彈打造菜刀，成為這裡的名產啦！

羅波：原來如此！可是這麼多年了，砲彈總該用光了吧？

高貴：是啊，不過也有人說「小金門」那邊還是有許多砲彈，因此現在金門的打鐵師傅都跑到小金門去收購呢！

邰克：當年中共沒打下台灣，卻平白送了金門這麼多把菜刀，應該很搥心肝吧！

羅波：那金門的另外兩寶是啥？
高貴：是「貢糖」和「高粱酒」。除此之外，這裡的麵線、一條根都很是名產喔！

邰克：沒錯，「金門縣陶瓷廠」是台灣唯一的「官窯」，金門的高粱酒就是裝在那裡所生產的瓷器裡，是很多外國人收藏的珍品喔！

羅波：嗯，這陳年特級高粱酒真的又濃又香，我要快遞一箱回台北啦！

高貴：那我買「一條根」好了。金門的水質、土壤、氣候特殊，配合之下才種出一條根，據說可以補氣血呢。

單字 ·····

- **tease**（**v.**）嘲弄
- **artillery** [ɑrˋtɪlərɪ]（**n.**）大砲
- **shell**（**n.**）殼
- **abound**（**v.**）大量存在
- **blacksmith**（**n.**）鐵匠
- **defeat**（**v.**）擊敗
- **regret**（**v.**）悔恨
- **tribute**（**n.**）貢品
- **spirits**（**n.**）烈酒
- **medicinal**（**adj.**）有藥效的
- **kiln**（**n.**）窯
- **porcelain** [ˋpɔrslɪn]（**n.**）瓷器
- **prize**（**v.**）看做非常有價值的
- **aged**（**adj.**）陳年的
- **special-grade**（**adj.**）特級的
- **crate**（**n.**）板條箱
- **express delivery** 快遞
- **nourish**（**v.**）滋養
- **qi**（**n.**）氣

片語與句型

❖ **use up**：用完；耗盡
例 He used up all his savings.（他花盡所有積蓄。）

❖ **hand out**：分發；分派
例 She was handing out drinks.（她正在發飲料。）

❖ **for free**：免費
例 He gave us the book for free.（他免費給我們書。）

發音小技巧 🔊

Kinmen-grown peanuts are big and sweet, and thus add to the flavor of peanut tribute candy.

金門出產的花生又大又甜，因此做成的金門貢糖十分美味。

● 趴趴走好用句

1.　金門的特產包括高粱酒、菜刀、貢糖、一條根、陶瓷器、海產等。

Kinmen's specialties include kaoliang, artillery shell knives, peanut tribute candy, Yitiaogen, china, and seafood.

2.　品質好的一條根是細長型的，且根部有紅土色。

Quality Yitiaogen is long and thin and has a reddish-brown root.

3.　一條根可以與豬腳、米酒一起燉，對風濕症很有療效。

Yitiaogen can be stewed with pig's knuckles and rice wine. It is effective in treating rheumatism.

4.　砲彈菜刀是金門最有名的特產之一，許多觀光客都會買回家做紀念。

Artillery shell knives are one of Kinmen's best-known specialties. Many tourists purchase them as souvenirs.

5.　金門的貢糖是將花生加上麥芽炒熟，再拍打輾碎，裹上花生粉。

Peanut tribute candy is made by adding malt syrup to peanuts and frying the combination; it is then broken into pieces and sprinkled with peanut powder.

6. 金門的高粱酒名滿天下,而「金酒」則泛指所有的金門酒類。

The kaoliang of Kinmen is known far and wide. The term "Kin drinks" refers to all Kinmen's alcoholic beverages.

7. 金門的酒類眾多,最令當地人珍愛的是具有清香味的「地瓜酒」。

Kinmen has a wide range of alcoholic drinks. The most treasured delight among locals is the faintly fragrant "sweet potato wine."

8. 金門的高粱酒酒精濃度很高,有一股很難抵抗的豪邁氣味。

Kaoliang contains a high concentration of alcohol and has an irresistibly bold feel to it.

9. 近年來金門酒廠不斷推廣高粱酒的各種喝法。

In recent years, the Kinmen Winery has been continually promoting different ways to enjoy kaoliang.

10. 金門盛產品質佳的高嶺土,因此陶瓷工業十分著名。

Kinmen produces quality kaoline in large quantities, which is the reason why its ceramics industry is very well known.

11. 2001年初，台灣政府開放「小三通」，當地人可由金門前往廈門。

In early 2001, the Taiwan government opened up the "Three Minilinks," allowing local residents to travel from Kinmen to Xiamen.

12. 「小三通」開放後，金門到廈門間的往返不論時間、路程或票價，都比以往經濟許多。

Following the opening of the "Three Mini-links," traveling between Kinmen and Xiamen has become more economical than ever in terms of time, distance, and ticket price.

CD
2-22

金門（二）
Kinmen（II）

Robert: Don't tell me that the land right across us is mainland China! That's **incredible**!

Kitty: You're right, though. Kinmen is only 2,100 meters off the coast of mainland China at the nearest point. You can see across with high-powered **binoculars**!

Robert: And… I also see a lot of birds.

Taike: That's right. Kinmen has a subtropical **monsoon** climate and is located on a **hilly terrain** composed of granite **gneiss**. In addition, due to its being near the edge of the mainland, it has become a stop for **migratory birds**.

Robert: But the birds must have been scared away from the many **bogies** that **scatter** the island. Right?

Taike: Hey! Show some respect! It's the well-known "Wind Lion God" you're talking about! It's a lion, not a bogie.

Kitty: He's right. In the past, **wind-borne** sand in Kinmen made it difficult for plants and animals to survive. The islanders later **erected** many statues of the Wind Lion God to **squelch** the wind-borne sand. After a long while, it became the **patron** saint of the place.

Taike: Right. What's more, people here are very **pious**. Aside from worshipping the Wind Lion God, they also worship such gods as Guan Yin, City God, and Matzu.

Robert: Sure, these are **battleground** islands. With worship comes **blessing**, especially with such dangers lying around.

Kitty: Yep. There are **underground air raid shelters** and buildings built because of the war everywhere in this place. Let's move on to the Mt. Taiwu Area, the **memorial** for the August 23 Artillery Battle!

羅波：別告訴我對岸就是中國大陸！太神奇了吧！

高貴：沒錯，金門離大陸最近的地方只有2,100公尺，你從高倍望遠鏡就可以看到！

羅波：而且……我也看到好多鳥耶。

邱克：對啊，金門是亞熱帶季風型氣候，是由花崗片麻岩構成的丘陵地形，又因為靠近大陸邊緣，所以成為候鳥遷徙的中途站。

羅波：不過鳥兒大概都被這島上處處可見的妖怪嚇跑了吧？

邱克：喂，放尊重點！那可是著名的「風獅爺」呢！人家是獅子，不是妖怪啦。

高貴：對啊，以前金門多風砂，使得動植物生長不易，後來島上的人在各處樹立風獅爺，用來鎮住風砂，長久下來，變成了這裡的守護神。

邱克：對，而且這裡的人很虔誠，除了祭拜風獅爺，也祭拜觀音、城隍爺、媽祖等神祇。

羅波：當然了，這裡是「戰爭之島」，危險多，有拜有保佑啊！

高貴：是啊，這裡到處都是因為戰爭所建構的地下防禦坑道和房屋。我們現在就去太武山區，那裡是「八二三砲戰」的紀念地！

單字 ‧‧‧‧‧

- ❖ **incredible**（**adj.**）難以置信的；令人驚訝的
- ❖ **binoculars** [bɪˋnɑkjələz]（**n.**）望遠鏡
- ❖ **monsoon**（**n.**）季風
- ❖ **hilly**（**adj.**）丘陵的
- ❖ **terrain**（**n.**）地形
- ❖ **gneiss** [naɪs]（**n.**）片麻岩
- ❖ **migratory bird** 候鳥
- ❖ **bogie** [ˋbogɪ]（**n.**）妖怪
- ❖ **scatter**（**v.**）分散；散布
- ❖ **wind-borne**（**adj.**）隨風飄移的
- ❖ **erect**（**v.**）使直立；矗立
- ❖ **squelch**（**v.**）鎮壓；鎮住
- ❖ **patron**（**n.**）守護者
- ❖ **pious**（**adj.**）虔誠的
- ❖ **battleground**（**n.**）戰場
- ❖ **blessing**（**n.**）保佑；幸福
- ❖ **underground**（**adj.**）地下的
- ❖ **air raid shelter** 空襲避難所
- ❖ **memorial**（**adj.**）紀念的；追悼的

片語與句型

✤ **compose of**：組成；構成

　例 Water is composed of hydrogen and oxygen.（水由氫和氧構成。）

✤ **move on**：前進

　例 Move on, please.（請往前走。）

發音小技巧

Kinmen's Wind Lion God statues are usually erected in front of temples and beside village roads.

金門的風獅爺多立於廟口或村莊的路口。

● 趴趴走好用句

1. 在金門的民間傳說中，風獅爺能鎮住風砂，保護居民的安全。

   According to Kinmen folklore, the Wind Lion God can squelch the wind-borne sand and protect the residents from harm.

2. 風獅爺大多是石雕的，造形各有特色，已成為特有的金門文化景觀。

   Most Wind Lion God statues are stone carvings, each different from the next. These have become a unique mark of Kinmen's culture.

3. 「金門民俗文化村」佔地面積1,230坪，建築採用閩南傳統式建築。

   The Kinmen Folk Culture Village covers an area of 1,230 "ping." Its buildings are built in traditional Southern Min fashion.

4. 太武山山頂豎立著「毋忘在莒」的碑石，此四字是金門軍民的精神象徵。

   There stands a rock on top of Taiwu Mountain with the inscription "Wu Wang Zai Ju" ("Don't forget the days in Ju"), a symbol of the spirit of the Kinmen military.

5. 要觀賞「毋忘在莒」石碑，必須由底下的登山口走約一公里的上坡路。

   To see the "Wu Wang Zai Ju" rock inscription for yourself, you will first have to walk about a kilometer uphill from the trailhead at the foot of the mountain.

6. 太武山為花崗岩，標高253公尺。

Taiwu Mountain is made of granite and rises to a height of 253 meters.

7. 金門與台灣雖然位置接近，但由於位於不同的候鳥遷移路線，鳥的種類與台灣的鳥有很大差異。

Although Kinmen and Taiwan are fairly close to one another, they are located on two different bird migration routes; thus, the birds that are found in the area are vastly different from those in Taiwan.

8. 金門的候鳥主要來自西伯利亞，台灣的候鳥則來自日本。

Kinmen's migratory birds mostly come from Siberia, while those in Taiwan come from Japan.

9. 金門鳥類眾多，種類將近兩百種。

Kinmen features a wide variety of birds, nearly 200 species in all.

10. 太武山區位於金門島的中央，是「八二三砲戰」重要的紀念地。

Taiwu Mountain in the central part of Kinmen Island is an important memorial ground commemorating the August 23 Artillery Battle.

11.　「八二三戰史館」是為了紀念八二三砲戰的英勇事蹟而建。

The August 23 Artillery Battle Museum was built to commemorate the brave souls who perished in the August 23 Artillery Battle.

12.　金門地區的國家級古蹟計有二十一處，島上有許多傳統聚落及歷史建築。

There are 21 national historical sites in the Kinmen area. The island features numerous traditional villages and buildings of historical significance.

緑島
Green Island

Robert: Wow! This is my first time on a **scooter**. I never thought that it could be this much fun. No wonder Taiwanese people love riding motorcycles!

Taike: Slow down. Although we got these scooters on a **rental**, we'd still have to pay for damages.

Kitty: Green Island was once known as the "Island on Fire." It is a **volcanic** island formed by volcanic action. Its area is a mere 16.2 square kilometers. However, **weathering** and wave erosion over the **eons** have given it an attractive **curved** coastline.

Taike: Yep. Green Island may have seemed **backward** in the past; but today, with its airport, fishing port, and round-the-island highway, it has become Taiwan's island travel **destination**!

Kitty: That's right. This is also the reason why so many Taiwanese come here to engage in water-based leisure activities!

Robert: So, where are we riding to now for skin diving and snorkeling **equipment** rentals?

Taike: I'll have to warn you first, I've heard that the **sea serpents** here are very **virulent**. Remember to refrain from touching them when you're skin diving, okay?

Kitty: Stop scaring him. Green Island belongs to the tropics and is surrounded everywhere by **marine** plants and animals, the most well-known of which are fish, **shellfish**, **crustaceans**, **coral**, sea turtles, etc. The view under the sea should be very **enchanting**!

Taike: Yes, and if time permits, we can go on an undersea tour aboard a tourist submarine **vessel** to take it all in!

Robert: In that case, I would also like to skydive so I can see Green Island's amazing scenery from the air!

羅波：哇，這是我第一次騎「小綿羊」，沒想到這麼好玩。難怪台灣人都愛騎機車！

邰克：你騎慢一點啦，這機車雖然是租的，騎壞了也是要賠錢啊！

高貴：綠島以前叫「火燒島」，是火山噴發後所形成的火山島，面積只有16.2平方公里。不過因為長時間受風化和海水的侵蝕，形成了曲折漂亮的海岸。

邰克：嗯，以前的綠島給人家落後的印象，但現在的綠島有機場、漁港、環島公路，已經成為台灣海上的觀光島嶼了！

高貴：沒錯，這也是為什麼這麼多台灣人會跑到這裡從事水上休閒活動了！

羅波：那我們現在要騎去哪裡租潛水和浮潛的用具？

邰克：我先警告你，聽說海裡面的海蛇有劇毒，你潛水時可不要亂摸它們喔。

高貴：你不要嚇他了啦。綠島地處熱帶，四周的海洋生物很豐富，最著名的有魚類、貝類、甲殼類、珊瑚、海龜等，所以海底的景觀應該很動人！

邰克：嗯，如果有時間，我們可以搭乘海底觀光遊艇，好好欣賞一番！

羅波：那我還要跳傘，從天空看綠島的美景！

單字

* **scooter**（n.）小輪摩托車
* **rental**（n.）租用物
* **volcanic**（adj.）火山的
* **weathering**（n.）風化
* **eon** [ˋiən]（n.）無限長的時代
* **curved**（adj.）彎曲的
* **backward**（adj.）落後的
* **destination**（n.）目的地
* **equipment**（n.）器具
* **sea serpent** 海蛇
* **virulent** [ˋvɪrulənt]（adj.）有毒的
* **marine**（adj.）海的
* **shellfish**（n.）貝殼類
* **crustacean** [krʌsˋteʃən]（n.）甲殼類動物
* **coral**（n.）珊瑚
* **enchanting**（adj.）迷人的
* **vessel**（n.）船隻

片語與句型

❖ **no wonder**：難怪
  例 You've drunk so much coffee, it's no wonder you can't sleep.（你喝那麼多咖啡，難怪睡不著。）

❖ **engage in...**：從事……
  例 He has engaged in farming for over 15 years.（他從事農作已超過十五年。）

❖ **refrain from...**：抑制……；忍住……
  例 She refrained from tears even though she was in great pain.（雖然很痛，她仍忍住不哭。）

❖ **if... permits**：如果……許可的話
  例 We will go out for a picnic if weather permits.（如果天氣好，我們會去野餐。）

發音小技巧

To get from Taiwan to Green Island, you can either ride a boat or hop on a plane.

從台灣到綠島觀光可以乘船或搭飛機。

趴趴走好用句

1. 綠島位於台東縣東方的海面上，面積約15平方公里，是台灣的第四大島。

   Green Island is located off the eastern shore of Taitung County. The fourth largest island in Taiwan, it has an area of approximately 15 square kilometers.

2. 綠島主要的風景點多分布在一條長約16公里的環島公路上，因此觀光十分方便。

   Most of the scenic spots on Green Island are found on the 16-kilometer highway that runs around the island, which makes it easy to get to them.

3. 綠島現有居民約3,000人，以漁業、畜牧業、觀光休閒業為主。

   Green Island currently has about 3,000 residents, most of whom make their living from the fishing, livestock, and tourism industries.

4. 綠島的觀光點包括南寮灣、綠島燈塔、綠島公園、將軍岩等。

   Green Island features such tourist spots as Nanliao Bay, Green Island Lighthouse, Green Island Park, and General's Rock.

5. 綠島的水上活動以浮潛、搭乘潛水艇為主。

   The main water activities in Green Island are snorkeling and submarining.

6. 機車是綠島最便利的交通工具，在當地有許多機車出租業者，價格便宜。

The best way to get around Green Island is by motorcycle. There are many low-priced motorcycle rental companies on the island.

7. 綠島的環島公路多彎道，騎士一定要謹慎行車，不要超速。

Green Island's round-the-island highway has many twists and turns. Drivers should practice great care when driving and should under no circumstances go over the speed limit.

8. 「綠島監獄」所關的罪犯多為重刑犯及一些幫派「大哥」級的人物。

Green Island Prison inmates are mostly serious offenders and gangster boss-types.

9. 到綠島觀光，盡量不要購買或食用珊瑚礁生物，以維護當地的海洋生物。

To protect the local sea creatures, avoid purchasing or consuming coral reef organisms on Green Island.

10. 綠島的傳統食物包括地瓜、花生和海產。

Traditional Green Island delicacies include sweet potatoes, peanuts, and seafood.

11. 綠島居民的傳統住屋為石屋，是以珊瑚礁砌成的閩南式建築。

Green Island residents traditionally live in houses built in Southern Min style from pieces of coral.

12. 綠島的海域溫暖又清澈，最適合珊瑚的生長。

The waters surrounding Green Island are warm and lucid, perfect for the growth of coral.

澎湖群島
Penghu Islands

Robert: The beaches here are **pristine**, the waters clear, and the sky **azure** blue. No wonder Penghu is also known as "Taiwan's Hawaii!"

Taike: This is why more and more Taiwanese **soap operas** are setting up their **sets** here!

Kitty: Penghu is an **archipelago** composed of 64 islands. It boasts different scenery in different seasons. The **peak season** for travel is between June and August. Since we're here during the **off-season**, we can better appreciate Penghu's **serene** beauty!

Robert: That's right. I hope that we'll have a chance to go to Wangan Island and see the green sea turtles today! It would be even better if we could also go skin diving and see the **coral reefs**, sea turtles, and **iridescent** undersea scenery.

Taike: But first, let's take a spin around Penghu's most **populous** city, Magong. Penghu was settled early, even earlier than Taiwan by four hundred years! Central Street here has a very long history. You can also find Taiwan's first Matzu temple, the Tianhou Temple, here.

Robert: Yep. There seem to be temples all over the place.

Taike: True. Penghu has the highest **density** of temples in Taiwan. It is said that there are about two hundred of them in all. They also hold a great many events to welcome the gods and pray for blessings.

Kitty: I also want to go to the **southernmost** tip of the Penghu Archipelago, Qimei Island, to see the Husband-Waiting Reef. It is said that once, a local woman missed her fisherman husband so much that she stood on that spot every day to look into the distance and eventually turned into a rock!

Robert: What a **tragic** yet beautiful story! In fact, it's more romantic than Taiwanese soap operas!

羅波：這裡的沙灘乾淨、海水清澈、天空湛藍，難怪這裡又稱「台灣的夏威夷」！

邱克：這是為什麼台灣越來越多的偶像劇都跑到這裡來拍攝了！

高貴：澎湖是個群島，由64個島嶼所組成，一年四季都有不同的景觀，不過觀光旺季在六月到八月。我們現在是淡季，更可以好好欣賞澎湖寧靜的美！

羅波：沒錯，我希望今天能到望安島看綠蠵龜！最好還可以潛水，欣賞珊瑚礁、海龜和繽紛的海底景觀。

邱克：不過我們要先逛逛這人口最多的馬公市。澎湖開發的年代很早，比台灣本島早了四百年呢！這裡的中央街年代久遠，有台灣第一座的媽祖廟「天后宮」。

羅波：對啊，這裡好像到處都是廟耶！

邱克：嗯，澎湖的寺廟密度居全台之冠，據說大大小小的寺廟共有兩百座左右，而且各種迎神祈福宗教活動也超多的。

高貴：我還想去澎湖群島最南端的七美島看望夫石，據說當地一個女生因為太思念捕魚的丈夫，每天到那裡去眺望，最後竟然變成了石頭！

羅波：好淒美喔！這故事簡直比台灣的偶像劇都還浪漫耶！

單字

✤ **pristine** [ˋprɪstin] (**adj.**) 原始的；清新的

✤ **azure** [ˋæʒɚ] (**adj.**) 天藍色的

✤ **soap opera** 偶像劇；肥皂劇

✤ **set** (**n.**) (電視或電影)場景

✤ **archipelago** [ˌɑrkəˋpɛləˌgo] (**n.**) 群島

✤ **peak season** 旺季

✤ **off-season** (**adj., n.**) 淡季(的)

✤ **serene** (**adj.**) 寧靜的

✤ **coral reef** 珊瑚礁

✤ **iridescent** [ˌɪrɪˋdɛsənt] (**adj.**) 燦爛光輝的

✤ **populous** (**adj.**) 人口稠密的

✤ **density** (**n.**) 密度

✤ **southernmost** (**adj.**) 最南的

✤ **tragic** (**adj.**) 悲慘的

片語與句型

✤ （take/ go for） a spin：兜風；逛逛

　⑩ Why not take your bicycle and go for a spin?（何不騎你的腳踏車去兜風一下？）

✤ **turn into...**：變成……

　⑩ He turned into a bad boy after his parents were divorced.（他父母離婚後，他變成了個壞孩子。）

發音小技巧 🔊

The Penghu Archipelago is composed of 64 small islands, but most of them are uninhabited.

澎湖群島是由64個小島所組成的，但多數的島嶼都沒有居民。

● 趴趴走好用句

1. 台灣除了本島，還有金門、馬祖、澎湖、綠島、蘭嶼等五大離島。

   In addition to the main island of Taiwan, there are five other outlying islands, namely Kinmen, Mazu, Penghu, Green Island, and Orchid Island.

2. 澎湖的產業以漁業、農業、礦業為主，其中漁業最為重要。

   The main industries in Penghu include fishing, farming, and mining; among them, fishing is the most important.

3. 「澎湖跨海大橋」連接白沙島和漁翁島，長度超過兩公里。

   The Penghu Trans-Ocean Bridge, spanning a length of more than two kilometers, connects Baisha Island to Yuweng Island.

4. 「七美島」古稱大嶼，是澎湖最南方的島嶼，島上建有環島公路。

   Qimei Island, formerly known as Dayu, is the southernmost island in Penghu. A highway circles the island.

5. 南滬港是七美島最繁榮的地方；南滬燈塔為澎湖群島最南邊的一座燈塔。

   Nanhu Port is the busiest part of Qimei Island. The Nanhu Lighthouse is the southernmost lighthouse in the Penghu Archipelago.

6.　「七美島」有著名的「望夫石」，據說是等待丈夫打漁歸來的婦人化身。

The famous Husband-Waiting Reef is located on Qimei Island. It is said to be the incarnation of a woman who once waited for her husband to return home from fishing.

7.　「吉貝嶼」位於澎湖海域的東北角，是旅客夏日度假及度蜜月的熱門據點。

Jibei Islet is situated off the northeastern shore of Penghu. It is a favorite destination for summer vacationers and honeymooners.

8.　「吉貝嶼」主要的水上活動包括浮潛、拖曳傘、迷你遊艇、水上摩托車等。

Water-related activities in Jibei Islet include snorkeling, parasailing, mini-yachting, and jetskiing.

9.　「望安島」位於馬公南方的海域上，可以浮潛、游泳、抓螃蟹、撿貝殼。

Wangan Island is located off the southern shore of Magong. Snorkeling, swimming, crab fishing, and seashell picking are possible activity choices here.

10.　澎湖的特產包括海產、花生酥，海苔酥、絲瓜、哈蜜瓜、文石、珊瑚等。

Penghu specialties include seafood, peanut cakes, seaweed cakes, loofahs, melons, aragonite, and coral.

11.　到澎湖一定要到「風櫃」看海蝕洞、海蝕溝，以及聽特殊的濤聲。

Fenggui is a mandatory stop in Penghu. The place offers a glimpse into sea-eroded caves and trenches and a chance to listen to the unique sound of the waves.

12.　根據考古學家的研究發現，澎湖群島在四、五千年前就有文化存在。

According to archaeological research, civilization existed on the Penghu Islands as early as four or five thousand years ago.

CD
2-25

蘭嶼
Orchid Island

Robert: The men here are so **open**. They're all dressed up like Taiwan's Ximending babes!

Taike: Please. The Tao dress like this to **facilitate** their fishing.

Kitty: But seeing old folks on Orchid Island wearing **thongs** and traditional **outfits** is pretty rare. Usually they can only be seen during such special events and ceremonies as the Flying Fish **Sacrifice Ritual** and the Ritual of the **Launching** of the New **Canoe**.

Robert: Truth be told, there seems to be a lot of old people here. There are also a lot more men than women!

Kitty: That is caused by population **outflow**. Many young people leave to work in Taiwan and end up staying there for good. What's more, many Tao women choose to marry husbands in Taiwan.

Taike: However, I have also heard of a number of **moving** stories about Taiwanese women marrying the local aborigines and staying here to work together for their future!

Kitty: Most people here fish for a living. And, in order to fight against the **humidity**, high **precipitation**, and typhoon-ridden weather, a lot of them **reside** in semi-**subterranean** houses.

Robert: The residents of Orchid Island are **optimistic**, **hospitable**, and full of tropical marine charm. The **tranquil** and **carefree** traditional way of life here makes me want to move in!

Taike: That's true. Orchid Island is a volcanic island, surrounded by coral on all four sides. In addition, because the Japan Current passes through here, it has become a sea fishing and skin diving heaven. No wonder some people say that Orchid Island is a **solitary** pearl in the Pacific **situated** off the southeastern coast of Taiwan!

羅波：這裡的男人好開放喔，竟然穿得跟台灣西門町的辣妹一樣！

邱克：拜託，這是達悟族人為了下海捕魚方便的穿著啦。

高貴：不過你平時要看到蘭嶼的老人穿丁字褲和傳統服裝可不容易，通常要在「飛魚祭」和「下水祭」等特殊的祭典儀式中才可以看到。

羅波：說真的，這裡的老人好多喔，而且男人也多過女人許多呢！

高貴：這是因為人口外流的結果。許多年輕人都到台灣工作、定居了，而且很多達悟族的女生也選擇嫁去台灣。

邱克：不過我也聽說台灣女生嫁給當地原住民，一起留在這裡打拼的動人故事！

高貴：這裡大部分的人以捕魚維生。而且為了抵抗濕熱多雨、颱風多的氣候，因此很多人住在「地下屋」。

羅波：蘭嶼當地的居民樂觀、好客，充滿熱帶海洋民族的魅力。這裡平靜悠然的傳統生活方式，讓我也想在這裡定居呢！

邱克：的確，蘭嶼是個火山島，島的四周珊瑚遍佈，又有黑潮流經，是海釣和潛水的天堂。難怪有人說蘭嶼是台灣東南方太平洋上遺世的珍珠！

單字

- **open**（adj.）開放的
- **facilitate**（v.）使便利；使容易
- **thong**（n.）丁字褲
- **outfit**（n.）服飾
- **sacrifice**（n.）祭祀
- **ritual**（n.）儀式
- **launching**（n.）下水（典禮）
- **canoe** [kə`nu]（n.）獨木舟
- **outflow**（n.）流出
- **moving**（adj.）感人的
- **humidity**（n.）濕氣；濕度
- **precipitation**（n.）降雨量
- **reside**（v.）居住
- **subterranean** [ˌsʌbtə`renɪən]（adj.）地下的
- **optimistic**（adj.）樂觀的
- **hospitable**（adj.）好客的
- **tranquil**（adj.）寧靜的；平和的
- **carefree**（adj.）無憂無慮的
- **solitary**（adj.）孤獨的；獨自的
- **situate**（v.）位於

片語與句型

❖ **dress up**：盛裝
   例 They were all dressed up for the big event.（他們全都盛裝參加盛會。）

❖ **for good**：永久地
   例 We decide to leave the city for good.（我們決定永遠離開這城市。）

❖ **for a living**：以……維生
   例 She writes novels for a living.（她寫小說維生。）

發音小技巧

On Orchid Island, mountain ridges abound and coasts curve this way and that, forming a superb landscape.

蘭嶼全島有許多山脈、海岸曲折，構成美不勝收的景觀。

● 趴趴走好用句

1. 蘭嶼位於台東市東南方約90公里處的太平洋海域，因盛產蘭花而得名。

   Orchid Island, named for the orchids that grow there in abundance, is located in the Pacific Ocean about 90 kilometers southeast of Taitung City.

2. 蘭嶼隸屬台東縣，面積約44平方公里，是台灣東岸最大的離島。

   Governed as part of Taitung County, Orchid Island, with an area of about 44 square kilometers, is the largest island off the east coast of Taiwan.

3. 蘭嶼每年七至十一月為颱風季節，常受暴風雨侵襲，島上的房屋及農作物常遭侵襲。

   From July to November each year is typhoon season on Orchid Island. Storms often batter the island, destroying houses and crops.

4. 蘭嶼長期以來人口外流嚴重。

   There has been a serious population outflow from Orchid Island for quite a number of years now.

5. 蘭嶼雖小，島上尚有中央氣象局的觀測站、國際燈塔、郵局、台電發電所、機場等。

   Although small, Orchid Island has a Central Weather Bureau observatory, an international lighthouse, a post office, a Taipower power plant, and an airport.

6.　蘭嶼有「海釣者天堂」之稱，經常有大型海釣比賽在此舉行。

Orchid Island is known as a sea fisherman's heaven. Large-scale sea fishing competitions are frequently held on the island.

7.　蘭嶼島上有六個村落沿海而築，交通只有一條全長約37公里的環島公路。

There are six villages along the coast of Orchid Island. The only way to get to them is via the 37-kilometer highway that circles the island.

8.　蘭嶼百分之九十的居民為達悟族人，以農業、漁業為生。

90 percent of the residents on Orchid Island belong to the Tao tribe. They make their living from farming and fishing.

9.　蘭嶼女性的主要工作是農耕，特別是種植水芋，漁撈則為男性主要的工作。

Women on Orchid Island work primarily in the fields, most often planting taro; men, on the other hand, focus on catching fish.

10.　飛魚（達悟語為alibangbang）是達悟人最重要的動物性蛋白質來源之一。

Flying fish, or alibangbang in the Tao language, are one of the most important sources of animal-based protein for the Tao people.

11. 每年春季，飛魚會隨著黑潮來到蘭嶼附近海域，此時達悟人開始捕捉飛魚。

Every spring, flying fish come to Orchid Island by way of the Japan Current. This is when the Tao start catching them.

12. 捕魚是蘭嶼男性的主要工作，因此捕魚技術的好壞可以決定男人社會地位的高低。

Catching fish is the main responsibility of the males of Orchid Island. It thus follows that their fish-catching skills will decide their place in society.

Linking English
用英文遊台灣

2007年9月初版　　　　　　　　　　　　　　定價：新臺幣380元
2013年12月初版第六刷
有著作權・翻印必究
Printed in Taiwan.

著　　　　著	黃　玟　君
總　編　輯	胡　金　倫
發　行　人	林　載　爵

出　版　者	聯經出版事業股份有限公司	叢書主編	何　采　嬪
地　　　址	台北市基隆路一段180號4樓	校　　對	Nick Hawkins
台北聯經書房	台北市新生南路三段94號		林　慧　如
電話	（02）23620308	封面設計	蔡　婕　岑
台中分公司	台中市北區健行路321號1樓		
暨門市電話	（04）22312023、（04）22302425		
郵政劃撥帳戶第0100559-3號			
郵撥電話	（02）23620308		
印　刷　者	文聯彩色製版印刷有限公司		
總　經　銷	聯合發行股份有限公司		
發　行　所	新北市新店區寶橋路235巷6弄6號2F		
電話	（02）29178022		

行政院新聞局出版事業登記證局版臺業字第0130號

本書如有缺頁，破損，倒裝請寄回台北聯經書房更換。　　ISBN　978-957-08-3192-4 (平裝)
聯經網址 http://www.linkingbooks.com.tw
電子信箱 e-mail:linking@udngroup.com

國家圖書館出版品預行編目資料

用英文遊台灣 / 黃玫君著 . 初版 .
臺北市 . 聯經 . 2007 年（民 96）
432 面；14.8×21 公分 .（Linking English）
ISBN　978-957-08-3192-4（平裝附光碟）
[2013年12月初版第六刷]

1.英語　2.會話　3.台灣遊記

805.188　　　　　　　　　　96016156